# MOUNTING FEARS

## BOOKS BY STUART WOODS

### FICTION

Hot Mahogany†

Santa Fe Dead§

Beverly Hills Dead

Shoot Him If He Runs†

Fresh Disasters†

Short Straw§

Dark Harbor†

Iron Orchid*

Two-Dollar Bill†

The Prince of Beverly Hills

Reckless Abandon†

Capital Crimes‡

Dirty Work†

Blood Orchid*

The Short Forever†

Orchid Blues*

Cold Paradise†

L.A. Dead†

The Run‡

Worst Fears Realized†

Orchid Beach*

Swimming to Catalina†

Dead in the Water†

Dirt†

Choke

Imperfect Strangers

Heat

Dead Eyes

L.A. Times

Santa Fe Rules§

New York Dead†

Palindrome

Grass Roots‡

White Cargo

Deep Lie‡

Under the Lake

Run Before the Wind‡

Chiefs‡

### TRAVEL

A Romantic's Guide to the Country Inns of Britain and Ireland (1979)

### MEMOIR

Blue Water, Green Skipper (1977)

*A Holly Barker Book †A Stone Barrington Book ‡A Will Lee Book §An Ed Eagle Book

# MOUNTING FEARS

## Stuart Woods

G. P. PUTNAM'S SONS
NEW YORK

PUTNAM

G. P. PUTNAM'S SONS
*Publishers Since 1838*
Published by the Penguin Group
Penguin Group (USA) Inc., 375 Hudson Street, New York, New York 10014, USA •
Penguin Group (Canada), 90 Eglinton Avenue East, Suite 700, Toronto, Ontario M4P 2Y3, Canada
(a division of Pearson Canada Inc.) • Penguin Books Ltd, 80 Strand, London WC2R 0RL, England •
Penguin Ireland, 25 St Stephen's Green, Dublin 2, Ireland (a division of Penguin Books Ltd) •
Penguin Group (Australia), 250 Camberwell Road, Camberwell, Victoria 3124, Australia
(a division of Pearson Australia Group Pty Ltd) • Penguin Books India Pvt Ltd, 11 Community
Centre, Panchsheel Park, New Delhi–110 017, India • Penguin Group (NZ), 67 Apollo Drive,
Rosedale, North Shore 0632, New Zealand (a division of Pearson New Zealand Ltd) • Penguin
Books (South Africa) (Pty) Ltd, 24 Sturdee Avenue, Rosebank, Johannesburg 2196, South Africa

Penguin Books Ltd, Registered Offices:
80 Strand, London WC2R 0RL, England

Library of Congress Cataloging-in-Publication Data

Woods, Stuart.
Mounting fears / Stuart Woods.
p.      cm.
ISBN 978-0-399-15547-5
1. Lee, Will (Fictitious character)—Fiction.    2. Presidents—Election—Fiction.
3. Washington (D.C.)—Fiction.    4. Political fiction.    I. Title.
PS3573.O642M68      2009                  2008034737
813'.54—dc22

Printed in the United States of America
1   3   5   7   9   10   8   6   4   2

*Book design by Stephanie Huntwork*

This is a work of fiction. Names, characters, places, and incidents either are the product of the author's imagination or are used fictitiously, and any resemblance to actual persons, living or dead, businesses, companies, events, or locales is entirely coincidental.

While the author has made every effort to provide accurate telephone numbers and Internet addresses at the time of publication, neither the publisher nor the author assumes any responsibility for errors, or for changes that occur after publication. Further, the publisher does not have any control over and does not assume any responsibility for author or third-party websites or their content.

*This book is for*
*Karl and Stephanie Walters.*

# MOUNTING FEARS

THE PRESIDENT OF THE UNITED STATES, WILLIAM JEFFERSON LEE IV, SAT STRAIGHT up in bed. It had been the nuclear nightmare wherein some unidentified country had launched missiles on the United States and he had to decide at whom to strike back. It was not the first time.

Will wiped the sweat from his forehead with the sleeve of his nightshirt, then tried to get out of bed without waking his wife. He was halfway to the bathroom when he remembered that Kate, who for the past four years had been director of intelligence, head of the CIA, had left for work two hours before, after an urgent phone call in the early hours.

Will stared at himself in the bathroom mirror while he waited for the water in the sink to get hot for shaving. How was he different from four years before? Considerably grayer, but Kate thought that lent him gravitas. His face was relatively unlined, still, and he took some pride in the fact that his waist size had not changed, in spite of only sporadic efforts to exercise.

He ran hot water onto the shaving brush, lathered his face, and began shaving while reviewing the high points of the day to come.

Most important was a nine a.m. with the vice president, George Kiel, and he thought he knew what the meeting would be about.

FORTY-FIVE MINUTES LATER, dressed in a standard chalk-striped suit and a red-and-blue-striped necktie, Will walked through the door of the White House family quarters to be greeted by the young naval officer who carried the "football," the briefcase containing the codes for a nuclear launch, and two Secret Service agents, who escorted him down the hallway and into the elevator.

Will had become accustomed to never being alone outside the family quarters and, sometimes, the Oval Office; he also had become accustomed to traveling to the airport in a large new helicopter, and from there in an outrageously well-equipped Boeing 747 with a bedroom and shower and conference room and telephones and Internet hookups and everything else that the minds of electronics experts could conceive. It had been harder to become accustomed to constantly being the most looked-at person in any room, up to and including Madison Square Garden. He had learned never to scratch his nether regions, because the video would be on the Internet within seconds.

The elevator reached the lower floor, and then, instead of being walked to the Oval Office, Will was walked to the press room in the basement of the White House. No preparation had been necessary, because the press had not been invited. Instead, the auditorium was filled with White House staffers.

Will stepped to the lectern. "My God," he said, "who's answering the phones?"

Tim Coleman, his chief of staff, stood up in the front row. "Nobody, Mr. President," he said, then sat down again. Everybody laughed.

"Well, good morning to you all," Will said. "As I expect you may have heard, I'm headed for New York today to accept the nomination tonight, and I wanted to say just a few words to you before I go." He looked around at the happy faces. "It may surprise some of you that I got the nomination." Everybody laughed again. "But I guess being the incumbent helps. What was even more of a help was the successful nature of our first term, and I use the pronoun advisedly. The people in this room had as much, maybe more, to do with that success than anyone else, and I wanted to thank you, personally, for that help.

"Now, assuming that I win a second term for us—and that's only an assumption at this point—I'm going to be faced with being called a lame duck for the next four years. It's my fervent hope that you will all be here to face that with me, but I understand that practically all of you have served for the past four years at a considerable financial sacrifice and that the call of the private sector, as the Republicans like to call the defense contractors and the Washington lobbying firms, will be ringing in your ears.

"It's my hope that you will all be here during the campaign, because *somebody* has to run the White House, and that you'll be here early in the next four years to help break in your replacements—should you choose to leave. I know, of course, that the last year of the next administration the rats will all be swimming for shore, and I can't blame them. I just want you to know that every one of you here has proved your value to the White House and to your country, and I would be delighted if you all decided to stay on for another four years.

"That said, be sure to tune in to the convention tonight to learn if any of your suggestions made it into the speech. Bye-bye for now."

Will walked off the platform and was followed by Tim Coleman and Kitty Conroy, his director of communications. These two had been his aides when he was in the Senate, and they were closer to him than anyone else on the staff.

Will walked through the reception room outside the Oval Office.

His secretary, Cora Parker, spoke up. "Mr. President, the director of Central Intelligence and the deputy director for operations of the CIA are waiting in the Oval Office."

This was a surprise. "Please send the vice president in when he arrives," he said. Kate and her DDO, Lance Cabot, were waiting for him, and they both stood as he entered. Will waved them to their seats and hung his coat on a stand by the door.

"What's up?" he asked.

"Mr. President," Kate said—she always addressed him formally in meetings with others—"we have a report that a Taliban group, possibly aided by Al Qaeda operatives, have captured a missile site in northwestern Pakistan, near the Afghanistan border."

Will stopped in his tracks. "A *nuclear* missile site?"

"Yes, sir," Kate said.

"Are the Taliban able to fire the missiles?"

"They also captured most of the technicians alive."

"So it's possible they could fire at something?"

"Just possible," Kate said. "Not likely, but possible."

"Have they made any demands?"

"No, but we're expecting that shortly."

"Has the story broken?"

"Not yet. The Pakistani president has clamped a tight lid on it, but I don't think we can count on that for long. When the occupiers of the site start making demands, they're very likely to make a lot of noise about it."

"Why are there no military people here?"

"They're on the way, sir," Kate replied. "Their departure from the Pentagon was delayed by what they hope is new information coming in."

Cora Parker's head appeared from behind a door. "Mr. President, the vice president and the chairman of the Joint Chiefs of Staff and the Army chief of staff are here with their aides."

"Send them right in," Will said, then stood up to receive the group. There was not a happy face among them.

Cora came back in behind them. "Mr. President, President Mohammed Khan of Pakistan is on the phone."

Will walked to his desk. "Excuse me, gentlemen," he said, "I'd better take this. Maybe he'll have something new."

## 2

WILL PICKED UP THE TELEPHONE AND PRESSED THE FLASHING BUTTON. "PRESI-dent Khan?"

"Yes, Mr. President."

"I understand that a nuclear missile site has been taken by the Taliban."

"That is correct, sir."

"And that Al Qaeda may be involved?"

"We expect so."

"How can we help?"

"I am meeting with my military staff in a moment, and I hope to have an answer to that question afterward."

"I understand that most of the technical staff were captured at the site?"

"Yes, that is true, I'm afraid."

"Have the occupiers made any demands?"

"No, and they are not responding to our communications."

"Is there anything I can do for you at this moment?"

"Not yet, sir, but I will be in touch. I just wanted to be sure that you had been made aware of the situation."

"I have, and my military and intelligence staff have just arrived. I hope to speak to you again when your meeting is over. Good-bye."

"Good-bye."

"That was Mohammed Khan," Will said to the others. "He seems to know little right now, but he's about to meet with his military staff."

"Mr. President," General Boone, the chairman of the Joint Chiefs, said, "I think it would be best if we moved this meeting to the Situation Room, since we have some electronic intelligence to display, and that room is best equipped for it."

TEN MINUTES LATER the group had settled in around the conference table in the Situation Room. "Who'd like to start?" he asked.

"I would," Kate said. "We have some satellite photos to show you." She clicked a remote control, and an image of mountains appeared; with a laser pointer she indicated a narrow valley. "This is the location of the installation," she said. "As you can see we have clear weather, so this is a very good photo." She clicked again and zoomed in until the missile site appeared clearly. "This is the view from about two thousand feet. You can see the cluster of buildings and the array of silos."

"No people?" Will asked.

"Everyone seems to be inside the buildings, but you can see dead bodies here, here and here, around the perimeter fence."

"What missiles are present?"

"I can answer that," General Boone said. "There are six silos, two of which contain nuclear-tipped missiles. The others are conventional high explosive."

"Do we know the tonnage?"

"We believe no more than ten kilotons each," the general said, "perhaps less."

"That's what, half the tonnage of the Hiroshima bomb?"

"Yes, sir."

"What range?"

"We think no more than a thousand miles. They could reach all of northwestern India, including Delhi."

"But not Israel."

"No, sir. But if they were able to move a missile to the southwestern corner of Afghanistan, they could just about do it."

"But they can't move them?"

"There are two mobile missile launchers inside one of the buildings, but it would be quite a job to load a missile onto one and truck it four or five hundred miles, then fire. We think that very unlikely, and if they tried it we could knock out the vehicle and the missile."

"If they were to attempt such a thing, how long might it take them?"

The general permitted himself a small shrug. "A week, ten days, perhaps."

"Let's keep that in mind during our planning."

The vice president, George Kiel, spoke up. "How far to the nearest Pakistani military base?"

"Thirty miles," the general replied.

"And what forces are present there?"

"An armored regiment."

Will spoke up. "I don't see how they could attack the missile site with that sort of force," he said, "without risking a launch. They could certainly hit any city in Pakistan."

"Correct, Mr. President," the general said. "The key would be speed, to get there before the invaders get a grip on how to fire a missile."

"That could be a very short time." Lance Cabot, the CIA DDO, had spoken for the first time, and everyone turned and looked at him.

"They would need time to persuade the staff to start firing missiles," the general said.

"Not if they had one or more men on the inside," Cabot said, "and we know there have been terrorist attempts to penetrate the Pakistani nuclear program."

"That's troubling," Will said.

"If it's true," the general countered. "Mr. Cabot, do you have any evidence of such a penetration or even an attempt?"

Cabot opened a folder in front of him. "Three weeks ago, we received a report from a source inside the Pakistani government that two technicians at this site had not returned from weekend leave on schedule. They still have not returned. Up to now, at least."

The room was silent for a long moment.

"General Boone," Will said, "have you had time to do any planning? And if so, do we have the relevant forces available?"

"Mr. President, we have a detachment of Navy SEALS deployed in the mountains, less than a hundred miles from the missile site."

"How many men?"

"Thirty, plus support people."

"Thirty doesn't sound like many."

"There may be no Taliban other than the invading party," Boone said.

"But we have no intelligence on the size of that party?"

"Correct, sir."

"Do we know which silos contain the nuclear warheads?" Will asked.

"No, sir, but the Pakistanis do. So that information should be available to us."

"Is it possible, if the SEALs could get into the compound, to destroy the missiles in their silos without setting off a nuclear blast?"

"Theoretically, sir."

"Certainly," Cabot said, interrupting. "The warheads are wired *not* to explode in the silos; they are armed by radio after firing."

"We don't know that for sure," the general said.

"*We* know for sure," Cabot replied. "We've known since before the missiles were deployed. I would have thought the Pentagon would know it, too."

"If we sent a few cruise missiles in there with conventional warheads," Will asked, "could we knock out the nukes before they could be fired?"

"In theory," Cabot said, looking at Boone. "General?"

Boone turned to the president. "Sir, the site was chosen to make that difficult, with high mountains surrounding it. An air strike would be more vertical—and more precise."

"What defenses would the site have against an air attack?" Will asked. "I presume that the surrounding mountains would reduce the effectiveness of radar until the aircraft were right on top of them."

"That's probable, sir," the general replied. "There are ground-to-air defensive missiles on the site. We don't know how many."

"All right," Will said. "We need more information. General Boone, I think you should contact your counterpart in the Pakistani army and get a full report on the defensive capabilities of the missile site, and then you should start plans for both an air strike and a ground assault immediately following."

"Mr. President, the Pakistanis are probably in a position to make both efforts before we could."

"For planning purposes, assume that they can't or won't do it in a timely manner," Will said.

"You understand, sir, that such a move on our part would constitute an attack on the soil of a friendly nation?"

"Of course, but I would rather deal with that than with the aftermath of a nuclear explosion," Will said. "Now Madame Director and gentlemen, the vice president and I need the room for a while, and

I assume you all would like to speak to your respective headquarters."

Everyone stood and filed out, except the president and vice
president.

"Now, George," Will said, "let's talk."

# 3

WILL LOOKED AT HIS VICE PRESIDENT. HE HAD NOT SEEN HIM FOR MORE THAN A week, and he seemed to have lost weight. "How are you, George?" he asked.

"Will, I'm not well. I've had a recurrence of the prostate cancer, and I'm scheduled for surgery this afternoon."

"I'm sorry to hear it. Have they given you a prognosis?"

"I'm afraid it has already spread. I know this is an awkward time to hear this, but I'm not going to be able to be on the ticket."

"George, you warned me when we teamed up four years ago that you would only serve one term, but I had hoped you might change your mind. Your advice on foreign affairs has been invaluable."

"Thank you, Will. I appreciate that. As a parting gift, may I give you my assessment of Mohammed Khan during this crisis?"

"I was going to ask you for that," Will said.

"He's an odd duck—strong in some areas, very weak in others. In the past, he has not performed well under this sort of pressure, not that anyone has ever had this sort of pressure weighing on him."

"What do you think he will do?"

"I think he will be forced to act immediately, perhaps rashly, in order not to appear weak. If he does, given the state of the Pakistani forces, I think he is likely to fail, and if he fails, it's going to be very bad, and his own military will want his head."

"He's been a good friend to us in a number of ways," Will said, "but I have to say I concur with your views. My immediate inclination is to send in our aircraft and the SEALs."

"That would be my view, as well," Kiel said, "but it's a move fraught with risk. We've never confronted a situation where a terrorist group has got hold of a nuclear weapon, and now these people have two."

"Yes," Will said. "I'm also inclined to think that this act was extremely well planned and executed, and I expect that they decided what they were going to do with the missiles before they attacked."

"I think you're probably right."

"God, I hope we have time to get a grip on it before they move further," Will said.

Kiel stood up and offered his hand. "A car is waiting to take me to Walter Reed," he said. "All I can do now, Will, is to wish you luck."

"Thank you, George. Good luck with the surgery and thank you for your exceptional service during our first term. Please give Doris my best, and know that you will be in our prayers."

The two men shook hands, and Kiel left.

Will picked up the phone and asked for Tim Coleman, his chief of staff.

"Yessir?"

"Tim, George Kiel is undergoing surgery for prostate cancer today and is out of the campaign. Ask Kitty to coordinate with his press secretary about an announcement."

"Sir, you might consider announcing it at the convention."

"Maybe. You get together with Kitty, Tom Black, and our leadership in the Congress and come up with some names. We all know who they're going to be, but it's important to consult."

"Do you have a top candidate in mind?" Tim asked.

"I'd appoint Sam Meriwether in a heartbeat, but we can't have both members of the ticket from one county." Sam Meriwether had been Will's own congressman before he had won Will's Senate seat in a special election. He had acted as Will's campaign manager when he first ran and was this time, as well.

"Yeah, well . . ." Tim said. "We'll get on this right away."

"I'm going to need some names before I get on that helicopter," Will said.

"I wish George had given us more notice."

"He didn't know himself, and, after all, he did tell me he would be around for only the first term." Will looked down and saw a light flashing on his phone. "I've gotta go." He pressed the button.

"Mr. President," the operator said, "I have President Khan of Pakistan for you."

"Good. Find everybody who was meeting in the Situation Room and get them back here, please." He pressed the relevant button. "President Khan?"

"Yes, Mr. President. I can give you some information now."

"Please, go ahead." He looked up to see Kate and Lance Cabot enter the room. "If you agree, I will put you on speaker, so that my people may hear you."

"Yes, please do."

The military people were entering the room as Will pressed the speaker button. "Please go ahead, Mr. President," he said.

"We estimate a detachment of forty to fifty in the initial assault," Khan said, "and they appear to be bringing in more people and fortifying the site now. There have been fatalities outside the building, but we have no knowledge of what happened inside. We suspect that the Taliban may have kidnapped two technicians earlier, so they may have launch capabilities."

"Excuse me, Mr. President," Will said, "but doesn't launching require codes?"

"Yes. In theory, only I can give the order, but the officer carrying the codes disappeared this morning, and we cannot locate him. We suspect that he may either have been taken by the Taliban or Al Qaeda or be in collusion with them."

"Please go on, Mr. President."

"I have given the order for an attack," Khan said, "and assault troops from a nearby base are moving into position as we speak."

"Mr. President, do you have shelter available that will withstand a nuclear attack?"

"I am leaving momentarily for my bunker," Khan replied.

"Good. Can you tell us which of the silos contain the nuclear warheads?"

"I will instruct my military staff to communicate with yours on that subject," Khan replied. "Now if you will excuse me, I must go."

"Good-bye, Mr. President, and good luck," Will said, but Khan had already hung up. He replaced the receiver and looked around the table. "Who has an update?"

General Boone spoke. "I have been in touch with the Pakistani military headquarters but was unable to speak with the commanding general. I got a feeling that the place was chaotic."

Kate spoke. "Our people on the ground suspect that at least some of the military command may have defected or revolted. A coup may be imminent."

"A coup in whose favor?" Will asked.

"We don't know," Kate said, "but Khan, of course, is a figure of hatred for fundamentalist Muslims. If he's replaced, it's not going to be with somebody we like."

Will turned to Boone. "General, how quickly could we attack the installation if the order were given now?"

"Given the logistics, not before midnight," Boone said, "but I've already placed the relevant units on alert and ordered the aircraft armed."

"Can you begin moving the SEALs closer to the installation?"

"They're less than an hour away by helicopter, so they're better off waiting where they are."

"Madame Director, please get in touch with Israeli intelligence. I don't know if they're aware of this situation yet, but I wouldn't be surprised. I don't want them jumping into this. Let them know that they're under no immediate threat. Also, please brief the secretary of state and ask him to call his counterpart in India and tell them what's happened. It's possible that Delhi might be a target for these missiles."

"Yes, Mr. President." She got up and left the room.

"General Boone," Will said, "what can we do that we haven't already done?"

"Militarily, nothing, Mr. President. Politically, well that's up to you."

"Lance, do we have any indication that anyone else knows about this yet?"

"No, Mr. President, but the lid won't be on it long, so I suggest we operate as if everybody knows."

"I'm not ready to announce this," Will said.

"No, sir, and you shouldn't, but you should be ready to respond to a leak immediately."

Will stood up. "All right, I'll leave you to your work, but I want to be notified of any change, good or bad, in the situation."

"Mr. President," General Boone said, "for the moment, it's pretty much out of our hands, but we'll do everything we can to be ready to move."

"Thank you, gentlemen," Will said. He left the Situation Room for the Oval Office.

# 4

WILL WALKED INTO THE OVAL OFFICE TO FIND TIM COLEMAN, KITTY CONROY, HIS campaign manager Sam Meriwether, his political consultant Tom Black, and the majority leader of the House and the minority leader of the Senate waiting for him. They all rose as he entered.

"Mr. President," Tim said, "is there something going on that we should know about?"

"You'll be briefed in a few minutes," Will said. "Now, have a seat and tell me whose names are on your list."

Tim began to read. "Senator Charles Watts of Idaho."

Will shook his head. "No—Idaho has a Republican governor, and we can't afford to give up the Senate seat."

"Congressman Tad Giddens of Nebraska."

"A good man, but green and a little impulsive. I need a grayer head."

"Governor Martin Stanton of California."

Will said nothing for a moment. "Good one. Who else?"

"Governor Bobby Breen of Texas."

"Two southerners on the ticket isn't good."

"Governor Eleanor Thomas of Oregon."

"A woman on the ticket would be a good thing, I think, but only if we believe she could credibly run for president after four years. What do you all think?"

Kitty Conroy spoke up. "She has a husband who runs his own large manufacturing business, and he isn't likely to come to Washington with her, which would be a problem for both of them. She has two teenaged children, too, and the girl could be a problem for us. She was arrested on a juvenile drug charge last year. She seems to be improving, but . . ."

"Who else?"

"Governor Elliot Sparks of Colorado."

"Twice divorced, and a reputation as a womanizer," Will said. "He'd be a time bomb. Anyone else?"

"That's all so far," Tim said.

"Marty Stanton is an appealing guy," Will said, "and he's finishing his second term as governor. He has an attractive family, grown children, and I think he'd be a serious candidate for president, if I weren't running, and he has a Mexican mother."

"I like him for the job," Sam said.

"So do I," Kitty chipped in.

The others made positive noises.

"Any women other than Betty in his life?"

Tom Black spoke up. "There were rumors about a woman in Los Angeles, before he was governor, but they both denied everything, and nobody had any real evidence. If there's been anybody since, Stanton has been very, very careful."

Will walked to his desk and picked up the phone. "Please find Governor Martin Stanton of California," he said into the phone, then hung up and looked around. "Last chance to bring up someone else," he said.

Nobody spoke. The phone rang, and Will picked it up.

"Hello? How are you, Marty? . . . I'm glad to hear it. Marty, I'm with Sam Meriwether, Tim Coleman, Kitty Conroy, Tom Black, Congressman Dan Tweed, and Senator Mike Hubbard. I'd like to put you on speaker so everyone can hear you. Here we go." Will pressed the button. "Can you hear me, Marty?"

"Yes, Mr. President."

"Marty, George Kiel has entered Walter Reed for prostate cancer surgery. The prognosis is unclear, and he's opted out of the race. All of us here think you'd make a great vice president, and a fine candidate for president in four years, and I'd be deeply honored if you'd accept George's place on the ticket."

Silence.

"You there, Marty?"

"Yes, but I'm stunned."

"I understand. Would you like to call me back?"

"May I put you on hold for a moment, Mr. President?"

"Certainly."

There was a click on the line.

"He's probably talking with Betty," Will said.

"It's going to be a short conversation," said Kitty.

Stanton came back on the line. "Mr. President?"

"I'm here, Marty. We all are."

"I'm very grateful for the opportunity, and I am delighted to accept."

"That's wonderful, Marty. Where are you now?"

"On my airplane, about two hours out of New York."

"Can we meet at the Waldorf Towers"—Will glanced at his watch—"at six o'clock?"

"Of course, Mr. President."

"And you'd better start drafting an acceptance speech. See you at six." Will hung up. "Well," he said, "that was easy. Tim, you'd better call the FBI and get them started on the background check. Tell them I want at least a preliminary report *fast*."

"Yes, sir." Tim started to leave but ran into Lance Cabot, who was on his way in.

"Stay, Tim," Will said. "Lance, anything new?"

"We've got the second wave of the attack on satellite now," Lance said. "They're going to be dug in by the time the Pakistani army arrives."

"Lance, will you brief everybody here on the situation, please?" Will asked.

"Yes, sir."

TEN MINUTES LATER, Lance had finished, leaving his audience nearly speechless.

"How do you want to handle the announcement?" Kitty asked.

"Write it, but keep it close. I'd like to wait until after the Pakistani army has finished its raid, unless we're forced to go sooner."

"Yes, sir."

"Who are we going to get to nominate Marty Stanton tonight?" Will asked.

"The speaker of the House is running the convention, and he's from California," Tim said.

Will nodded and picked up the phone. "Get me the speaker of the House," he said. "I believe he's at the Waldorf Towers." He waited the ten seconds it took for the White House operator to find the man.

"Yes, Mr. President?"

"Tank, George Kiel is in surgery and won't be running. I've asked Marty Stanton to replace him."

The speaker gave out a low whistle. "I'm sorry about George, but Marty is wonderful news."

"I agree, and I don't want you running for governor; I need you where you are."

"Yes, sir."

"I'd like you to place his name in nomination before my speech and get a vote by acclamation from the convention."

"I'd be delighted."

"My speech is televised at nine, so get it done by seven-thirty, then give Marty a few minutes for an acceptance speech. He can introduce me."

"Sounds good, Mr. President."

"I'm meeting with Marty at six at the Towers, and if you're available, I'd like you to be there."

"Of course, Mr. President."

"See you then, and keep all this under your hat until tonight." Will hung up and looked at the group. "Any loose ends?"

"Mr. President," Lance Cabot said, "I think you might describe Pakistan as a loose end."

"I can't do any more about that now. Is the helicopter ready, Tim? Everybody's luggage aboard?"

"Yes, Mr. President."

"Then let's go to New York."

# 5

WILL DIDN'T BOTHER WITH *AIR FORCE ONE*; THE HELICOPTER WOULD GET HIM TO New York just as fast, and it would land on top of the old Pan Am building, very near the Waldorf.

Halfway to New York, the copilot's voice came over the intercom system to Will's headset. "Phone call for you, Mr. President. The speaker of the House, Mr. Wainwright."

Will picked up the phone. "Tank?"

"Mr. President, I'm getting a lot of press questions about some sort of trouble in Pakistan."

"If you don't hear from the Joint Chiefs, I'll tell you about that at our six-o'clock meeting," Will said.

"Is anybody making an announcement about George?"

"I assume his press secretary will handle that."

"I've had a couple of calls about that, too, from the press."

"Refer them to the office of the vice president," Will said. "Anything else?"

"Are you going to mention this Pakistan thing in your speech?"

"I'll know more about that at six o'clock," Will said. "See you then, Tank." He took off the headset. "Kitty, give George's press secretary a call and see how they want to handle the announcement of his surgery. Also, ask her what time I can call the hospital and get an answer on the results and speak to Nancy Kiel."

"Yes, sir," Kitty said, taking the phone from Will.

Will sat and watched Philadelphia and New Jersey pass under them. Half an hour later they set down gently on top of the office building. They took an elevator down to the street, where a motorcade awaited, then drove to the Waldorf on the traffic-cleared streets. Will hated driving in New York because of the inconvenience it caused so many people, but at least this was a short trip. They arrived at the garage entrance to the Waldorf and were whisked up to the Towers, to the Presidential Suite. By the time Will had opened a bottle of water, his valet was already unpacking his and Kate's clothes and sending them to be pressed.

Will opened his briefcase and began reading the morning traffic, as his mail was called.

AT PRECISELY SIX O'CLOCK, Governor Martin Stanton of California arrived, followed closely by the speaker of the House, William Wainwright, known as "Tank" because of his considerable bulk.

Tim shook their hands and offered them seats and coffee. "Marty, I'm delighted you'll be on the ticket, and I'm sorry I couldn't give you more notice, but George told me only this morning."

"I understand, Mr. President, and I'm delighted to be on the ticket."

"Tank, has anybody briefed you on the Pakistani incident?"

"Yes, Mr. President, an aide from the Joint Chiefs came over. Marty was there, too, so we're up to date. I gather we're still waiting for the results of the army raid on the missile site."

"That's right," Will said. "We've got Navy SEALs and the Air Force on standby, in case they're needed."

"I hope to God the Pakistani army is successful."

"So do I, Tank. Marty, do you have a draft of your acceptance speech?"

"Yes, sir," Stanton said, handing over a copy. Will handed it to Kitty. "Tank, what's the schedule for the convention?"

"The platform is being adopted now—it's a final vote, so the debate is over. I'll make the announcement about George at seven and introduce Marty for his acceptance speech, then he'll introduce you at exactly eight-oh-one p.m. That'll give the networks a minute for their commentators to appear wise."

Kitty answered a ringing phone. "It's Walter Reed, Mr. President."

Will picked up a phone. "This is Will Lee."

"Mr. President, this is Dr. Brad Hardy. I am the vice president's surgeon."

"Good evening, Dr. Hardy. How is the vice president?"

"Not very well, I'm afraid. His condition was even worse than we had suspected, and there's a chance he won't survive. He's in the ICU now, and we'll know more in a few hours, tomorrow morning at the latest."

"I'm sorry to hear that, but thank you for letting me know. Is there anything I can do for him or you?"

"No, sir."

"Then good evening." Will hung up. "Kitty, find Nancy Kiel for me, please. She'll be at Walter Reed."

"Yes, sir." Kitty got on the phone. "Mr. President, I have Mrs. Kiel."

Will picked up the phone. "Nancy?"

"Hello, Will."

"I've just spoken to the surgeon."

"I know. It doesn't look good, I'm afraid."

"Nancy, how did he get this far along before the surgery?"

"He wouldn't do it, Will, and I couldn't make him, and his doctors couldn't, either. He wanted to finish out his term first. If only he'd done this last summer . . . but he just wouldn't."

"Is there anything I can do for you or George?"

"No, I think everything that can be done has been done. When will the announcement be made?"

"Tank Wainwright will announce it to the convention at seven o'clock and introduce Martin Stanton, who's replacing George on the ticket. I know this seems rushed, but we don't really have a choice."

"I agree. That's the way to do it."

"I'll have Kitty speak to George's office about it."

"Thank you for calling, Will."

"When George wakes up, tell him I'm praying for him."

"I will."

"Good night." Will hung up the phone.

"How is he?" the speaker asked.

"Not good," Will said.

WILL WAS BACKSTAGE at Madison Square Garden in the reception room that had been arranged for him. Kate arrived from Washington with his stepson, Peter, in tow.

Will kissed them both. "Any news on the Pakistani thing?"

"The counterattack should be in progress now," she said. "I don't know when we'll have the result."

Kitty came over. "Excuse me, Mr. President, but I think we should get Mrs. Lee and Peter to their box now, before the speaker introduces Governor Stanton."

"Right," Will said. He kissed them good-bye, then sat down to watch the proceedings on television, like everyone else.

"LADIES AND GENTLEMEN," Martin Stanton roared, "the once and future president of the United States of America!"

Will entered from the wings, and a roar went up in the huge

arena. The band was playing "Happy Days Are Here Again," but nobody could hear. The pandemonium continued for a good five minutes, while Will plastered a smile on his face, put an arm around Stanton, and waved like an idiot until they quieted.

As the roar expired, Will stepped forward to the lectern and checked the TelePrompTers on both sides of where he stood.

"The first thing I should tell you is that I've just spoken to the vice president's surgeon and to Nancy Kiel, and George is out of surgery. I hope we'll have more news of him before the night is over.

"I know that having a new vice-presidential candidate came as a surprise to you, but I didn't know about it myself, until George came to see me this morning. I hope you'll all mention him in your prayers tonight.

"Martin Stanton is going to be a great vice president!" he said, and the roar came again, while Stanton waved from the sidelines. Then, as Will was taking a breath to begin his acceptance speech he heard two cell phones begin ringing behind him on the stage. Then he heard more cell phones, some from the audience, and two Secret Service agents came running down the aisles and stood at the foot of the podium, facing the audience.

Will looked over his shoulder and saw Tim Coleman striding toward him from the wings, his cell phone in his hand.

Will stepped away from the microphones. "What's happened?" he asked as Tim reached him.

Tim leaned in close to Will's ear. "There's been a nuclear explosion in Pakistan," he said.

# 6

WILL FOLLOWED TIM COLEMAN BACK TO THE GREEN ROOM, JUST OFFSTAGE. KITTY Conroy was waiting, and a moment later Kate walked in with Peter in tow.

Will turned to his Secret Service agent. "Please find Peter a safe and private place to wait for us," he said. "Be sure there's a TV set." He turned to Peter. "Peter, please go with the agent. We have to have a meeting here." Peter left the room with the agent without a word. It was not the first time he had been asked to leave a room.

Will looked at the large-screen TV set on the wall of the room. It was divided into four areas with a different network on each screen. None of them appeared to have the story.

"What kind of communications do we have here?" Will asked.

"One secure line to the White House switchboards, Mr. President. Other than that, only ordinary phone lines, four of them. They've been checked repeatedly for bugs."

"Where's the nearest command center?" Will asked.

"At the Waldorf, sir."

"Clear me a path to the Waldorf and let me know when the motorcade is ready to go."

"Right away, sir," the agent said. "It shouldn't take more than ten or twelve minutes." The man went to work on his cell phone.

"Kate," Will said, "do you know anything I don't?"

"No," Kate said, "but I have a secure cell phone, and I can call Lance at Langley."

"Please do so." Will picked up the secure phone, and a White House operator answered immediately. "This is the president. Please connect me with the duty officer at the Pentagon."

"Yes, sir." The line was picked up on the first ring.

"Duty officer, Colonel Bird."

"Colonel, this is the president speaking."

"Yes, sir?"

"Where are the secretary of defense, the chairman of the Joint Chiefs of Staff, and the other chiefs of staff?"

"The secretary is still on vacation at his home in Aspen, sir. The others are all en route to the Pentagon, Mr. President," the colonel said. "The earliest will arrive in twelve minutes and the latest in twenty-one minutes."

"What information do you have on the nuclear explosion in Pakistan?"

"Only that it has occurred, sir. We caught it on satellite, about forty miles east of the missile site from which it was fired."

"Thank you, Colonel. Please tell the chairman to call me at the Waldorf command center as soon as he has assembled his group and to arrange to feed video to me there and to the secretary in Aspen." He hung up the phone and looked at the Secret Service agent. "How soon can we leave for the Waldorf?"

"In about five minutes, sir."

"I'm going back to the podium," Will said. "Tell the speaker to call for order now." Will went and stood in the wings while the speaker quieted the arena, then he walked to the lectern.

"Ladies and gentlemen, please excuse my brief absence. I have some important news for you that has not been broadcast on the networks yet." Silence fell over the arena. "Early this morning, eastern time, an attack was made by elements of the Taliban, with the possible assistance of Al Qaeda, on a missile launch site in northwestern Pakistan. The site was captured, and among the six missiles stored in silos there, two had uranium-235 nuclear warheads of about ten kilotons each, or about half the size of the Hiroshima bomb.

"I spoke twice this morning and this afternoon to President Khan of Pakistan, and he assured me that preparations were under way to retake the missile site and that the attack would be made this evening. President Khan assured me that all precautions were being taken to secure other missile sites.

"As a precaution, I gave orders to put on alert an Air Force squadron of fighter jets, armed with conventional missiles, and a unit of ground troops, in case they were needed to assist the Pakistani army.

"A few minutes ago, we learned from satellite observations that a nuclear device had detonated in a remote area of northwest Pakistan. We do not know yet whether this was deliberate or accidental.

"As I speak, the Joint Chiefs of Staff are assembling at the Pentagon, and shortly I will be speaking to them and to the secretary of defense, who is in Colorado, from a command center in New York City. I must leave now to go to that site, but I want to assure you that we have no intelligence at this time to indicate that any other place in the world is being threatened. Every indication we have so far is that this disturbance is highly localized, so you have nothing to fear.

"Before I go, please let me say that I am honored to accept your nomination to once again lead my party in the race for president and that I look forward to campaigning all over the United States. Thank you and good night."

Will turned and walked toward the green room and was met by the speaker on the way.

"What should I do now?" the speaker asked.

"Our business is done here, Tank," Will said. "Close the convention as planned and send these people home."

"Yes, sir."

TWO MINUTES LATER, Will, Kate, and Peter, along with Martin Stanton, were in the presidential limousine bound for the Waldorf. Eight minutes later they were in the Presidential Suite in the Waldorf Towers, sitting at the dining room table, watching an array of screens that had been previously installed in the room. The phone on the table rang, and, simultaneously, the Joint Chiefs of Staff appeared on one screen and the secretary of defense, Charles Quarry, on another.

"Good evening, gentlemen," Will said. "Mr. Chairman, what do you have to tell us?"

"Mr. President," the chairman said, "there is precious little information coming in at this time."

"One moment, please," Will said. "Tim, get President Khan on the telephone as quickly as you can. General, please go ahead with your report."

"We know from satellite observations, Mr. President, that the attack by the Pakistani army took place and that, during heavy fighting, a missile was fired—we don't know whether that was accidental or not. Shortly after that, when the missile was around forty miles downrange in a southeasterly direction, on a course that would have taken it toward Islamabad, it exploded at an altitude of approximately thirty thousand feet."

"That's much higher than if an airburst attack had been planned," Will said.

"Yes, sir. A more effective altitude for an airburst would be three to five thousand feet, depending on the throw weight of the missile."

"Does it seem likely that the target was Islamabad, then?"

"Yes, sir, it does."

"We are trying to contact President Khan now. Do you have any information from him or from the Pakistani army at this time?"

"No, sir. We have been unable to reach either the Presidential Palace or army headquarters."

"The president told me earlier that he was removing himself from the palace to a bunker. Have we had any communication with that place?"

"No, sir. We are unable to reach anyone in authority at this time."

The secretary of defense spoke up. "General, I believe you have a standing plan to take out the other Pakistani nuclear missile sites."

"Yes, sir. We do."

"Do you need to move forces or aircraft to get that done?" Will asked.

"No, sir. We have attack submarines present in the Arabian Gulf and the Gulf of Oman as well as in the eastern Mediterranean that can hit the sites with multiple cruise missiles."

"I want it clearly understood that, should it become necessary to hit the missile sites, all our missiles will be armed with conventional, non-nuclear warheads."

"That is confirmed, Mr. President. Our plan calls for staggered firings, dependent on the distance of each sub from the targets, so that we get simultaneous strikes, thus giving no opportunity for a retaliatory nuclear attack. We have allotted four cruise missiles for each target."

"What sort of casualties would such an attack engender?"

"All the sites are on military bases, except the one captured, which is thirty miles from a base. Large numbers of Pakistani troops man the bases, and there are some military dependents there, too, as well as civilian employees. However, the missiles are accurate to within three meters and can be programmed to explode after entering the ground at the sites. Virtually every person manning the sites would be killed, but those in the surrounding area would have a better chance of survival."

"Can you put a number on the fatalities?"

"Likely several hundred at each of the five remaining sites. Do you wish us to target the site from which the missile was fired?"

"Plan for it, but I'll make that decision after I speak with President Khan."

"Yes, sir."

"Stand by. Madame Director?" Kate was on a phone at the other end of the conference table.

"Yes, Mr. President?"

"Have you been able to obtain any information from your sources in Islamabad?"

"Sir, we have reports from our station there and from our resources on the ground that the blast was seen in the sky from Islamabad, but at the moment the city is reasonably calm. The streets are full of people waiting for news from the president, but no official announcement has been made, except to request calm and that people remain in their homes, which many are not doing."

"General, did you hear that report?" Will asked.

"Yes, Mr. President, and with that I believe you have everything we can now confirm, until you speak with President Khan or we speak with Pakistani army headquarters."

"Thank you, General. Please call when you have further information, we'll be here." Will hung up. Kate was still on the phone.

"Kate?"

She put her hand over the phone. "Yes?"

"Is there any indication that the attack on the missile installation was part of a planned coup d'état?"

"No, not at this time."

She continued to talk on the phone, presumably to Lance Cabot, and Will sat and tried to think if there was anything he could do that he had not already done.

7

WILL FIELDED CALLS FROM AIDES, THE JCS, AND CABINET MEMBERS FOR THE NEXT hour; then Tim Coleman came into the room. "President Khan for you, Mr. President."

Will picked up the phone. "President Khan?"

"Yes, President Lee."

"I'm very glad to hear from you; we were all very concerned. What is your situation?"

"We have put down a small rebellion in the military—fewer than fifty officers, none of them ranked above colonel."

"That's good. What is the status of your nuclear capability?"

"When we attacked the northwestern missile site someone inside managed to fire one missile before we could disable it, but we were able to detonate it electronically a few seconds later."

"What about the second missile?"

"Once at close range, our troops were able to disable it electronically."

"Was there damage to the facility?"

"Some of the aboveground buildings were knocked down by the

shock wave, but everything belowground was undamaged. We managed to pump an odorless gas into the tunnels, rendering everyone inside unconscious. We captured all of them."

"What about the other installations around your country?"

"All the nuclear missiles have had their guidance systems and other essential systems removed, so that they cannot be fired. All sites but one are now neutralized."

"What about the other one?"

"There is a fight in progress there now, and I hope to have a favorable report within minutes."

"What is the situation in the country at large?"

"Calm has been restored in most places, and by tomorrow things should be quite normal. We will proceed with elections on schedule."

"May I release this information to the American press, Mr. President?"

"Yes, but please do not mention the final facility until I have confirmation from there."

"As you wish. Is there anything I can do for you at this time?"

"Thank you, Mr. President, no. Everything is well in hand."

"Mr. President, may I ask, where is the final missile site that remains unsecured?"

"It is southeast of Islamabad about one hundred miles."

"Have you had any damage reports from the northwest?"

"Only at our military base in that region, which suffered much damage to structures. Also, a number of our troops were blinded, temporarily, I hope, by the blast. We do not expect much in the way of radioactive contamination, since the blast occurred at a high altitude. If you will excuse me, President Lee, I must go and attend to some things."

"Of course, President Khan. Please let me know the moment the final missile is secured. As you can imagine, my administration is in touch with many world leaders who are concerned about the situation."

"Yes, Mr. President."

"And don't hesitate to call me if I can be of any help." Will hung up and looked around the room. "Everybody hear that?"

He got a chorus of affirmation from around the table and from the TV screens. Everyone seemed vastly relieved, and Will was not an exception.

"Tim," Will said, "I think we should be getting back to Washington. I'll hold a press conference as soon as we get word on the securing of the final missile."

"I'll alert the Secret Service and the helicopter, Mr. President," Tim replied, then left the room.

"General," Will said to the figure on the TV screens, "please lower you alert level; the worst seems to be past."

"Yes, sir, Mr. President," the man said.


WILL TOOK ALONG his new vice-presidential candidate and his luggage. "We have a lot of campaign planning to do, Marty," he said. "And I want you to meet members of the vice president's staff. You'll be seeing a lot of them on the campaign trail."

"I've already canceled the rest of my schedule," Stanton said. "Most of my staff are returning to Sacramento to handle things there."


THEY WERE TEN MINUTES out of Washington when Will got a phone call from Walter Reed. He listened briefly, then hung up. "George Kiel died five minutes ago," he said to the people on the copter. "Tim, I want to speak to Mrs. Kiel as soon as we're at the White House. Marty, I'm afraid you're not going to be able to serve out your term as governor of California. I'm appointing you vice president as soon as the FBI completes its background check, and I'm sure we can get a quick confirmation from the Senate."

"Well, Mr. President," Stanton said, "it's been quite a day."

"There are going to be a lot of those ahead, Marty. You'll get used to it."

# 8

WILL WAS WATCHING THROUGH THE HELICOPTER WINDOW AS THE WHITE HOUSE got closer, when Kitty Conroy gave him a sheet of paper with hand-written notes.

"Mr. President, a clutch of press will be waiting when the helicopter lands, and when we land, I think you should make an on-the-run statement along these lines."

Will quickly read the notes and handed them back. "Right, I'll do that."

"Don't stop for more than a couple of seconds, say your piece, and get out."

"Right, Kitty."

The big helicopter settled onto the White House lawn, and everyone poured out. The knot of waiting press ran toward Will, shouting questions.

Will stopped, held up a hand to quiet them, and spoke rapidly. "Naturally, we are all saddened by the unexpected death of Vice President George Kiel, and our hearts and our prayers go out to his loved ones. On another subject that I'm sure will interest you, I spoke with President Khan of Pakistan a little over an hour ago, and he tells me that his military exploded the missile shortly after it was fired and that little loss of life or damage resulted from the explosion. The Pakistani military has moved quickly to secure all the other missile sites in that country, and I'm waiting for a final report. I'm optimistic that all will be well shortly. I'll address the subject when all reports are in, and that's all I have for you now." He walked quickly toward the White House, ignoring shouted questions.

"Marty," Will said, "you stay with me. The staff will put your things in an upstairs bedroom, and by tomorrow we'll have you in Blair House."

"Yes, Mr. President."

The two men walked into the Oval Office, and Will noted the flashing lights on his telephone. "And Marty, it's 'Will' when we're alone or with top staff. You can use the title in public or larger gatherings."

"Yes, Will."

Will took a brief call from the Pentagon and hung up. "No further word from President Khan," he said to the small group. Kate was on another phone talking with her people. She hung up.

"We've been able to confirm the location of the site with the remaining missiles," she said. "I suggest you allow me to give the Pentagon the coordinates, in case we have to knock it out."

Will nodded. "Tell them only on my direct and explicit order," he said. "I want to keep us out of this, if at all possible." He turned to Kitty. "Call the secretary of state and tell him I want him in constant touch with the Pakistani ambassador," he said.

"Will," Martin Stanton said, "does it worry you that we've heard nothing from Khan about the securing of the final missile site?"

"Yes, it does," Will said, "but Khan has, in the past, sometimes been slow to respond to communications. I hope this is just one of those times."

"I hope so, too," Stanton said. "I don't think you should say anything else publicly until that situation is fully clarified."

"I'll put it off until tomorrow morning," Will said, "but if we haven't had a positive response from Khan by then, I'll just have to report what I know. I can't allow this to drag on."

"I understand."

The phone rang, and Will picked it up. "Yes?"

"President Khan for you, Mr. President."

"Put him through. President Khan?"

"Yes, President Lee. I am calling to tell you that the final missile site has been secured. Also, I wish to express my condolences and those of my government on the death of Vice President Kiel. I knew him well, and he was a fine man."

"Thank you, President Khan."

"If you will forgive me for being brief, I have matters to attend to."

"Of course, Mr. President," Will said, "and I am glad to have your news." He waited for a response, but Khan had hung up. Will turned to the group. "Looks like we're out of the woods," he said. "The final site has been secured. Kitty, release that to the media and tell them I'll hold a brief news conference in the morning. No address to the nation. Let's not make too big a deal of this—it's over."

"Yes, Mr. President." Kitty ran for her office.

"I think that's it for the night," Will said. "Everybody get some sleep. Marty, you come upstairs with Kate and me."


UPSTAIRS, WILL TOOK a call from the secretary of state, who said he had gotten Khan's message from the Pakistani ambassador.

"Tom," Will said, "we've got to use these events as a tool for forging a new agreement with Pakistan on the handling of nuclear weapons. Let's make it our goal to have them all disabled and secured at a single location. We may not get that, but let's try. Get started on that first thing tomorrow, and make it your highest priority."

"Yes, Mr. President, and may I say that everyone at State is very sad about the death of George Kiel. He knew his foreign policy, and we had great respect and affection for him."

"Thank you very much, Tom, and good night," Will said, and hung up.

"Would you two like a drink?" Kate asked.

Both men nodded. "The usual," Will said. He allowed himself a drink or two a day at his doctor's suggestion.

"A single malt, if you've got it," Stanton said.

They settled in with their drinks.

"This was a close one," Will said. "There are a hundred ways it could have been a lot worse, and I think we've gotten off easy."

"So far," Kate said. "Do you really think that Khan will agree to tighter controls on his warheads?"

"If not, I'm going to tighten as many screws as I can think of," Will said. "He knows how bad this could have been, and I hope it's shaken him to the core."

"I've met the man twice," Stanton said, "but I don't think I know him well enough to offer advice."

"Nobody expects you to be an expert on foreign policy, Marty," Will said. "Not yet, anyway. Defer any questions from the press to Kitty or me. After all, you're still the governor of California."

"Perfectly true, Will."

"What kind of governor do you think Mike Rivera will make?"

"He's been a good lieutenant governor," Stanton said, "and I think he would have had a good shot at my job in November. It should be easier for him, now."

"Maybe you should give him a call before you go to bed," Will said.

"Yes, I will."

Stanton looked pensive. "This is the first nuclear explosion in the atmosphere since . . . the sixties? The French?"

"Since 1980," Will replied. "The Chinese."

The phone rang, and Kate picked it up. She listened for a minute or so. "Stay on it," she said, then hung up. She turned back to Will and Stanton. "We've had a report from an operative that something important was taken away from that last missile site," she said. "In a helicopter."

"What was taken?"

"No confirmation, but the helicopter probably means that the military took it away."

"I hope to God it was the warhead," Will said.

"I hope to God it was the military," Kate replied.

9

WILL SAT WITH MARTIN STANTON AS THEY FINISHED THEIR DRINKS. KATE HAD GONE to bed.

"Will," Stanton said, "there's something I have to tell you. I know I should have spoken about this sooner, but I couldn't until I had talked to Betty, and what with the events of today, the situation was resolved only earlier this evening."

"What is it, Marty?"

"Betty and I are divorcing."

Will sat and stared at the man, saying nothing.

"We had talked about this before but hadn't come to any conclusions. The vice-presidential nomination was the final straw—she doesn't want to come to Washington. It's amicable, I assure you. There's only the settlement to be worked out, and we're both reasonable people. I want her to be happy with it."

"You're right, Marty. You should have told me sooner, but I don't think it would have eliminated you as a candidate. Of course, we'll never know about that."

"I'm sorry."

That's enough punishment for the man, Will thought. "I'll get together with my staff, and we'll figure out when to make the announcement."

"I'll need to know that, so that I can inform Betty beforehand."

"Of course. It's not a time to make her angry." Will paused and took a sip of his drink. "Now there's the other question."

"The answer is no," Stanton said. "There's no other woman."

"I'm glad to hear it," Will said. "Does Betty have another man?"

Stanton looked surprised at the question. "Of course not. Betty's not given to that sort of thing."

"Are you sure about that, Marty? How much time have you and Betty spent together lately?"

"More than you might think, in the circumstances. We still sleep in the same bed, or at least we did until now."

"Then I'll take your word for it, Marty. But I don't want any more surprises. If there's anything else you want to tell me, now is the time."

Stanton shook his head vigorously. "No. There's nothing else."

Will polished off his drink and stood up. "Good, then I'm off to bed."

"I, too," Stanton said.

The two men shook hands and went to their respective bedrooms.

Will found Kate in bed reading a novel. He sat down on the bed and shucked off his shoes. "All these years, and I don't know how you do that," he said.

"Do what?"

"Go from a nuclear crisis to a novel in a heartbeat."

"It keeps me sane to be able to live in a book for an hour." She turned the page.

"And you can read while talking to me," Will said.

"In my novel, you're not the president."

"Maybe I won't be on January twentieth, either," he said.

"Fat chance," she replied, turning another page.

# 10

WILL CONVENED A MEETING WITH KITTY CONROY, HIS CAMPAIGN MANAGER SAM Meriwether, his chief of staff Tim Coleman, his political consultant Tom Black, and Moss Mallet, his pollster. He began by telling them of his conversation with Martin Stanton.

The reaction was, at first, a thoughtful silence. Finally, Tom Black spoke. "This is going to come out," he said. "Perhaps during the campaign, perhaps sooner."

"Only Marty and his wife and the people in this room know about it," Will said.

"Marty and his wife and his mistress," Tom said.

"There was no mention of a mistress," Will said.

"That doesn't mean he doesn't have one, or that his wife doesn't have another man, or both."

"Kitty," Will said, "see that the FBI adds those questions to their questionnaire and the background check."

"Yes, sir," Kitty replied, making a note.

"Whatever there is, it's going to come out," Black repeated, "even if only God knows. Even He would mention it to *somebody*."

"What do you suggest we do?" Will asked.

"One of two things: either find yourself another running mate, or announce it soon, while we can still control it."

"I'm convinced Marty is the best choice," Will said, "even with a pending divorce."

Moss Mallet spoke up. "You all know Governor Stanton has a Mexican mother. That's going to help us in California and the Southwest and in Florida, too, and that is a very great deal of help. Your immigration policy has cost you some Hispanic support, Mr. President, but no Republican is going to have even a part-Hispanic running mate. We have to capitalize on that."

Will nodded. "Sam?"

"Keep him, but get the news out."

"Tim?"

"Stick with him," Tim replied.

"Kitty, are you on board?"

"I'm scared, but I'm on board," she replied.

"So be it," Tom Black said. "Are you going to appoint him vice president soon?"

"Yes," Will said.

"Then I think he should bring it up in his opening statement at the Senate confirmation hearings."

"That will grab all the headlines," Tim Coleman said.

"For a day," Tom replied. "Then we'll have it out in the open and out of the way."

"It will get more play than that in California," Coleman pointed out.

"Nothing we can do about that," Sam said, "and California is where we can most afford the coverage. Stanton was reelected with nearly seventy percent of the vote."

"Tim," Will said, "you work on the opening statement with Marty's people. Don't finish the statement with the announcement—put it somewhere in the middle. In the meantime, nobody in this room is authorized to tell any other person, living or dead, about this, and don't mention it in your prayers; you never know who's listening. What's next?"

Black spoke up. "Henry King Jackson." Jackson was the African-American mayor of Atlanta who had left the Democratic Party and had been elected as an independent. A large, handsome man with a voice to match, he had become the most prominent national spokes-man for black Americans.

"What about Henry?" Will asked.

"I'm hearing rumors that he's considering launching a third-party candidacy," Black said.

"How substantial are the rumors?" Will asked.

"Not very, but they're from fairly inside sources."

"I know him about as well as any white guy," Sam said, "and I don't think he'll do it. He'll use the threat to get something from Will, but in the end, he won't run."

There were murmurs of agreement from the others.

"We have to have a plan to deal with him, anyway," Black said, "just in case he does."

Will turned to Kitty. "What can we offer him? Something in the new cabinet?"

Kitty shrugged. "King Henry has a pretty high opinion of him-self. It would have to be something bigger than HUD. You want to make him secretary of state?"

Will smiled and shook his head.

Sam spoke up. "Why don't you make him an ambassador-at-large to Africa?"

"Too grandiose a title and not substantive enough," Will said. "The man is not stupid. How about assistant secretary of state for African affairs?"

"That's a career diplomat's post," Kitty said. "Still, if he had a top-notch State Department officer at his side and in his hair, it might work. And it would keep him out of the country a lot, and that's a plus."

"Are you going to keep Tom Rodgers on at State?" Sam asked.

"Yes," Will said, "and he's already said he'll stay on."

"You'd better feel him out about it before you talk to Henry," Kitty said. "I'm not sure how he'll react."

Will smiled. "Neither am I."

"Henry's going to be in D.C. for an NAACP conference pretty soon," Sam said.

"Maybe I'll invite him to lunch," Will replied.

"No witnesses," Kitty cautioned. "None of his people, anyway."

"You're a cynic, Kitty. If Tom Rodgers buys into this, maybe I should have him there. It would lend weight to the offer."

Kitty nodded and made a note.

"Moss," Will said, "how are we looking in the polls this week?"

"You've got a fifty-eight percent approval rating nationwide—up a point. Your ratings on foreign affairs and defense remain at that level, too. Forty-seven percent on immigration, which is more than I expected."

"How about against the Republican candidate?"

"Tell me who he or she will be, and I'll tell you," Moss said, laughing. "There's a close, three-way contest among the opposition party. But, you're ahead of them all by at least ten points."

"So things aren't bad, then?"

"They're better than not bad, they're very good."

"Have you done any polling on a possible Henry Jackson run?"

"I've thought it better to let sleeping dogs lie, but I haven't seen anything from the papers or the networks that gives him more than eight percent. Of course, most of those would be black folks who would otherwise be voting for you."

"Would he take any votes at all from a Republican?"

"Maybe a few black Republicans, but not anybody else. Jackson could only matter in a tight race."

"Still," Will said, "I'd rather have him in Africa than on the campaign trail."

"Who wouldn't?" Kitty asked.

"Henry is a smart guy," Will said. "Let's not underestimate him."

"I hope he's smart enough to take the African job," Kitty said.

ROBERT KINNEY, DIRECTOR OF THE FEDERAL BUREAU OF INVESTIGATION, LOOKED across the desk at Assistant Director Kerry Smith, the youngest AD every to hold that office. Kerry looked back at him expectantly.

"Kerry, you've been supervising the background check on Governor Martin Stanton, haven't you?"

"Yes, Director, but just oversight, not direct participation."

"There's an interview with the governor scheduled this afternoon."

"That's correct, Director."

"I want you to conduct it personally."

Smith's eyebrows went up.

"Don't question, just do."

"I take it this interview is of a special nature to the White House?"

"This *appointment* is of a special nature, Kerry. We've got a dead vice president, not even in the ground yet, and an appointment of a new one by the president on the fly in the middle of a nuclear event halfway around the world. There've been a lot of distractions for the president. He's ordinarily a careful man by nature, but I don't want him to miss something that's going to rise up and bite him on the ass later, like in the confirmation hearings in the Senate."

"Then he's going to appoint Stanton vice president to serve out Kiel's term?"

"You have to ask?"

"No, sir. Is there anything in particular that should be brought into this interview, apart from the draft of the information you've already seen?"

"Yes, two things: First, the governor has told the president that he and his wife are divorcing quite soon and that she will not be participating in the campaign."

"And the president is keeping him as his running mate? Wow."

"They intend for Stanton to announce this during his opening statement to the Senate Judiciary Committee. They figure it will blow over quickly."

"That seems like a good plan," Smith said.

"It's a good plan, if the governor has told them everything. It's my experience that no one ever tells anyone, let alone a Senate committee, *everything* about the circumstances of a pending divorce."

"I agree."

"What I want you to find out is *everything*, or at least everything the governor is willing to tell anybody."

"What methods do you wish me to employ to secure this information, Director?"

"I want you to *ask* him."

Smith blinked. "Oh."

"And then I want you to check out everything he says and, in addition, everything he *doesn't* say. I want you to do it fast, and I want you to do it good, because when I report to the president that his candidate is squeaky clean or, at least, highly unlikely to get caught doing anything that isn't squeaky clean, I want to be telling my president the truth. Do I make myself clear?"

"Yes, Director." Smith held up a folder. "I have his questionnaire, and there are some points in there that I will raise with him. Ah, you said there were two things you wanted me to raise with the governor. What was the other one?"

"I want you to ask him where he was born. That is, *exactly* where he was born."

"Exactly?"

"Get a street address, if you can."

"May I ask the relevance of this information, Director?"

"Not yet."

Smith flipped through the pages of his file on Stanton and came up with a sheet of paper. "His birth certificate says he was born at San Diego Women's Hospital, in California. Isn't that good enough?"

"Look just under the hospital name, Kerry. What does it say?"

Smith looked at the information. "It says 'in transit.'"

"I want you to find out exactly what that means."

"I expect it means in an ambulance, on the way to the hospital."

"I can tell you the governor wasn't born in an ambulance, and what the birth certificate doesn't tell us is where his mother was in transit *from*."

Smith shook his head. "I'm sorry, Director, but you're going to have to tell me what you're talking about, because I'm not getting it."

Kinney sat back in his chair and tossed a file across his desk. "Read this," he said. "I'll wait."

Smith read quickly through the two sheets of paper.

"Are you getting the drift, Kerry?"

"Having read his questionnaire, I can see how there may be problems. Is the governor aware of these circumstances?"

"From my reading of his questionnaire and the preliminary report, he is either not aware of them or is concealing them. I want to know if either of those things is true."

"Director, forgive me for asking, but if this information is not known to the governor, how did you come by it?"

"I had a phone call from someone who, if not in a position to know, was at least in a position to ask some questions."

"Was this person a member of the Republican Party?"

"That's enough questions, Kerry. Now get out of my office."

Smith gulped. He now realized that the file in his hand and what he would add to it in his investigation and interview of the governor might determine who the next vice president and, therefore, a potential future president would be.

Kerry Smith stood. "Sir, I will find out what you want to know."

"Thank you, Kerry," Kinney said. "And don't keep me waiting for information about this."

Kerry Smith got out of there fast.

## 12

MARTIN STANFORD CLOSED THE DOOR OF THE LITTLE OFFICE HE HAD BEEN ASSIGNED in the family quarters of the White House and sat down. He figured a president's secretary had once worked in this room; it was too small for a visiting dignitary. He unlocked his briefcase and removed a cell phone that had been purchased for him at a grocery store in Los Angeles, one containing a prepaid phone card and no GPS chip, then he dialed the number, which he had committed to memory and not stored in the phone, of a duplicate cell phone.

"Hi there," she said.

"Hi there, yourself."

"How did it go this morning?"

"Well, I think. At least he didn't immediately dump me. My guess is, the way he thinks, he'll want me to make it public soon, to get it out of the way."

"How is the gargoyle going to feel about that?"

"She'll be good with it. She thinks she wants it even more than I do."

"How about your kids?"

"They're grown-ups. They'll take it well, and they probably won't be very surprised."

"Is there any suspicion of us?"

"Not that I've detected. How about on your end?"

"Nope. We've been very careful, and it's paying off."

"Are you still willing to move here?"

"You bet I am. Your successor and I don't really get along all that well, and I don't want to work for him when you're gone. And there's some news: I've heard through the legal grapevine that the AAG for criminal stuff is not going to be around for the next term, and he wants to leave as soon as his boss can find a replacement."

"That would be a great job for you, after your years as an ADA and state justice, before you came to work for me."

"You bet your ass it would, and I've already made some calls. They're sending me an application to start the process."

"Listen, baby, I can't have anything to do with your application; I can't even write a letter, unless the AG asks me to."

"How about if I give the big guy as a reference. I've known him since he was a Capitol Hill aide, worked with him a couple of times on justice issues."

"Good idea. He'll ask me, and I'll give him my highest recommendation."

"Then I'll get started on the application as soon as it comes. When do you want me to resign?"

"We talk almost every day on state business. During the next call, tell me about your plan, then send me a letter saying that you want to start looking for something, but you'll stay on until you've nailed down a new job. That'll get it on the record, and be sure to log the content of our conversation. I'll do the same."

"Can we get together when I'm in town?" she asked.

"Baby, you know we can't do that. I've got the whole process to go through, and I've got a security detail on my back now. But announcing this means we can start the proceedings immediately, and I've already talked with my people about how to divvy up, so that shouldn't take long. I'm sure she has a list of what she wants. I'll give her the house at home, of course, and she'll pretty much get half. Don't worry, there'll be enough for us, especially if I get the job. And after that, who knows?"

"How are we going to handle it when I get there?"

"After everything's over, we'll arrange to bump into each other at some public event, then we'll do a few dinners, or something, just to let people get used to seeing us together, and after that, we'll be home free. I think you might like that very nice house over at the Naval Observatory."

"I might at that," she said.

"I wish you were here, now, babe," he said.

"I want to fuck you," she said.

"How would you like it?"

"Every which way."

"That's a promise, but we have to be patient. If you get a chance, be seen with other men around town. That would be good for us."

"What if I fall in love?"

"You're already in love," he said, "and so am I. We're going to make this work. Bye-bye, now. We won't be talking for a while, and always let me make the call."

"Will do, and I'm holding you to that promise."

Stanton hung up and tried not to think about her body.

A BLOCK AND A HALF AWAY, a man in an extremely well-equipped car was fiddling with a very illegal scanner that operated on cell-phone frequencies. He had caught only snatches of that conversation, since in this neighborhood he couldn't park where the reception was best and listen without attracting Secret Service attention. He didn't know who the parties were, but he knew there was a story in this, probably a big one. He would just have to keep listening. He shut off his recorder and made a note of the time and place where the reception had been best, then he took the memory chip from the recorder and slipped it into his pocket. He'd go over it later with Marlene; she was very good at figuring out this stuff.

# 13

FBI ASSISTANT DIRECTOR KERRY SMITH, ALONG WITH A RECORDING TECHNICIAN AND the agent who was nominally in charge of the background investigation, Shelly Bach, presented himself at the reception desk at the White House.

Smith gave his name and title. "I have an appointment with Governor Martin Stanton," he told the uniformed Secret Service officer behind the desk.

"Yes, Director Smith," the officer replied, "we've reserved the Map Room for you, and you'll have half an hour to set up your equipment before the governor arrives."

Smith and his little group followed another officer down hallways until they were admitted to a handsome room.

"This is called the Map Room," the officer said, "because during World War Two all the theater operations maps were displayed here and kept current so that President Roosevelt could consult them at any time."

"That's very interesting," Kerry replied, because it was. "Thanks for your help." The man left, and the technician began setting up the equipment around the conference table.

_____

WILL LEE STOOD as Governor Stanton was shown into his private study, off the Oval Office. They shook hands and sat down.

"Good morning, Marty," Will said.

"Good morning, Will."

"I've talked with all the relevant people about your situation, and there's a general agreement that you should remain on the ticket. Whatever light flak we might receive about your domestic situation would be less than the difficulties involved in choosing a new running mate, and we all agree that you're the best man for the job."

Stanton heaved an audible sigh. "Thank you, Will, I'm very pleased to hear that."

"We're able to proceed as before, largely because of your candor in bringing up the situation now, instead of later, and I want you to know we're all grateful to you."

"I'm looking forward to the campaign," Stanton said. "Just let me know what you want me to do."

"Right now my staff are putting together a schedule for you, Marty, and, of course, they'll want your approval before it's all set. Roughly, the FBI expects to conclude its background check this week, perhaps as early as tomorrow, and the day after the National Cathedral service for George Kiel, I'll announce that I'm appointing you to his unexpired term. Barring any hiccups, we should have Senate approval inside of a week."

"That's moving fast," Stanton said.

"We're going to need every day between now and the election," Will said. "The Republican Convention starts Monday, and we'll all be interested, of course, to see who they pick. They're going to get a big television audience, because of the closeness of their race. No one candidate has the delegates to sew it up yet."

"I think you can beat any one of them handily, Will."

"Together, I think we can." Will's phone buzzed, and he picked it up. "Thank you," he said, and hung up. "The FBI people are ready for you in the Map Room."

Cora Parker, the formidable African-American woman who was Will's personal secretary, came into the room. "Governor, if you'll follow me, please," she said.

"We'll talk more later," Will said, waving him off.

KERRY SMITH STOOD as Governor Martin Stanton walked into the room. "Good morning, Governor," he said, with a smile. "I'm Assistant Director of the FBI Kerry Smith. This is my associate, Special Agent Shelly Bach, and our technician, Danny Miller."

The governor shook hands all around.

"Please have a seat there," Kerry said, indicating a chair on the other side of the table. "As you can see, you and I and Shelly each have a microphone before us." He pointed to the other items on the table. "These small objects are high-definition television cameras. It's customary to record all background-check interviews, so that we can review transcripts for accuracy, if necessary. When the interview has been completed, the tapes will be secured in an FBI vault. At a later date to be determined, they will either be destroyed or given to you for your collection of personal papers, whichever you desire."

"That's fine with me, Director Smith," Stanton said.

He was an impressive man, Kerry thought, handsome, with a fine baritone speaking voice, and he exhibited no signs of nervousness, as many men in his shoes would have.

"If I may, I'll begin by going over the answers on the questionnaire you completed, to be sure we have your answers correct and to your satisfaction."

"Fine."

"Let's begin with your birth," Kerry said, getting right to the point. "Where were you born?"

The governor smiled. "I was born in the backseat of a 1957 Cadillac Sedan de Ville, on the way to the San Diego Women's Hospital, where both my father and maternal grandfather were born."

"Can you tell us the circumstances surrounding that event?"

"My family have had business connections with Mexico for three generations," Stanton said. "My grandfather was a Coca-Cola bottler in San Diego, and my father, after his graduation from Oxford University, in England, and with his father's help, bought the franchise to bottle Coca-Cola in Tijuana, Mexico, along with a Mexican business partner with whom he had roomed at Eton and Oxford. My father fell in love with and married his partner's sister, and they built a home in Tijuana, so that he could closely supervise the business activities and advertising while his partner managed the bottling plant.

"My parents had planned for the birth to occur in San Diego, since there was no equivalent to Women's Hospital in Tijuana. The day before my mother was to move to my grandparents' home in San Diego to prepare for the birth, which her doctors had predicted would take place two weeks later, my father was about to leave for work when my mother went into labor. She later told him she had had mild contractions during the night but had thought nothing of them.

"He panicked, of course, and hustled her into the rear seat of the car, while his regular driver got the car started and headed for San Diego.

"My father was, like most American men of that day, unacquainted with the details of the birth process, and as my mother tells it, when my birth drew very near, his panic gave way to hysteria. He had a slightly different version of the story, of course, but the result was that my father and his driver, Pedro Martínez, a family employee, changed positions, and my father drove while Pedro, coming from a society where births were not always accomplished in hospitals, delivered me. He did a good job, apparently, and when we all arrived at the hospital, the doctors and nurses praised him for his skills."

"That's a delightful story," Kerry replied, laughing, "but can you tell me exactly what time and where, geographically, you were born?"

"Well, I was pretty young at the time, so I've had to rely on my parents' accounts and that of Pedro, of course, who has told me the story more than once, and they were all pretty busy for half an hour or forty-five minutes. As I understand it, I drew my first breath only a minute or so after crossing the border."

"Are your parents still living?" Kerry asked.

"My father passed away more than twenty years ago. My mother is still alive, but she is ninety-two and suffers from Alzheimer's disease. She's in a residential facility in San Diego."

"What about Mr. Martínez?"

"Pedro is still alive and living outside Tijuana on a bottling company pension. I last saw him early this past summer, when he and I were both in San Diego, and, although his health is not good, he is alive."

"Can you give us his address?"

"The bottling company in Tijuana will have it," Stanton replied. "Why? Are you looking for confirmation?"

"Frankly, Governor, yes. It's not that we doubt your account, but as you say, you were pretty young at the time, and the question of whether you were born on American soil has become pertinent."

Stanton frowned. "You mean my citizenship? My father was an American citizen, so I am, as well. I have an American birth certificate and an American passport."

"I understand, Governor, but a vice president must be a native-born American, and a potential problem exists in the legal definition of what is native-born." Kerry produced a sheet of paper. "This is what Section 1401 of the U.S. Code says about aliens and nationality:

"'The following shall be nationals and citizens of the United States at birth: (a) A person born in the United States, and subject to the jurisdiction thereof.' (b) This one is not relevant, it's to do with Indian tribes and Eskimos. '(c) A person born outside of the United States . . . of parents both of whom are citizens of the United States.'

"I believe your mother was a citizen of Mexico at the time of her birth?"

"That's correct," the governor replied.

"There is another situation that might apply: one born to a foreign national and a U.S. citizen who, prior to the birth, was present in the United States for periods totaling not less than five years, at least two of which were after the age of fourteen.

"Now, according to the form you completed, your father's early years were spent almost entirely in Mexico, and from the age of eight, he was educated at Eton, then Oxford, in England, and he was twenty-two years old at your birth. We've combed through this very carefully, and the most we can put him in the United States, conforming to the statute, is three years and two months, so that part of the statute does not seem to apply to you. Finally, there is a circumstance where the citizen parent has been physically present in the United States for a continuous period of one year, and you do not qualify under that circumstance, either."

"But I was born in California," the governor replied.

"Governor, if our investigations can confirm that, you will have no problem meeting the qualification."

The governor was frowning. "So where do we go from here?"

"We'll interview Pedro Martínez, and that should do it. In the meantime, let's keep working our way through the questionnaire."

14

KERRY SMITH AND SHELLY BACH WERE ON THE WAY BACK TO THE HOOVER BUILDING
after the interview with Governor Stanton.

"I think the governor is looking pretty good," Shelly said.

You're looking pretty good, yourself, Kerry thought. Shelly was
a long-legged blonde who dressed better than a female FBI agent
had any business dressing. "I think so, but we've got to clear up this
birthplace question. I want it thoroughly documented for the file,
because, believe me, this is going to come up at his confirmation
hearing."

"Sounds like this Pedro Martínez is the man we have to talk to,"
she said.

"How's your Spanish?" Kerry asked.

"Pretty good, actually. I minored in it at college, and I had three
months at the Army language school in Monterey, California, as
preparation for working in the Albuquerque office. Then I got trans-
ferred here."

"I want you to call the Coke bottling plant in Tijuana, find out
exactly where Martínez lives, and interview him. Be sure and get an

audio recording of the interview. I'll authorize a jet for your trip, so get out there, interview the old man, and get back here. We've got to have this thing wrapped up by the end of the week, or the director will eat us both alive."

"Yes, sir."

"SO?" THE DIRECTOR ASKED.

Kerry told him how the interview had gone. "I'm sending Shelly Bach to Tijuana to interview Pedro Martínez," he said. "I've authorized a jet for her."

"You go, too," Bob Kinney replied. "'Assistant director' will look better on the passenger manifest. We're not in the habit of authorizing Citations for special agents."

"Yes, sir," Kerry said, surprised, but he could not regret spending ten or twelve hours in a small jet with Shelly Bach.

MARTIN STANTON WAS BACK in his family-quarters office and reaching for his throwaway cell phone.

"Hello!" her surprised voice said.

"Hello."

"You don't sound so good."

"I'm a little tired. I've just spent three hours with two FBI agents who are exploring every nook and cranny of my life."

"How'd it go?"

"Pretty well. You remember when we were in San Diego last summer, when I was speaking at that thing?"

"Yes."

"You met an old family friend from Mexico?"

"Yes."

"I want you to find him and talk with him as soon as possible."

"Why?"

"You remember the story about my birth?"

"In the backseat of the car? Sure."

"Get him to tell you that story, and make sure he states clearly that I was born on the U.S. side of the border. And get it on tape."

"You want me to do this myself?"

"I wouldn't trust anybody else with this job."

"I think I'm getting the picture here—geography is important?"

"You're getting the picture. Call the Coke plant and get his address. Go by private airplane and pay cash. You know where to get the money. Don't use your own name, except with immigration."

"I understand. I'll go down this weekend."

"Go tomorrow, and as early as possible."

"As you wish."

"Tell the old man some other people may visit him, and it's important that he tell them the right story."

"I understand."

"I love you."

"I love you, too."

Stanton broke the connection.


HALF A MILE from the White House, Felix Potter pulled the tape from the recorder and tucked it into his shirt pocket. This was the second recording of these two people, and it wasn't much better than the first. He called Marlene.

"Hey," she said.

"I got those two people on tape again," he said. "I think either from the White House or the Executive Office Building, next door."

"Did you get everything this time?"

"No, it's a lot like the last recording. Get this, though—they said something about a coke plant."

"You're thinking drugs?"

"What else?"

"You think someone in the White House or the EOB is doing drug deals?"

"Shit, I don't know, but there's always the possibility. Do you have any idea where the woman in the conversation is?"

"I assume in D.C., but she could be anywhere."

"Still no caller ID came through?"

"Nah, they're probably talking on throwaways."

"Well, if they're going to those lengths to not be identified, there must be something weird going on."

"Yeah, I thought it was just two people fucking on the sly, but if they're talking about a coke plant, then I don't know."

"When I get home from work, we'll listen to both tapes together and see if we can figure out what's going on."

"See you at home, then." Felix hung up. As he did, a blue light started flashing in his rearview mirror, and a whooper went off. He pulled over and checked out the car in the mirror: black and apparently unmarked. He spread an unfolded city map over his radio installation and set his camera on the dash to anchor it, then rolled down his window.

A man in civilian clothes walked up to his car, holding out an ID. "Federal officer," the man said. "Step out of the car, please."

Felix got out and reached for his wallet.

"Easy," the officer said, grabbing his arm.

"I thought you'd want to see my license," Felix said.

"Slowly," the man said.

Felix retrieved his wallet from a hip pocket, fished out his license, and handed it to him.

The man looked at it, then produced some sort of electronic device and appeared to scan the license. "You've been driving around and around the White House for over an hour," the officer said. "What are you doing?"

"I'm a photographer," Felix replied. "Freelance. I get shots of people visiting the White House, when I'm lucky."

"What's in your camera now?"

"Nothing. I haven't been lucky today. I was about to go home when you stopped me. I'm not breaking any laws."

The officer handed back his license. "See that you don't," he said.

"But you'll see me around here again, doing the same thing. I'd appreciate it if you'd pass the word that I'm harmless."

The agent snorted, got back in his car, and drove away.

Felix breathed a sigh of relief. He was going to have to work on concealing the equipment in his car.

15

KERRY SMITH AND SHELLY BACH HANDED THEIR OVERNIGHT BAGS TO THE PILOT and boarded the airplane.

"What kind of plane is this?" Shelly asked as they buckled in.

"A CitationJet Two," Kerry responded. "The government has caught on to using smaller, single-pilot jets for a lot of flights—saves them a lot of money. We have the range to make it nonstop if the headwinds aren't too bad. Otherwise, we'll refuel somewhere."

"I've never been on a private jet before," she said.

"It will be especially time-saving in avoiding the airport scene," Kerry said. "No security lines, no hordes. There'll be a car and driver waiting for us on the ramp when we land."

"Wow."

"I'm sorry I can't offer you a drink, but the Bureau isn't that enlightened. There'll be soft drinks and water in the fridge up front, though."

The airplane rolled onto the runway at Washington National and accelerated. A moment later they were climbing fast, headed west.

An hour later, Kerry finished making a list of phone calls and looked at Shelly. She had fallen asleep, her lips parted, her chin on her shoulder. The top button of her blouse had somehow come unbuttoned, and he appreciated the glimpse of breasts. Her shoes were off, and her feet were surprisingly small for a tall woman. She must be, what? Thirty? He'd read her jacket, and she had done nothing but excel for her whole life—school, college, sports, the works. The Bureau was lucky to have her, he felt, and he was lucky to have time to look at her thoroughly without getting busted for sexual harrassment.

Kerry had recently broken up with his girlfriend of two years, or, rather, she had dumped him. She wasn't up for his schedule—the broken dates and missed vacations—and it had annoyed her that he couldn't talk about his work after he got promoted. When he had been an ordinary special agent, he could tell her most things, entertain her with stories of busts, but not when Bob Kinney got the director's job, noticed him, and started promoting him. Shelly would understand that.

While strictly enforcing the sexual harassment rules, Director Kinney had quietly let slide any notion of a nonfraternization policy in the Bureau. He figured, he had said to Kerry, that with more and more women agents in the Bureau, attractions would exist, liaisons would form, and some marriages would result, and that might be a good thing, since agents would understand each other's problems. Kerry thought so, too, but he had not been tempted until now. He was her supervisor on this job, of course, but that would end when they turned in their report, and he would be free to ask her out.

She opened her eyes and looked at him across the table between them. It was as if she had known that he had been watching her as she slept. She gave him a little smile, and the effect ran directly from his eyes to his crotch, as though a wire existed for that communication.

BARBARA ORTEGA TOOK OFF from Mather, a general-aviation field ten miles east of Sacramento, in a Beechcraft Baron, a twin-engine air-craft being used for air-taxi work, at ten o'clock Pacific time. She was in Tijuana and in a rental car three and a half hours later. She had a road map and the address the woman at the Coca-Cola bottling plant had given her. Pedro Martínez lived near Baja Malibu, on the coast, not far from the U.S. border. Following directions, she turned left off the coast road and climbed a hill. A couple of turns later she came to a small adobe house that looked old but in good repair. She remembered the old man from San Diego, and he now sat on the front porch, looking out across the sea, a couple of miles away. A small duffel bag rested beside him on the porch. She got out of the car and switched on her Spanish.

"Pedro," she said, "my name is Barbara. We met in San Diego last spring, do you remember?"

Martínez fixed her with his gaze. "Ahhh," he said, "you are the friend of Martin. Yes, I remember you—you gave me champagne." He smiled broadly, revealing perfect dentures.

"May I sit down?" she asked, reaching into her purse and switch-ing on her recorder.

"Of course, señorita. What brings you to visit me?"

"I came because you told me a story in San Diego, and I wanted to hear it again."

"A story?"

"The one about how you delivered Martin in the backseat of the Cadillac."

Pedro threw back his head and laughed. "Oh, yes, it is true. I brought Martin into this world." He began the story, starting when he drove to the Stanton home to drive the señor to work. "Then we got to the border crossing," he said, "and we were stopped for inspection. Big Martin said to me, 'Pedro, you have to help her. I don't know what I'm doing.' So I got out of the car and got into the backseat, and Big Martin got behind the wheel, and little Martin was born. Then he drove us to the hospital in San Diego."

Barbara switched off the recorder. "Pedro," she said, "where were you, exactly, when Martin was born?"

"At the border, the guard, who was very young, was scared when he saw what was happening, and he yelled, 'Get out of here!' and waved his arm, and Big Martin put his foot down."

Barbara switched off the recorder. "Pedro, this is very important: Were you in the United States when Martin was born or in Mexico?"

"Between, I think. I don't know exactly."

"Pedro, you are Martin's friend, are you not?"

"Oh, yes, for his whole life."

"Some people are going to come here soon and ask you about this, and it is very important to Martin that you tell them the car was already in the United States when he uttered his first cry. Do you understand?"

Pedro looked at her for a long moment. "Little Martin will be your vice president, is it not true? This is what I am told."

"Yes, Pedro, he will be the vice president if he was born in the United States. Do you understand?"

"Ah, yes, I see," Pedro said. "Let me think. Ah, yes, I remember."

Barbara turned on the recorder again.

"We came to the border, and I got into the backseat with Magdalena, and the young border guard looked inside and said, 'Get out of here!' so Big Martin put his foot down, and we drove into El Norte, and two or three minutes later, Little Martin uttered his first cry."

"And is that what you will tell everyone from now on?"

Pedro spread his hands. "But it is the truth, señorita. I must tell the truth, mustn't I?" He gave her a big smile.

A car driven by a young woman pulled up, and Pedro stood. "You will please excuse me, señorita," he said, "but I am to go now to Tecate, to the birthday of my youngest sister." He picked up his little duffel, got into the car with the woman, and they drove away.

Barbara waited a moment, taking in the view, then she got into her car and drove back toward Baja Malibu. As she turned onto the main road, a black car driven by a man in a suit turned onto the road toward the Martínez house. Another man in a suit sat in the rear seat with a blonde woman.

Barbara had the feeling she had not been a moment too soon.

16

KERRY WAS SURPRISED THAT HIS CELL PHONE WORKED AT THE MARTÍNEZ HOUSE, but soon he had Bob Kinney on the line.

"Where are you, Kerry?"

"At the home of Pedro Martínez. He left the house only a few minutes before we got here. A woman here says he went to someplace called Tecate, to his sister's birthday party. I don't even know where Tecate is."

"When is he coming back?"

"He'll be here by lunchtime tomorrow, according to the woman."

"Go to Tecate and question Martínez there."

"The woman doesn't know where the sister lives, or even her name."

"So you're stuck there for another twenty-four hours?"

"It looks that way."

"All right. Check into a hotel, and get it done tomorrow."

"Yes, sir," Kerry said, but the director had already hung up. He and Shelly walked back to the car and got in. "Driver . . . What's your name again?"

"José, señor."

"Do you know of a decent hotel near here? Not in Tijuana?" Kerry was nervous about Tijuana; he had heard too many wild things about it.

"Oh, yes, señor. There is a very good hotel in Baja Malibu, on the beach. I have the number in my cell phone."

"Will you please call and book two rooms for us? Just one night."

"Of course, señor." The man made the call. "They have the rooms, señor. Shall I drive you there?"

"Yes, and you'll need to pick us up at, say, eleven o'clock tomorrow morning, drive us here, then back to the airport in Tijuana."

"Of course, señor." He put the car into gear and headed to Baja Malibu.


KERRY CHECKED IN at the desk and told the desk clerk they wouldn't need a bellman, since they had light luggage. The clerk gave him two keys and directions to the rooms, on the top floor.

They took the elevator upstairs, and Kerry found the rooms. He unlocked the door of the first one and handed Shelly the key. "Would you like to have dinner later?"

"Yes, thank you."

"I'll book a table in the restaurant. Seven o'clock?"

"That will be fine."

"I'll knock on your door." He walked down the hall and let himself into the next room. It was nicely furnished with a flat-screen TV, and there was a terrace overlooking the sea. He heard a knock at the door and walked back into the room and opened it, but no one was there. Then the knocking came again, and he found that it was coming from another door in the room. He opened it and found Shelly waiting.

"It's not two rooms," she said, "it's a suite." She was standing in a sitting room.

"I'm sorry," Kerry said, walking into the sitting room and picking up the phone. "I'll call down and fix this."

"Yes, señor?" the clerk said.

"I asked for two rooms, but you gave me a suite, instead."

"Señor, a suite is two rooms."

"But I wanted two bedrooms."

"Ahhh," the clerk said. "Just a moment."

"I'm on hold," Kerry said to Shelly.

She nodded.

The clerk came back. "Señor?"

"Yes?"

"I'm sorry, señor, but the hotel is fully booked. You got the last suite."

"You don't have even one more bedroom?"

"No, señor."

Shelly was waving at him. "It's all right," she said.

"Thank you," Kerry said to the clerk, and hung up.

"I'll sleep in here," Shelly said.

"No, I'll sleep in here. You take the bedroom. I insist," he said, holding up a hand. "There's a comfortable-looking sofa."

"Oh, all right," she said. "I'll go freshen up."

"Would you like something to drink?" he asked, opening the refrigerator behind the bar.

"I don't suppose there are any margaritas in there?"

He held up a can. "Actually, there are." He poured them each one. "No salt, I'm afraid."

"That's all right. I don't like salt on my margaritas, anyway. Excuse me for a minute." She picked up her bag and, taking her margarita, walked into the other room.

Kerry hung up his jacket, took off his tie, and rolled up his sleeves, then he grabbed his drink and walked out to the terrace. He arranged himself on a lounge chair and closed his eyes for a moment.

"There," he heard Shelly say, "that's better."

He opened his eyes and found her spreading a towel on her chair. She was wearing a very small bikini, and the effect was riveting.

"Why don't you put on your swimsuit and relax?" she said, arranging herself on the lounge chair.

"I didn't bring one," he replied, with regret.

She regarded him coolly. "Boxers or briefs?" she asked.

"Uh, boxers."

"Same thing as a swimsuit," she said. "You'll burn up in those clothes." She closed her eyes.

Kerry sat there, uncertain.

"Oh, go on," she said, without opening her eyes.

He went back into the sitting room, hung up his trousers and shirt, and walked back to the terrace in his boxers, snagging another can of margarita on the way.

He refilled her glass, and she opened one eye. "*Mmm,* you've been working out."

"Most days," he said, holding in his belly. "There's a gym in my building."

"Good for you. Most of the agents in the Hoover Building are pretty dumpy-looking, except the youngest ones, and they're . . ."

"Callow?"

"The perfect word," she replied. "Are you seeing anyone back in D.C.?"

"No. I recently broke up with someone. You?"

"I'm about to break up with someone," she said.

He wondered what she meant by that, but he was afraid to ask.

## 17

BOB KINNEY PICKED UP THE PHONE. "GOOD MORNING, MR. PRESIDENT."

"Good morning, Bob. When can I expect your report on Martin Stanton?"

"Sir, I anticipate completing that early this afternoon, when the final detail should be in place. I'll messenger it over the moment it's in my hands."

"E-mail it, Bob. It's faster and cheaper."

"Yes, sir."

"I'll look forward to receiving it." The president hung up.


KERRY SMITH LOOKED UP into the eyes of Shelly Bach, who was astride him, moving rapidly.

"I love it that you look at me when we're fucking," Shelly said.

"Looking at you is fun," Kerry panted, massaging her breasts.

She began moving faster, and they were at the peak of their mutual orgasm when the phone began to ring.

"Shit!" Kerry yelled. "Sorry, that was for the phone, not for you."

He picked up the phone, while Shelly laid her head on his shoulder. They were panting in unison. "Hello?"

"Good morning, Kerry. What do you have for me?"

"Good morning, sir. Nothing just yet. It's three hours earlier out here, and we're planning to be at the Martínez place at eleven a.m., local. He's due back for his lunch."

"Why are you breathing so hard?"

"I was working out, sir, doing sit-ups, when you called. I was just about to get into a shower."

"I see. At what hour can I expect your report?"

"Sir, if Martínez returns on time, we should be done by one p.m. and on the airplane by two. I'll e-mail it to you from the airplane, so you should have it between five and six your time."

"Call me the minute you have confirmation from Martínez, so I can call the president. He's on my case about this."

"Yes, sir. I will."

"How's Special Agent Bach?"

"I haven't seen her yet this morning, but I'm sure she's fine. She certainly was at dinnertime. She's just next door, if you'd like to speak to her."

"I'll take your word for it," Kinney said, slyly. "Call me." He hung up.

"You're very quick," Shelly said.

"Maybe not quick enough."

"You think Kinney thinks we were fucking?"

"I can't read his mind, but it's probably best to assume he does."

"You want to do it again?" she asked.

"We did it three times last night and again this morning," Kerry sighed. "I think that is the maximum performance level for an assistant director. If you want an improvement on that, you're going to have to start seeing the new agents."

She rolled over and lay beside him, her hand holding his balls. "I wouldn't want to seem greedy," she said.

"Good, because if you were greedy, you'd be flying me back to D.C. in a coffin."

She kissed him on the ear. "You were wonderful," she said.

"Once I sign off on your report and e-mail it to Kinney, this won't be against agency policy anymore."

"Does that mean we can do it on the plane?" she asked.

Kerry groaned.

THEY GOT INTO THE CAR at eleven sharp, showered and pressed, if sore, and were at the Martínez *casa* fifteen minutes later. Kerry was about to knock on the door when he heard a car coming.

An elderly Toyota pulled up, and an old man got out.

"Señor Martínez?" Shelly asked in her best Spanish.

"Yes, señorita," he replied in his best English. "What can I do for you?" He climbed the stairs to the porch and indicated that they should sit.

"I'm Kerry Smith, and this is Shelly Bach," Kerry said. "We work for the FBI in Washington, D.C., and we've come to ask you a few questions." He surreptitiously switched on a recorder in his pocket.

"Ohhh," Pedro said with mock fear, "am I under arrest?"

Kerry laughed. "No, Señor Martínez, nothing like that. I believe you're acquainted with Governor Martin Stanton of California."

"Yes, I am," Pedro replied. "In fact, you could say I am the first person he ever met. We have been acquainted that long."

"Could you tell me how you first met?" Kerry asked.

"Oh, yes, señor. It is my favorite story. I was the driver for his father, you see. Every morning I would come to his house in Tijuana and drive him to the Coca-Cola bottling plant in his new Cadillac. I liked to drive the Cadillac."

"They're very nice cars."

"Oh, yes. Well, on the morning I first met Little Martin, as all who worked for Big Martin would call him, I came to the house to drive the car, and Big Martin and his wife, Magdalena, were coming from the house in a hurry, because her time had arrived a little sooner than expected." He made a big belly motion with his hands. "You understand?"

"She was pregnant," Kelly said.

"Yes, señor, but not for long. We get in the car, the two of them in back and myself behind the wheel, and we head for San Diego, where the hospital is where Big Martin and his father were born. There is a little delay at the border, but when the guard saw what was happening, he waved his arms and yelled for us to get going! Then Big Martin said to me, 'Pedro, I can't do this. You do it, and I will drive.' So we changed places, and I got in the back and we are racing for the hospital. Two or three minutes later, Little Martin's first cry was heard. Soon we were at the hospital, and the doctors told me what a fine job I had done. Then Big Martin and I went to a bar across the street and got very drunk."

Kerry laughed. "I don't blame you—that was quite an experience. You say two or three minutes after you left the border crossing, Little Martin was born?"

"Yes, señor, about that. Of course, I was pretty busy at the time; it could have been longer."

"And which country were you in when the baby was born? Mexico or the United States?"

"Oh, the United States, señor. We were halfway to the hospital by then."

"That's a wonderful story, Señor Martínez, and I thank you for telling it to us. Now we must be going back to Washington."

"I'm very glad to have had you as my guests," Pedro said.

They got into their car and, with a wave at Pedro, drove away.

Kerry breathed a sigh of relief and called Bob Kinney.

"What happened?" Kinney asked.

Kerry told him the story, blow by blow.

"And Martínez is certain they were on U.S. soil when the boy was born?"

"He's absolutely certain, sir, and I have him on tape saying so. I'll e-mail you the report as soon as we're in the air."

"See you tomorrow, Kerry, and thank Special Agent Bach for me, will you?"

"Yes, sir, I'll thank her."


WILL PICKED UP THE PHONE. "Yes, Bob?"

"It's confirmed, Mr. President. Martin Stanton was born on U.S. soil. I'll be e-mailing you Assistant Director Smith's report in just a few minutes."

"Thank you, Bob," Will said. "And thank Assistant Director Smith and Special Agent Bach for me."


IN THE AIR, Kerry closed his computer. "The report is submitted," he said.

Shelly looked over her shoulder at the closed cockpit door. "Since there's only one pilot, he can't leave the controls, can he?"

"No," Kerry replied, taking off his coat, "he can't."

"Oh, good," she said, shucking her panties.

# 18

WILL STOOD AT A LECTERN IN THE WHITE HOUSE ROSE GARDEN WITH MARTIN Stanton by his side. The funeral of Vice President George Kiel had been held at the National Cathedral the day before, followed by burial at Arlington National Cemetery.

"Good morning," he said to the knot of press, White House staffers, and dignitaries gathered there. "It gives me great pleasure to announce that I am appointing Governor Martin Stanton of California to the office of Vice President of the United States of America. You may have heard that I had already selected Governor Stanton as my running mate last week"—he paused for scattered laughter—"and since the office has become vacant, I didn't think it was necessary to keep him waiting." More laughter. "I regret only that Mrs. Stanton is unwell in California and unable to be here today, but I'm sure she is watching us on television. The customary FBI background check has been completed, and the director has informed me that there are no grounds on which to arrest the governor, so there was no reason for delay. As you know, the Constitution requires that the appointment of a vice president must be ratified by the Senate, and the leadership has informed me that the confirmation hearing will be held the day after tomorrow. Governor, would you like to say a few words?"

Stanton stepped forward to a round of polite applause. "Thank you, Mr. President. I am deeply honored by this appointment, and I am grateful to you for this opportunity. I know that Vice President Kiel's shoes are large and will be difficult to fill, but I will do my best to fulfill the requirements of the office and the hopes of the American people."

THAT EVENING, Felix and Marlene sat before their big-screen flat-panel television set sharing a pizza and watching the little ceremony on CNN.

Felix took a swig of his beer and belched. "Y'know," he said, "that guy sounds like the guy on the tape."

"Which guy? Oh, *that* guy?"

"*That* guy. He has that deep voice, y'know?"

"Felix, how many beers have you had?" Marlene asked.

"Not that many," Felix replied, defensively.

"That guy is going to be the vice president," she said.

"Yeah, I figured that out. I'm just telling you, he sounds like the guy on the tape."

"So, if that's true, this Stanton guy has a girlfriend stashed somewhere?"

"Sounds like it."

"So, how do we prove that his voice is the one on the tape?"

Felix scratched his head. "I could record that speech he just made off the TiVo and compare the two voices."

"Compare them how?"

"Well, you know, there are ways you can compare two recordings electronically."

"I know that the National Security Agency can do that," Marlene said, "but I don't know that *you* can do it."

"I know a guy that might have the equipment to do it," Felix said.

"Hang on just a minute," Marlene said.

"Okay, I'm hanging."

"We need to look at what we're getting into here. What you usually do with the recordings you make is get a leg up on the story, get there first."

"Yeah, well, that's what I'm doing here."

"Felix, this is different. If you sell this story to somebody based on these tapes, you're going to have to give them the tapes, and even if the two voices are the same, those tapes have a lot of gaps in them. The Feds would find out where the tapes came from, and they would be all over you. You really want to go through that for a few grand, which is what you're going to get for the tapes?"

"All that, just because I taped a guy and his girlfriend on the phone?"

"You taped him at the White House."

"Well, I don't know that. He could have been sitting on a park bench in the neighborhood, you know?"

"It's still illegal to tape somebody on a cell phone, and if you sell the story, you'll have to admit that's what you did. Also, if all of this stuff was somehow confirmed and became believable, you'd be blowing a vice president out of the water. Hellfire would rain down on you, if you did that."

"Just because he's fucking somebody?"

"You just heard them say he's married. Remember what happened to Gary Hart?"

"Who?"

Marlene sighed. "He was a guy running for president who got caught with a girl on the side—then he wasn't running for president anymore. And he *invited* the press to follow him around. Stanton has not issued you an invitation to record his personal telephone calls. Do you *want* him to get blown out of the water?"

"What the fuck do I care—I don't even know him."

"My very point."

"Look, all these guys are crooks. Why would you care what happened to him?"

"Well, putting aside simple human decency for a moment, I care what happens to you. Are you willing to trade the possibility of prison time and your face all over the news for the few grand you'd get for the tape?"

"I might like being famous," Felix said.

"There's famous good, and there's famous bad. Nobody would ever buy a story from you again."

"They might. The publicity might even improve my business."

"You can't operate your business, if that's what you want to call what you do, from a jail cell, and when you get out, you'll be Felix the ex-con that nobody wants to know, let alone buy dirt from."

"I think you're overreacting, Marlene."

"I'm just trying to be real, here."

"Well, how about this: I get this guy I know who has the equipment to compare the tape with a recording of what we just saw?" He began rewinding the TiVo.

"If you give this guy the two tapes, what's to keep him from selling the story himself?"

"He's a good guy—he wouldn't do that."

"Felix, there's a real scarcity of good guys where money is concerned, especially money made this way."

"Well, I'm just going to look into it, that's all. I'll talk to you about it before I do anything."

Marlene opened another beer and went back to her pizza. She didn't speak to him again that evening.

## 19

WILL SAT IN HIS OFFICE ABOARD *AIR FORCE ONE*, DICTATING RESPONSES TO correspondence into a recording machine. The letters would be typed and ready to mail by the time the big Boeing arrived in Los Angeles. His phone buzzed.

Will picked it up. "Yes?"

"Moss Mallet would like to see you."

"Send him in."

Moss, his pollster, rapped on the door and opened it. "Okay, Mr. President?"

"Come on in, Moss," Will said, and pointed to a chair. "Have a seat."

Moss took a deep breath. "My office has just faxed me the raw data on our first poll since the convention. I haven't finished all the analysis yet, but I thought you should know what the raw data are before you speak in L.A."

"Shoot," Will said.

"The appointment of Governor Stanton as your running mate, bumped you up a point in the poll, but—and this is weird—your appointment of him as veep knocked you down a point."

"I don't get it," Will said. "People want him as my running mate but not as vice president?"

"The one-point bump seems to have come from Democrats, who like the appointment by seventy percent or so. Eight percent didn't like it, and the rest are undecided. The one-point drop seems to have come from independents, mostly."

"So the net result is flat, no change?"

"That's right."

"I thought we'd get a six- or seven-point bump in the polls, based on Marty's popularity in California."

"We did get that in California but not nationally."

Will shrugged. "Okay, the rest of the country will like him better as they get to know him, see him on more Sunday morning shows and in campaign appearances."

"He's doing *Meet the Press* this Sunday," Moss said. "I hope you're right." He shuffled some papers. "But there's something else."

Will looked at Moss closely. "What's the problem?"

"You took a hit on the A-bomb explosion in Pakistan: down four points nationally."

"I don't understand. I didn't explode the bomb, the Pakistanis did."

"As I said, I haven't had time to analyze all the data yet, but it seems that four percent of Americans somehow hold you responsible, at least in part, for the incident."

"That's nuts," Will said.

"Yes, it is, but that's how they feel."

"Four percent of all Americans feel I'm partly responsible for a nuclear explosion halfway around the world?"

"That's about the size of it."

"So after the convention and the arrival of Marty Stanton in the campaign, I'm down four points net?"

"That's right."

"That's depressing," Will said. "Any indication of *how* they think I'm partly responsible?"

"No, sir. This is raw data."

"So a chunk of the American people think the president is omnipotent and feel he should be able to stop bad things from happening before they happen?"

Moss shrugged. "I know it sounds crazy, but it's there."

"In a tight race, four percentage points could cost me the election."

"Fortunately, you're not in a tight race. The Republicans are voting at their convention tonight, so tomorrow we'll know who their candidate is, and we can do a head-to-head comparative poll. That will tell us better where we stand."

"Okay. Let me know what that poll says."

There was a knock at the door, and Kitty Conroy stuck her head in. "Got a minute, boss?"

"Sure. Come in. Anything else, Moss?"

Moss shook his head and left.

"What's up, Kitty."

"They've put Charlene Joiner at the head table for your speech tomorrow night."

Will felt a flash of annoyance. This went back years. He had represented the woman's boyfriend at his trial for the rape and murder of a black woman in his home county seat, and the boyfriend had been convicted and sentenced to death. Charlene was a knockout blonde, and he had, before he was married, slept with her on one occasion, and she had managed to parlay the press reports of that incident into instant fame and a career as an actress. She had also turned out to be a very good actress and had built a huge career, winning an Academy Award, while maintaining her place as America's foremost sex symbol.

Charlene had also conducted a campaign to get the boyfriend's death sentence set aside, badgering Will for a presidential pardon, and, incredibly, she had succeeded, apparently by seducing the governor of Georgia, who had commuted his sentence to life. And every time Will turned up in California, she had been there, finding a way to be at his side for a photo op.

"My very clear instructions to the committee," Will said, "were that Charlene would not be seated anywhere near me. Did someone not get that message?"

"They did, but this morning, Charlene made a million-dollar contribution to the Democratic National Committee."

*"A million dollars?"*

"It's not unprecedented, but it happens rarely enough that they don't want to make her angry by seating her somewhere else. The contribution is already on the AP wire, and it will be all over tomorrow morning's papers. If she's seated anywhere but on the dais, it will ignite a story that will make headlines for a week."

"Then cancel the dinner," Will said petulantly.

"Will, come on. She's nailed us on this one, and there's nothing we can do about it without making things infinitely worse."

"All right, then, tell them I want her as far as possible from me at the head table. And I mean that!"

Kitty sighed. "There's more: Charlene wants to present the million-dollar check to you before you speak, and she wants to say a few words."

"This is insane," Will said. "I can't accept the check—it's against the campaign funding laws."

"Not if it's made out to the Democratic National Committee. After all, you're the head of the party."

"Kitty, are you telling me that I can't stop this from happening?"

"Not without causing a huge rumpus in the press."

"Then tell the Secret Service to shoot her."

"Now *that's* the best idea I've heard yet," Kitty said, "but I don't think I can talk them into it."

"I want that head table packed with people who are more important than Charlene is," Will said, "and I want all of them between her and me."

"I'll see what I can do," Kitty said.

"And if you can't get this done, *you're* going to have to shoot her."

Kitty beat a hasty retreat.

# 20

MARTIN STANTON CHECKED HIMSELF IN THE MEN'S ROOM MIRROR ONE LAST TIME. His suit was perfectly pressed, his necktie centered, his graying hair neatly combed.

"Time to go, Governor," his lawyer said.

They walked from the men's room out into the hallway, where they were joined by two Secret Service agents, then down the hall and into the grand Senate hearing room. Flashbulbs did not pop, since no photographer had used flashbulbs for decades, but the dull whomp of strobes firing filled the room, raising the light level to a point where a blind man could read the fine print.

Stanton, followed by his lawyer, strode down the center aisle, and stopped before sitting down. "Good morning, ladies and gentlemen," he said.

"Good morning, Governor Stanton," the chairman replied. "The clerk will administer the oath."

Stanton raised his right hand and chanted the words, then took a seat, his lawyer beside him.

"And good morning, Mr. Roberts," the chairman said to the lawyer. "I trust your presence here will be superfluous."

"As do I, Mr. Chairman," Jacob Friedman said smoothly. "Good morning."

"Governor," the chairman said, "I take pleasure in welcoming you to the Senate this morning, as I am sure do all the members of the committee. I understand that you have an opening statement; please proceed."

Stanton took the statement from his pocket and laid it on the table before him, though he was sure he would not need to refer to it. He began to speak, fixing a small smile on his face, and as he did, something behind the row of senators moved, catching his eye. Stanton relied on his peripheral vision to watch an aide rush from a door behind the senators to the side of the junior senator from Arizona, a famously right-wing Republican, and hand him a small black box and some earphones. The man put on the earphones and listened, and he appeared to enjoy what he heard.

Stanton did not miss a beat, and he did not refer to his written statement. He finished and sat waiting.

"I have a few questions," the chairman said, "and then we will take turns to question the witness." The chairman's questions were benign, not to say bland, and they offered Stanton the opportunity to make a few free points. The chairman then said, "The junior senator from Arizona, Mr. Melfi."

Melfi smiled broadly, perhaps too much for the subject of his questioning. "Governor, I once heard you tell the story of your birth, and I wonder if you would relate it once more for the benefit of us all?"

"Of course, Senator," Stanton said, and he launched into the tale he had told at a thousand political meetings and dinner parties. When he had finished, he waited for the next question.

"Mr. Chairman," Melfi said, "I apologize for this departure from procedure, but it was brought to my attention only moments ago that a witness has come forward with information highly pertinent to my questioning of the governor. I request the opportunity for the committee to hear this witness now, before we continue with the governor."

"Mr. Melfi," the chairman said, "this is highly irregular. I am sure you know that witnesses must be vetted by staff before appearing before the committee."

"And the witness has been vetted by staff," Melfi replied. "They completed their process only four or five minutes ago. I assure the chairman that this will take only a very few minutes, and, as I said, his testimony is highly pertinent."

A staffer came over, handed the chairman a sheet of paper, and whispered something in his ear. The chairman asked a brief question, then turned back to Stanton. "Governor, I apologize for this interruption, but I think we should hear this witness."

"Of course, Mr. Chairman," Stanton replied. "Please call him."

The chairman consulted the sheet of paper in his hand. "The committee calls Mr. Marvin Sheedy."

Stanton turned and looked up the aisle to see a small, elderly man using a cane walk slowly forward to be sworn. He took a seat at the other table, next to where Stanton sat.

"Mr. Sheedy," Senator Melfi began, "would you state your full name and address for the record?"

Sheedy cleared his throat and leaned into the microphone. "Marvin Ellis Sheedy, 101 Sun Terrace, Phoenix, Arizona."

"And what is your occupation, Mr. Sheedy?" the senator asked.

"I retired fifteen years ago from the United States Border Patrol," Sheedy replied, "after thirty-five years of service."

"Mr. Sheedy, do you recall where you were on January 9, 1958?"

"Oh, yes, sir," Sheedy replied. "I was on duty at the border station between Tijuana, Mexico, and San Diego, California. I remember, because that was my first day on the job."

"I see. Mr. Sheedy, was that day memorable for any other reason, besides its being your first day in the Border Patrol?"

"Well, yes, sir, it was."

"Can you tell us why?"

"Well, it was a little before nine o'clock in the morning. I had been on duty only since eight o'clock, when this Cadillac car came racing up to the border station—it cut off another car—and screeched to a halt right in front of me."

"Can you describe the car?" Melfi asked.

"It was a four-door, real new, painted yellow, with a black fabric top. I was told later that it belonged to a Mr. Stanton, who crossed the border often and was well known to several of the officers."

"What happened then?"

"Well, there was a man and a woman in the backseat, and she was lying down. The man in the back yelled something at the driver, then both of them got out of the car and changed places. When they did, I saw the lady was having a baby."

"And then what happened?"

"Well, the fellow in the backseat with the lady held it up and slapped it, and it started crying."

"And what did you do?"

"I yelled at the driver to get the hell out of there. I guessed he was going to a hospital, you see. The driver, who I later found out was Mr. Stanton, stomped on the gas and got the hell out of there."

"And you're sure, Mr. Sheedy, that while the car was stopped at your station, the baby was born?"

"Oh, yessir," Sheedy said. "That was the first time, before or since, I saw a baby born."

"Mr. Sheedy," Senator Melfi said, "where, precisely, was your station located?"

"My station was about fifty yards south of the border. You see, we were located there, so in case we found somebody trying to cross the border illegally, we could stop him before he entered the United States."

"You're certain about the location?"

"Oh, yes sir," Sheedy said.

"Mr. Chairman," Melfi said, "that concludes my questioning of the witness. I would like to point out that his testimony affirms that Governor Stanton is not a *native-born* American citizen, as the rules of the Immigration Service define that status, and so, because of that and other circumstances in Governor Stanton's father's life, he is not eligible to serve as vice president of the United States of America."

All hell broke loose in the hearing room.

# 21

WILL LEE WAS SITTING UP IN BED IN THE PRESIDENTIAL SUITE OF THE HOTEL Bel-Air in Los Angeles when his phone rang. It was six forty-five a.m. He picked it up. "Yes?"

"I'm sorry to disturb your breakfast, Mr. President," Kitty Conroy said, "but there's been something of a bombshell in Governor Stanton's confirmation hearing." She related the events of a few minutes before.

"Where the hell did *that* come from?" Will demanded.

"Right out of left field, sir. Apparently Senator Melfi has been doing some digging."

"You get on the phone to Bob Kinney. His people have already checked out Marty's story, and they have the testimony of the man who delivered Marty in the car. Get moving!"

"Yes, sir," Kitty replied and hung up. She went to her laptop, found Bob Kinney's direct line, and called it.

THE SENATE COMMITTEE reconvened after a lunch break, and Jacob Friedman, Stanton's attorney, rose. "Mr. Chairman, since Governor

Stanton was pretty young at the time of the events described by Mr. Sheedy, I would like to call a rebuttal witness on the events of January 9, 1958."

"You may do so, Mr. Friedman," the chairman replied.

"I call Special Agent Shelly Bach of the Federal Bureau of Investigation," Friedman said.

There was a stir in the audience and many strobes firing as the tall blonde agent walked purposefully down the aisle and stopped to be sworn. Then she sat down where Mr. Sheedy had sat.

"Good morning, Special Agent Bach," Friedman said, rising.

"Good morning, sir, and Mr. Chairman," Shelly replied with a fetching smile.

"A little background first, please," Friedman said. "How long have you been an agent of the FBI?"

"For seven years," Shelly replied. "I was recruited out of Yale Law School."

"And what are your current duties?"

"I'm assigned to the office of Assistant Director Kerry Smith for general duties in the Washington, D.C., area."

"And what was your most recent assignment?"

"I was assigned to the background check of Governor Martin Stanton after the president selected him. This is a routine examination of persons appointed to high office in the government."

"And what did your review of Governor Stanton's background reveal?"

"Nothing of a derogatory nature, but the full report could be released only by the director of the FBI."

"Let me be specific: Did your investigation reveal the birthplace of Governor Stanton?"

"Yes. Governor Stanton was born between the United States border and Women's Hospital in San Diego, California."

"And how did you learn this?"

"First from Governor Stanton's own account of his birth, as related to him by family members and a staffer."

"And how did you substantiate this account?"

"At the direction of Director Kinney, Assistant Director Smith and I traveled to Mexico, where we interviewed Mr. Pedro Martínez, who was an employee of Martin Stanton, Senior, and who actually delivered the baby who is Martin Stanton, Junior, while the elder Mr. Stanton drove the car."

"Did you find the account of Mr. Martínez convincing?" Friedman asked.

"Yes. He confirmed every detail of the story Governor Stanton had told us and in a most convincing manner."

"So we have an accurate account of events from the only person still living who knows every detail of that morning's events?"

"That is correct."

"And as a result of your investigation, you have determined beyond any doubt that Governor Stanton was born on United States soil?"

"Yes, sir. That is correct."

"I've no further questions at this time, Mr. Chairman," Friedman said, then sat down.

The chairman turned toward Melfi. "Does the junior senator from Arizona have any questions for this witness?"

"Yes, Mr. Chairman, just one or two." Senator Melfi leaned into his microphone. "Special Agent Bach," he said, "are you aware of the testimony given this morning by retired Border Patrol Agent Martin Sheedy as to the actual birthplace of Governor Stanton?"

"Yes, sir, I have read the transcript."

"And that is from direct testimony before this committee?"

"Yes, sir."

"But your testimony is secondhand, isn't it? This Mr. Martínez has not appeared here today."

"That is correct." Melfi smiled and took a deep breath. "But," she said, interrupting him, "I have a tape recording of the interview that we conducted with Mr. Martínez three days ago, and I would be happy to play it for you."

"Please do so, Special Agent Bach," the chairman said, before Melfi could react.

Shelly removed a CD from her briefcase and handed it to a committee staffer, who inserted it into a machine and pressed a button. The voices were clear, as Pedro Martínez told his story.

When the recording had ended, Shelly said, "Mr. Chairman, I spoke with Mr. Martínez by phone this morning, and he has expressed his willingness to come to Washington and repeat his story in person should the committee ask him."

"I don't think that will be necessary," the chairman responded.

"Mr. Chairman," Senator Melfi cut in, "I have another question or two for Ms. Bach."

"Proceed."

"Special Agent Bach, you have told us of the investigation of Mr. Martínez's story, but have you also investigated the story of the retired Border Patrol agent, Mr. Sheedy?"

"Since we heard of Mr. Sheedy's account of events only this morning," Shelly said, "we have not had time to fully investigate his assertions." Melfi was smiling again. "Except," Shelly said, "that I spoke to the gentleman who was Mr. Sheedy's commanding officer at the time, Mr. Ronald Wicks, who is now retired and living in San Diego. He told me that when Mr. Sheedy was in training, in December 1957, his account of the position of the U.S. Border Control Station in Mexico was accurate. However, he also told me that on January 1, 1958, both the Mexican and American Border Patrol stations were moved onto their respective soils, and that the U.S. station was several yards inside the United States. Mr. Sheedy's first day on duty at the border was eight days later, and apparently, he was not aware of the change."

Melfi sat, staring at her, speechless.

The chairman spoke up. "Mr. Melfi, do you have any further questions for this witness?"

"Ah, no, Mr. Chairman, not at this time."

"Do you wish to recall your previous witness, Mr. Sheedy, for rebuttal testimony?"

"No, Mr. Chairman," Melfi replied.

"Special Agent Bach," the chairman said, "you are excused, with the committee's gratitude."

Shelly closed her briefcase, rose, and left the room, followed by the lens of every camera.

"We will continue with the questioning of Governor Stanton," the chairman said.

## 22

WILL, NOW UP AND DRESSED, SWITCHED OFF THE TV IN HIS SUITE, WHICH HAD BEEN tuned to C-SPAN. "That was very satisfying," he said to Kitty. "Good work."

"Thank you, sir."

"Have you the seating chart for the dinner this evening?"

"Not yet, sir, they're still working on it. All the guests have given at least one hundred thousand dollars to the Democratic National Committee, so they're being very careful about the seating arrangements."

"Did anyone besides Charlene Joiner give a million dollars?"

"Yes, sir. Helene Branley, the widow of William, former head of Branley Industries. She's ninety years old."

"Will she be at the dinner?"

"That's in doubt, sir; she's a bit frail."

"I want her there, even if she's in a wheelchair," Will said, "or, if that doesn't work for her, a gurney. And get me the chairwoman of the event on the phone."

"Yes, sir."

———

BACK IN HIS BORROWED OFFICE at the White House, Martin Stanton made a cell-phone call to Sacramento.

"Hello?"

"Did you watch this morning?"

"Every minute of it. You were superb."

"It did go well, didn't it. What's-his-name looked like a complete ass."

"What's-his-name certainly did."

"How are you?"

"Horny."

"Tell me about it."

"I'd love to. When?"

"In a few months."

"Oh. I made a formal application to the potential employer yesterday."

"Good. I expect I'll hear about it soon, but I'll have to keep the whole business at arm's length. You understand, don't you?"

"Of course. It's better for both of us."

"I'll be in town for a day, you know that?"

"Of course."

"We have to be very careful while I'm there; we can't act on our feelings."

She sighed. "I know. You can depend on me."

His phone began ringing. "Hang on. I've got a call." He picked up the phone. "Yes?"

"The president for you, Governor Stanton," the White House operator said.

"Of course." He whispered into the cell phone. "Gotta run." He cut off the cell call.

"Marty?"

"Yes, Will."

"I watched the second half of the hearing, and I thought it went brilliantly."

"Yes, it did. I don't know who that agent was, but she was perfect."

"I'd never heard of her, either, but I suspect Bob Kinney sent her for a reason."

"A very apparent reason. How's it going in L.A.?"

"Ask me tomorrow. I've got to get through this fund-raiser tonight."

"I know, all the heavy hitters."

"I'm not sure I've ever been in a room with that much money," Will said.

"I'm sure it won't be the last room like that. How do you feel about running against Bill Spanner?" The Republicans had nominated the comparatively young senator from Ohio the evening before.

"I think he could turn out to be a handful," Will said. "Since he doesn't expect to be elected, he can say and do anything he wants, and, from what I know of him, he will. The disadvantage is, next to either of the other two, I'd look young, but next to Spanner, I look old."

"Not old, wise."

"By the way, Marty, I had a call from Joe Tracy at Justice, and he tells me that your chief of staff in Sacramento, Barbara Ortega, has made a bid for head of the Criminal Division."

"Yes, she told me about it, but I'm staying at arm's length from the process, and she knows that. I don't want any appearance of any improper influence."

"I guess that's why she gave me as a reference instead of you," Will said.

"Did she? Do you know her?"

"Oh, yes, I've met her a few times. It was clever of her to use my name; that got Joe's attention."

"She's a very smart woman," Stanton said.

"I take it she has your wholehearted support?"

"Off the record, yes, of course. And if Joe Tracy should walk in front of a bus, I think she'd eventually make a fine AG."

"Well, on that recommendation, I'll write Joe a note, just to formalize my support."

"I'm sure Barbara would appreciate that."

"Marty, I'm sure Tom Black's people grilled you about any of your personal relationships that might jeopardize your candidacy."

"Yes, of course. You need have no fears on that account. Oh, were you referring to Barbara?"

"Well, yes."

"Our relationship has been very close but entirely professional. She has nothing to do with my divorce."

"I'm glad to hear it. Again, my congratulations on the hearing. I hear they're voting today, and your nomination will go to the full Senate tomorrow. I don't anticipate much of a debate."

"Anything I can do, anyone I can talk to, let me know, Will."

"You've already done your footwork. Let's have dinner in the quarters tomorrow night and celebrate."

"I'd love to. Good luck tonight."

"Thanks, Marty. Good-bye."

Stanton hung up and heaved a sigh of relief. He had not been kidding when he had told Barbara how horny he was. He was having wild dreams about her, and when he was back in Sacramento it was going to be very difficult to keep his hands off her.

# 23

AT SEVEN-FIFTEEN, WILL LEFT HIS SUITE WITH KITTY CONROY AND FOUR Secret Service men to walk to the meeting room where the dinner was being held. More agents would be stationed along his route through the gardens, he knew. The Secret Service didn't like him walking through hotels or their gardens, even one as upscale as the Bel-Air.

Will had spent the last hour going through a three-ring binder filled with photographs and short bios of the dinner guests, who were the hundred biggest contributors in California. It was his habit at the smaller dinners to rule out name tags and impress everybody with his memory of names.

The guests had been drinking since six-thirty, so they would be well oiled by the time he began to move among them. This was the kind of event the Secret Service liked, where every guest was known to them and had been vetted for criminal records or threats against the president. This was a "soft" event, except for Charlene.

Kitty spoke as they walked. "The committee chairman has followed your instructions to the letter," she said. "Mrs. Branley will be seated on your right, perhaps in a wheelchair, we're not sure yet, then Ralph Braden, the new CEO of Branley Industries, then Charlene, and boy-girl after that. Rivera, the governor-to-be will be on your left, then his wife, then boy-girl."

"Charlene will try to change the place cards," Will said.

"I'm on that, and so is the Secret Service."

"How am I going to avoid an embrace with Charlene?"

"Frankly, I don't know," Kitty replied, "but even with no press or photographers there, you're going to have to avoid the appearance of pushing her away. She's a very popular lady with this crowd, and she has probably slept with half of them."

"There'll be a photographer there to take pictures of me with everybody," Will said. "See that he leaves the room before the presentation of Charlene's check."

"Don't worry, there's only one, and he's on my staff," Kitty replied.

"See that no photos of me in the same frame as Charlene are released to the press."

She opened the door to the meeting room for him. "Don't worry."

Will strode into the room and grabbed the first outstretched hand. "Hello, Mike," he said. "How are Alice and the girls?"

The astonished man, whom he had never met before, managed to say, "Just fine, Mr. President," before Will grabbed another hand. The photographer stayed at his elbow, getting at least one shot with every contributor. Then, out of a corner of his eye, Will could see Charlene Joiner elbowing her way through the crowd toward him. He tacked to his left, allowing the crowd to fill in between them, giving Charlene a cheerful wave.

A minute later, however, she appeared before him, wearing a dress that reminded him of the one Marilyn Monroe had worn when she sang "Happy Birthday" to Jack Kennedy, but lower-cut.

As she held out her arms to him, Will grabbed her hands and pulled them in front of her as he pecked her quickly on the cheek.

He could feel the backs of his own hands pressing against her impressive breasts. "How are you, Charlene? Good to see you!"

"Will . . . ah, Mr. President, I need a moment of your time," she was saying, but Will had already turned to another guest and his wife and was posing for a quick photo with them.

God only knew what cause Charlene wanted to buttonhole him about, he reflected. Larry Eugene Moody, her murderous ex-boyfriend, already had had his death sentence commuted. What the hell did she want now?

Will worked his way forward in the room, making progress, shaking hands, making eye contact, hugging and kissing wives, occasionally unable to block a hug from a male guest. Mentally, he counted, and when he was at ninety-two he had made the dais. Mrs. William Branley was being pushed in a wheelchair toward her seat next to his. Charlene was standing on the other side of her, and he managed to keep the wheelchair between them. Then, as he was about to take his seat, Charlene made her move and was deftly blocked by a large Secret Service agent who pretended to adjust Mrs. Branley's chair, while another agent held Charlene's chair. Reluctantly, she sat down next to the Branley Industries CEO, who immediately engaged her in conversation.

Will sipped lightly from a glass of champagne and conversed with Mrs. Branley until the first course arrived. Then he turned to Lieutenant Governor Rivera. "Mike, congratulations on ascending to the throne."

"Thank you, Mr. President," Rivera replied, smiling broadly, "but it may be more of a hot seat."

Will laughed. "I expect you've got a pretty good handle on the job by now. After all, you've had a great role model in Marty."

"That I have," Rivera said, "though we disagree on a few issues."

"I hope they're local, not national," Will said. "We can't have any public squabbling between you two until after the election."

Rivera seemed under no illusions about the seriousness of Will's little joke. "You can rely on me, Mr. President."

Will finished his first course, and when the filet mignon was served, he cut it in two and ate only half and a few vegetables. He avoided dessert and drank only a few more sips of his champagne. When coffee was being served he excused himself for a moment and used a backstage men's room. "Don't let anybody near here," he said to an agent as he went inside. He had visions of Charlene barging in and holding his dick for him while he peed.

When he left the men's room he stood in the wings and pretended to consult some notes while the little lectern was placed on top of the dinner table and the microphone rigged. The Secret Service used the opportunity to herd all the waiting and bussing staff out of the room and guard the doors against any premature return. Finally, when only guests and guards were left in the room, Miguel Rivera stood, welcomed the audience and, eventually, after what sounded like a campaign speech for his next term, introduced Will. As the crowd leaped to their feet, an aide exchanged the California seal for the presidential seal on the lectern, then Will stepped out.

He stood there waving and pointing at people until the applause slowly died, then began to speak. "As I was saying twenty-five million dollars ago . . ." The crowd roared and applauded again.

WILL FINISHED HIS SPEECH, then turned to Mrs. Branley to receive her check for a million dollars. As he thanked her profusely, he saw Charlene remove an envelope from her purse and push her chair back; then Kitty Conroy appeared from nowhere, plucked the check from her hand, and surreptitiously used a hip to shove her chair back in.

Will took the check from Kitty and put both checks in his inside jacket pocket. "And I also want to thank the beautiful and talented Charlene Joiner for her continuing support of our party and her generous donation of a million dollars to the Democratic National Committee. I'll bet no Academy Award winners are doing that for the Republicans!"

Charlene tried to get up, but Kitty was standing behind her chair, blocking her move.

Finally, with a wave, Will was escorted from the room by a rear entrance and was whisked back to his suite in a golf cart with Kitty. "Nice work," he said to Kitty as he opened the two envelopes and gave the checks to her. Then he noticed a note in one of the envelopes.

"Remember how good it was between us?" Charlene had written. He did. "I'll be at the back entrance to the Presidential Suite twenty minutes after you leave the dinner."

Will tore the note into small pieces and handed them to Kitty for disposal. "Tell the Secret Service to double the guard on the back door," he said to her, "and to be careful. I wouldn't be surprised if Charlene knows jujitsu."

## 24

THE FOLLOWING MORNING WILL WALKED WITH HIS SECRET SERVICE DETAIL THROUGH the gardens of the hotel to the parking lot where his limousine was to be waiting. The Secret Service would have much preferred the car to come in the back way to his suite, but the driveway had been torn up by workmen repairing a water main.

He walked over the bridge that straddled the little pond with the swans and came to the end of the awning. The car was not there.

A Secret Service agent was on his radio immediately. "I'm sorry, Mr. President, there was an accident on Stone Canyon Road, and the car was held up for a couple of minutes. It will be right here."

"It's all right," Will said. Then he heard the click of running high heels on the bridge behind him and a female voice, shouting.

"Mr. President!"

He turned to see Charlene Joiner running toward him. A Secret Service agent stepped in front of her, and she ran into him with a sound like a deer striking an oak.

"Will!"

Will sighed. "It's all right," he said to the agent. "Let her through."

Charlene strode quickly toward him, and he held up a hand. She grabbed it and pressed it to her considerably exposed bosom. "Please, Will, I just need a moment."

"What is it, Charlene?" he asked, attempting to disengage his hand from her left breast.

"It's Larry," she said. "I know it's early to be talking about this, but once you're reelected, you can pardon him."

*"Pardon him?"* Will asked, incredulous.

"Yes, you can do it without political consequences, once you're reelected."

"Charlene, the man is a rapist and murderer, and I will never, *ever* loose him upon an unsuspecting citizenry."

"Will, Larry has done nearly ten years," she said, and a tear trickled from the corner of an eye and down her cheek. "*Please* do the humanitarian thing. I'm going to set him up in a little business, and he can live a quiet and respectable life."

"Charlene," he said, finally recovering his hand from her bosom, "I will *not* pardon Larry Moody, and if you *ever* so much as mention him to me again I will not speak to you further, under any circumstances, and I don't care how much money you give the party. I hope that's perfectly clear." The car rolled up, and an agent quickly had the door open. "Good-bye, Charlene," Will said with a wave, and dove into the car. He looked back through the darkened glass as they drove away, and she was standing there, waving.

*AIR FORCE ONE* TOOK OFF half an hour later from Van Nuys Airport, and Will was very happy to be putting the entire country between himself and Charlene Joiner, though he was not sure it was enough. He had a long day's travel ahead, with campaign stops in Denver, St. Louis, and Indianapolis on the way back to Washington, and there was work to deal with in his office between stops. It was dark when *Marine One* set down on the White House lawn.

"Where's Kate?" he asked Kitty as they got off the copter.

"On the way in from McLean," she said. "She should be here in twenty minutes."

"Call her and tell her we're having Martin Stanton to dinner in the quarters this evening," he said. "Tell her she can take her shoes off."

"Will do," Kitty replied, flipping open her cell phone.

Will's own cell vibrated on his belt, and he opened it. "Yes?"

"It's Sam Meriwether, Mr. President," his campaign manager said. "The Senate confirmed Martin Stanton as vice president a couple of minutes ago. We kept them here late to get it done."

"That's great news, Sam. Thank you for calling."

"He's at the White House now. I suggest a swearing-in ceremony in the East Room tomorrow morning, then Marty can head west for Mike Rivera's swearing-in. We're lining up half a dozen stops in California for him after that. There's a real celebration going on among Hispanics in L.A. and San Diego, and we want to take advantage of that mood."

"Good idea. Have you cleared my schedule for the swearing-in?"

"We have to move only one half-hour appointment with the Pakistani ambassador and the secretary of state to tomorrow afternoon."

"Have the secretary call the ambassador personally about that. I don't want him to feel shunted aside when we shunt him aside."

"Right. That's all. Talk to you tomorrow."

"Bye-bye." Will put away his cell phone and continued to the family quarters.

Martin Stanton was sitting before the fire when Will walked in. "Congratulations, Mr. Vice President," Will said, shaking his hand. "That went about as smoothly as we could have hoped for. Have you talked to Sam Meriwether?"

"Yes, Will, and thank you again for the appointment. Where's Kate?"

"She'll be here in a few minutes. Can I get you a drink?"

"I'll have some of that bourbon you like," he replied.

Will tossed his jacket on a chair, loosened his tie, and went to the bar.

"I hear you handled Charlene Joiner nicely last night."

"Yes, but not so well this morning." Will told him about the early-morning encounter."

"She really expected you to pardon the son of a bitch?"

"Charlene is a force of nature," Will said, "and she's accustomed to getting what she wants. Did you know she went to Atlanta and screwed the governor of Georgia to get Moody's death sentence commuted?"

"I'd heard that, but I thought it was just a bawdy joke."

"Nope. The embarrassing thing is, I facetiously suggested she do that, just to get her off my back. I was astonished when she actually pulled it off . . . ah, so to speak."

Stanton laughed. "That's unbelievable."

"So is Charlene," Will said, sipping his drink. "Oh, don't mention her when Kate gets here."

"Right."

"Don't mention who?" Kate said, closing the door behind her and kicking off her shoes.

"Never mind," Will said.

"Congratulations, Marty," Kate said, pointing at the bar. "Will, I've got to talk business for a minute. You want to go down to the double O?" They had a rule about not talking business in the family quarters.

"Oh, go ahead," Will said.

"It's not good news. We've got a report from a previously reliable source in Pakistan that the nuclear warhead taken from the last of the missile sites, south of Islamabad, has disappeared and has, possibly, fallen into the wrong hands."

"Oh, shit," Will muttered.

# 25

THE PRESIDENT AND VICE PRESIDENT OF THE UNITED STATES AND THE DIRECTOR OF
the Central Intelligence Agency dined on the coffee table, sitting on
the floor. The White House kitchen had sent up rack of lamb, new
potatoes, and haricots verts, with apple pie for dessert.

"I suppose," Will said to Kate, "you've alerted the Joint Chiefs
about this warhead, so they can alert their intelligence people."

"Yes, and I have an eight-o'clock meeting with them tomorrow
morning," she said. "I don't think you should attend yet. If word got
out, it would get the media all stirred up. As it is, we can call it an
unsubstantiated rumor, which it pretty much is."

"Then let's say no more about it this evening," Will said, "and
just enjoy our dinner." He tasted the California cabernet and poured
them all a glass.


THEY HAD FINISHED their dinner and were on brandy when the phone
rang. Will picked it up. "Yes?" He punched the hold button and
turned to Stanton. "For you—your wife."

"I'll take it in my bedroom," Stanton said, getting to his feet.

---

"HELLO?"

"Marty?"

"Yes."

"I hope I've called at an inconvenient time," she said, and there was acid in her voice.

"I'm having dinner with the Lees. What's wrong?"

"I had a meeting with my lawyers this afternoon. They want me to hire a forensic accountant."

"What's a forensic accountant?" Stanton asked, and he had an idea he wasn't going to like the answer.

"That's who a party in a divorce hires when she believes the other party is hiding money from her."

"Betty, have I ever lied to you?"

"I'm beginning to wonder about that."

"Why do you think I'm hiding money?"

"My lawyer says that, because you have family ties in Mexico, it's very likely that you have money hidden there."

"I've never lied to your lawyer, either. I gave him a complete and highly detailed financial statement, accompanied by all the backup documents, and nothing was omitted."

"How about that vintage Cadillac you were born in? I'm told that's worth a lot of money. California is a community-property state, you know."

"Yes, I know that, and that car is not community property. It's been in my family since a year before I was born."

"How about brokerage accounts?"

"You have my brokerage statements. And by the way, the market is way down at the moment, so we'll have to get current values when we sign the settlement."

"So you're going to try to screw me out of even more money?"

"Betty, you get half of my net worth. If you'd signed the settlement a month ago, when my net worth was higher, you'd have gotten more money. Even your lawyer advised you to sign then."

"I wasn't ready," she said.

"Then you'll have to accept the responsibility for that. I've done all I'm required to do, all I've agreed to do."

"Then why didn't you announce the divorce at the hearing, the way you said you were going to."

"The president's people decided it would be better to wait until I'm sworn in."

"And when is that?"

"Tomorrow morning."

"And, of course, I'm not invited to Washington for that."

"You told me you didn't want to come to Washington."

"So I can't change my mind?"

"It's too late now."

"So what about this money you've hidden? Where is it?"

"Betty, neither you nor your lawyer has the slightest reason to think I've hidden money. Why would I put money in a Mexican bank?"

"Because you could."

"Betty, I can only give you my word that I have no money that isn't included in that financial statement. If you aren't willing to accept that, then there's nothing more I can do. I'll ask my lawyer to call your lawyer. Now, if you'll excuse me, I have to get back to dinner. Good-bye." He hung up, and he was sweating. He was glad he wasn't in Sacramento, so that he wouldn't be tempted to strangle his wife. She had been reasonable up to now, but she seemed to have become deranged. Perhaps it was that she was being egged on by a mercenary divorce lawyer. He hoped that was all there was to it.

# 26

WILL WAS WAKENED FROM A SOUND SLEEP BY A HEAVY OBJECT BEING DROPPED ON his abdomen from what seemed like a great height, making a *whomp* noise. "Huh?" he managed to say after he had gotten his breath back.

Kate was fully dressed. "Got your picture in the paper," she said. "Enjoy!" She slammed the bedroom door on her way out.

Will struggled to sit up in bed. The object that had struck him was the combined weights of *The New York Times*, *The Washington Post*, *The Wall Street Journal*, the *Los Angeles Times*, and the New York *Daily News*. A headline from the *News* screamed at him: PREXY PAWS STAR. This was accompanied by a half-page full-color photograph of him with his hand on Charlene Joiner's left breast. Will flung the newspaper across the room, just as the butler was entering with his breakfast on a tray.

The butler dodged the paper just in time. "Good morning, Mr. President," he said, setting the tray in Will's lap.

"Good morning," Will replied. "Sorry about the newspaper."

"Quite all right, sir. Will there be anything else?"

"No, thank you."

The man left, and Will began searching for the TV remote control among the covers. By the time he found it and turned on the set, his breakfast was getting cold. He looked at the tray: a single, poached egg on dry toast, a small glass of orange juice, and a pot of coffee. He began eating as the *Today* show popped onto the TV screen.

". . . and the president managed to get himself photographed in a compromising situation with Charlene . . . "

Will switched to *Good Morning America*. ". . . Joiner, Hollywood's biggest sex symbol," the program continued. Will switched off the TV set and attacked the lonely egg.

WILL ENTERED the Oval Office at the stroke of eight o'clock. His top campaign staff were waiting, sipping coffee and eating Danish. Will grabbed a cheese Danish and poured himself some coffee. "Morning, everyone," he said.

"You've seen the papers?" Tom Black asked.

"You mean the picture of me with Charlene Joiner's breast in my hand?"

"That's the one."

"I put out my hand to hold her off," Will said. "She walked right into it."

"Funny there was a photographer on station at that very moment," Sam Meriwether said.

"Yeah, funny," Will said.

"I wouldn't worry about it," Moss Mallet said. "In the past, every time your name has been linked with Charlene's, your polls have gone up."

"This time my hand was linked with her breast," Will said. "That ought to make me the most popular man in the country."

"With men," Kitty Conroy said. "Women will want to kill both of you."

"I can't argue with that," Moss said.

"As long as they get Charlene first," Will said. "We're going to have to take further steps to see that she doesn't get near me again between now and the election."

"What sort of steps?" Sam asked.

"I ordered Kitty to tell the Secret Service to shoot her, but Kitty failed me."

"Mea culpa," Kitty said.

"Charlene has this new thing," Will said. "She wants me to *pardon* Larry Eugene Moody."

There was laughter in the room.

"It's funny to everybody but Charlene," Will said. "And when she wants something, it's very hard to stop her."

"What is it you want done?" Tom asked.

"The first thing is, we have to be sure she is not on the guest list for any White House dinner. If she turns up here, Kate will shoot her and save the Secret Service the trouble."

"Done," Kitty said, making a note.

"It's not enough just to screen the guest lists for her name," Will said. "She's perfectly capable of sneaking in here on the arm of some invited guest. In those circumstances it would be very hard to stop her."

"I think what we have to do," Tom said, "is to start a sort of Charlene Watch. If we know where she is at every moment, we can sound the alarm if she gets within a mile of you."

"Within a hundred miles of me," Will said. "But don't go hiring any private detectives. That would not look good on the campaign fund's reporting forms."

"We'll do it with volunteers," Tom said.

"That might work," Kitty said, "if they're male volunteers."

"Please, *please*," Will said, "don't let the press track this back to the campaign. Tell the volunteers that if they get caught, they'll have to plead to stalking her."

"I'll take care of it," Tom said. "If she gets close, we'll head her off at whatever pass she's riding in from."

"Thank you," Will said, "I feel better now."

Kitty held up a sheet of paper. "Here's the veep's statement." She read it aloud. "Vice President Martin Stanton and his wife, Elizabeth, announced today that they are divorcing after twenty-nine years of marriage because of irreconcilable differences. The parting is mutual and amicable, and Mr. and Mrs. Stanton request that the media respect their privacy in this matter."

"First question they'll ask," Tom interjected, "is, Why was the announcement not made during the hearings or before the swearing-in?"

"The delay was at the request of Elizabeth Stanton," Kitty said. "She didn't want their personal differences to overshadow an important time for the country."

"Is that true?" Will asked.

"I spoke with her myself," Kitty said. "She was very reasonable about requesting that, after I suggested she request it."

Moss spoke up. "I give the story one news cycle," he said. "Unless there's another woman."

"What about another man?" Kitty asked.

"Is Stanton gay?"

"You know what I mean: What if Betty Stanton has something on the side."

"That would be the very least of our problems," Moss said. "The question is still on the table: Does Stanton have something on the side?"

There was silence in the room.

Will broke it. "Surely, someone asked him."

"I asked him the more general question," Tom Black said. "You know: 'Is there anything in your life we should know about?'"

"Well," Moss said, "if it happens, it happens, and we'll just have to deal with it."

"I hope not," Will replied.


AT TEN O'CLOCK, a cast of media, congressional leaders, White House staff, and invited guests assembled in the East Room and watched as a Supreme Court justice swore in Martin Stanton as vice president of the United States. Hands were shaken all around, and, after the president and his new vice president and the justice had left the room and the president had walked the vice president to a waiting helicopter, the press secretary distributed the release concerning the divorce of the vice president.

There was, of course, a clamor of questions from the press, but the press secretary reminded them that the vice president and his wife had requested privacy, and that, anyway, the vice president was already in the air and unavailable for comment.

## 27

VICE PRESIDENT MARTIN STANTON HAD HOPED FOR *AIR FORCE TWO* TO WING HIM
west, and he got that, but not in the form he had expected. *Air Force
Two* turned out to be not the Boeing 747 he had anticipated but a
Gulfstream III. His disappointment must have been apparent when
he alit from his limousine, because the Air Force pilot had rushed
over, introduced himself, and apologized.

"Mr. Vice President," the man said, "I'm very sorry about the
equipment today, but one of our 747s is down for an unscheduled
engine change and the other, of course, has to be held for the president, should he require it."

"Of course, Colonel," Stanton replied. "I understand perfectly,
and I'm sure I'll be quite comfortable." Stanton walked up the stairs
to the airplane, turned, and waved to the crowd, which consisted of
two mechanics in coveralls and a pool television cameraman, there
in case he should die on the way to the airplane.

Stanton briefly inspected the tiny private cabin at the rear of
the airplane, which contained a single bunk and an uncomfortable-
looking chair, then took a seat at a desk just outside the cabin. At

least, he thought, this was an improvement over his California State aircraft, a short-legged Citation that had to stop and refuel on its way across the country.

Stanton took a look at the papers. Then, as the jet climbed to cruising altitude, he learned that he was not, even in the smaller airplane, incommunicado. The phone on the desk in front of him rang. He hesitated, then picked it up. The pilot must be calling him.

"Vice President Stanton, this is the White House operator," a woman's voice said.

"Good morning," Stanton replied, surprised to be in touch with Earth.

"I have a gentleman on the line named Jacob Friedman, who claims to be your attorney and who insists on speaking with you."

"I know him, I'll take the call," Stanton replied.

There was a click, then a male voice said, "Hello?"

"Hello, Jake," Stanton said.

"Oh, Governor?"

"Not anymore."

"Sorry, Mr. Vice President."

"Yes?"

"I'm sorry to disturb you when you're . . . Where are you, anyway?"

Stanton looked out the window. "I guess that's Virginia down there."

"Then you're on *Air Force Two*?"

"In a manner of speaking."

"Wow, that must be impressive."

"What's going on, Jake?"

"Henry Wilcox—that's Mrs. Stanton's attorney—has just written to me, saying that they're appointing a forensic accountant to go over your finances."

"Yes, Betty told me that last night."

"This is not a good thing, Gov . . . Mr. Vice President."

"You can call me Marty, Jake."

"It's not a good thing, Marty. This could hold up a decree for months while this guy runs up as many billable hours as he can, all to no avail, of course, since you reported all your assets and liabilities on your financial statement." He paused. "You did report all your assets, didn't you?"

"I did. If I think about it hard, though, I might be able to come up with a few more liabilities. Tell Wilcox that Betty can have half of those."

"Heh-heh, very good. I'll put that in my petition."

"What petition?"

"My petition to the court to suppress the appointment of a forensic accountant."

"On what grounds?"

"Ah, too late in the process, no evidence of hidden assets, harassment, unreasonable delay, that business about new liabilities, and, of course, malice. A woman scorned and all that."

"Don't mention malice and a woman scorned. Let's not make her angrier than she already is."

"Frankly, Marty, I think what's behind this is Wilcox is trying to get more for her than they had agreed to in the draft settlement. Maybe if we give them something else they'll go ahead and sign, and we can get this thing over with."

"Did you have something in mind?"

"Well, Wilcox obliquely referred to that old Cadillac, the one you were born in."

"Betty said something about that last night. She seems to think it might be worth a lot of money."

"I did some checking around. A mint Cadillac of that vintage might bring as much as fifty grand at the right auction."

"I was going to donate it to a car museum in L.A. and get a tax deduction of twenty-five grand," Stanton said.

"So all it would cost you would be whatever the tax savings would have been. That would be a good deal to get us out of this."

"Oh, hell, if it will get her off my back, give it to her, but be cagey. Tell Wilcox how reluctant I am to part with it and how it might bring a hundred grand at auction, because of the connection to a vice president."

"Gotcha. I'll call him back as soon as we're off the phone."

"Don't be hasty, Jake. Let him stew until tomorrow."

"Okay, Marty. I'll get back to you when I know more. In the meantime, do I have your permission to file the petition?"

"Sure, go ahead whenever you think the time is right."

"Bye-bye, Marty. Say, does *Air Force Two* have a bedroom?"

"In a manner of speaking," Stanton replied. "Good-bye, Jake." He hung up.

Stanton, for the tenth time that morning, thought about Barbara Ortega—specifically, Barbara Ortega naked in his bed. He reflected that the past few weeks had been the longest time in his life that he had gone without sex, but he had suspected that Betty had put detectives on him, so he had been good, as much as it had hurt. Now he was going to see Barbara at Rivera's swearing-in, and he was going to have to work hard not to seem to want her. It was going to be tough.

He hoped to God that Betty took the Cadillac; he had been paying five hundred bucks a month to garage it, since there wasn't room for it at the mansion, and he couldn't afford it anymore.

# 28

BARBARA ORTEGA LOOKED AROUND THE ROOM THAT HAD BEEN HER OFFICE FOR THE past three years. The walls were bare of her diplomas, her law license, and the collection of photographs that had followed her life from childhood through high school and college and through law school. Four boxes of files stood ready for transfer to the state archives, and another two held her personal files. Everything was ready for the movers, so when Mike Rivera's swearing-in ceremony was over, his chief of staff could move immediately into the office.

Barbara sat down on the sofa and began remembering the first time she and Marty Stanton had made love—on that very sofa. Not that it was making love; it was just straight fucking, and she had loved every second of it. Lovemaking came later, at a friend's apartment and various other locations, none of which they had used more than once. God, she thought, they had been careful. No one had twigged their affair, least of all Betty Stanton.

Now she would be on her way to Washington, to start the new job, if she was lucky, and to look for another, if she wasn't. If Justice didn't work out, Marty would help her find something else good, she was sure of it. Her apartment looked pretty much like her office, she reflected. She had thrown away or donated everything she could do without, sold her furniture, and arranged for the utilities to be disconnected soon.

Barbara Ortega had burned her bridges.

MARTIN STANTON'S ARRIVAL in Sacramento was much better covered than his departure from Washington. Every political reporter who had covered him for seven years was there, cameras were pointed, TV lights switched on. He paused at the top of the boarding stairs and tried to look surprised, then he walked quickly down to where a microphone had been set up.

"Good afternoon," he said to the crowd, and they hushed. "It's great to be back in Sacramento, even if only for the day. After I left to go to the Democratic Covention in New York, events took a sudden turn, and my feet have hardly touched the ground since then. In the space of a very few weeks I have become the Democratic candidate for vice president, then appointed to the unexpired term of the great George Kiel, then confirmed by the Senate, then, this morning, sworn into office. No politician has ever had such a roller-coaster ride. I want to thank all my friends in Sacramento and in all of California whose unwavering support of me over the years made all this possible. Any questions?"

"Gov . . . Mr. Vice President, have you resigned from the governorship?"

"I faxed my resignation to the secretary of state early this morning, and I'm delivering the original document to him today," Stanton replied, patting his inside pocket.

"How long have you and Mrs. Stanton been planning the divorce, sir?"

"That's a private matter, not connected to my government service, either in Sacramento or Washington, and I won't be answering any questions about it. Neither will Mrs. Stanton, whom I hold in high regard."

Barbara Ortega suddenly appeared at his side. "That will be all the questions," she said. "The vice president has an inauguration to attend." She guided him into the governor's limousine, and once the doors were closed, pressed the button that closed the window between the driver and passenger compartments.

"It's good to see you," Stanton said, reaching across the seat and squeezing her hand.

"And you, baby," she replied.

Stanton glanced at the driver, as if to warn her.

She nodded and handed him a sheet of paper. "Here's your schedule: first the swearing-in, then some dinner and an appearance at Mike's inaugural ball, which will be at a downtown hotel, then this limo will whisk you to San Francisco, where you're in a big suite at the Ritz-Carlton for the night. I'd like to join you there."

Stanton shook his head. "This is the only time we're going to have alone. It's important that you be seen at the ball tonight after I've gone."

She nodded. "I know, I was just dreaming. I've packed up your office and shipped your personal files to the house at the Naval Observatory. I've packed my things, too."

"You've already resigned?"

"Simultaneously with you. Mike has his own chief of staff, and, anyway, he wouldn't want me around here. I've sublet my apartment, and I'm leaving for Washington on Monday."

"You got the job already?"

"I've been told I'm a serious candidate, but if I don't get it I'll find something else. I've got a pretty good résumé, you know."

"Don't I know it."

"You'll help me, if I need it, won't you?"

"I'll do everything I can without being seen to do it. I've already talked to Will Lee about you, and he's sent a recommendation to the AG."

"Oh, thank you, Marty. I'm more confident than ever now."

"After the election, when I've got my feet on the ground in Washington, we'll bump into each other somewhere."

"I know the plan."

"It'll take me a while to get settled into the office, since I'll hardly be in Washington at all between now and the election. They've got a schedule for me you wouldn't believe."

"What's with the G-III?" she asked.

"The big Boeing was down, and they have to keep one ready for the president. I was comfortable, though."

"You make them be nice to you, or I'll have to come straighten them out."

"Don't worry. I'll be traveling in a campaign plane, a Boeing Business Jet, which will have room for press and staff."

"What are you going to do about a chief of staff?"

"You know, I haven't had a moment to think about it. I don't know what I'm going to do without you running things for me."

"All in good time," she said. She looked out the window. "We're here. You get out, and I'll take the car on to the garage. I'll see you at the ball. I have a date with Jimmy Saxon, the Silicon Valley guy."

"I hope he's gay."

"Don't tell anybody, but he is."

Stanton got out of the car and began shaking hands.

# 29

WILL WRAPPED UP HIS DAY A LITTLE AFTER SEVEN P.M. AND WENT UPSTAIRS TO THE quarters. Kate was sitting on a living room sofa reading a newspaper.

"Not the *Daily News*, I hope," he said.

"Somebody had tacked it to a bulletin board at Langley this morning," she replied, not looking at him.

"I was ambushed," Will said. "Surely you understand that."

"I don't like it when you're ambushed," she said.

"Neither do I."

"I don't like it when you *let* yourself be ambushed."

"It was the crack of dawn. I was half asleep, and she came at me from behind."

"From behind was not where you were grabbing her."

"I told you, I was fending her off. Obviously, the whole thing was planned. She wants me to pardon Larry Moody."

Kate dropped the newspaper. "I don't believe it!"

"Neither do I, but that's what she wants. The campaign has instituted a Charlene Watch to make sure she doesn't get near me again."

"Good luck with that," Kate said. "She's a very determined bitch."

Will went to the bar, mixed her a martini and poured himself a bourbon. He sat down on the sofa next to her and handed her the drink. "Look at me," he said.

"I'd rather look at the martini."

He held on to the glass when she reached for it. "Look at me."

She looked at him. "All right."

"That's enough about this incident."

She blinked rapidly a few times. "Is it?"

"It is. Let's not refer to it again."

"All right," she said.

Will released the martini to her, and they clinked glasses.

"I know assassins who could fix this problem," she said.

"I'm not supposed to know you know assassins," he replied.

"Well, I'm not absolutely certain about it, but I think I could scare up an assassin, if I had to."

"You don't have to. Have your people found that nuclear warhead?" he asked.

"You're changing the subject."

"I am."

"We're not supposed to talk business in the quarters."

"I take it if there were any new developments, you'd apprise me."

"I'd apprise you. How did Marty's ceremony go?"

"Just fine. He's in California for Rivera's inauguration. He had to ride out there in a G-III, instead of *Air Force Two*."

"I'll bet he loved that."

"He has to get used to being number two. He'll like his campaign plane better."

"I had a meeting with somebody from Justice today, and he said that Marty's chief of staff has applied for a big job over there."

"That's right. She gave me as a reference."

Kate laughed. "Not Marty?"

"Marty is being very careful to remain hands-off," Will said.

"Uh, oh."

"What do you mean by that?"

"I mean, I think it would be a perfectly normal thing for a vice president to do, to help his former chief of staff get a Washington job."

"I suppose so. What are you getting at?"

"Doesn't he strike you as being a little too careful, if he's not willing to recommend her himself?"

"You mean you think he's been screwing his chief of staff, and that's the reason for the divorce?"

"Would you be shocked if he were, Will?"

"Surprised, maybe, but not shocked. I'm a lot harder to shock than I used to be."

"Nonsense. You're shocked every time somebody does something the slightest bit venal or unethical."

"Shocked, maybe, but not surprised."

"If anybody knew the width and depth of your straight-arrowness, they'd be shocked."

Will laughed. "Don't ever tell anybody—it would impair my effectiveness. The press would start comparing me to Jimmy Carter."

"There are more similarities than differences," Kate said.

"There are more similarities between men and women than differences," he pointed out. "Same number of fingers and toes, eyes and ears, et cetera, et cetera."

"Sure. Different only in the important areas."

"What time is dinner?" he asked.

"Any minute. You have something in mind?"

"After dinner," he said.

"Hold that thought," she replied.

---

MARTIN STANTON WAS ENSCONCED in his hotel suite in San Francisco, plugging in his secret cell phone, when it vibrated.

"Yes?" he said.

"I'm downstairs," Barbara said, her voice husky. "Can I come up?"

"Listen, baby, I've got Secret Service protection now, you know?"

"You think they'd shoot me?"

"I think I don't want to ask them to look the other way while you and I fuck each other's brains out."

"Oooh, I love it when you talk dirty," she said.

"Okay, come on up. I'll switch off the security."

"You really mean that?" she asked. "I'm shocked."

"I love shocking you."

"Now I have to shock you."

"Go ahead."

"I lied. I'm not downstairs. I'm in my Sacramento apartment, or what's left of it."

"Awwww."

"Yeah, eat your heart out."

"Why are you toying with me?" he asked plaintively.

"I just wanted to see how far you'd take this celibacy thing, and I guess I found out."

"I was kidding about calling off the Secret Service," he said.

"Yeah, sure."

"I was, really."

"Well, in any case," she said, "you're going to have to sleep with your hand under the covers tonight." And she hung up.

Stanton whimpered, then hung up, too.

# 30

TEDDY FAY ADJUSTED HIS GRAY COMB-OVER HAIRPIECE AND COMBED HIS VERY real, very gray mustache and his not-so-real thick eyebrows. As a final touch he slipped on a pair of heavy black-rimmed spectacles, then stood back from the mirror and took in his full length. In the months he had been in Panama he had lost twenty-five pounds, and given his exercise program, he felt fitter than he had in years. This look was one of three he had adopted, so that he could move around Panama City without becoming familiar to very many people.

He slipped the jacket of his white suit over his open-necked white shirt, took one last look in the mirror, and went out the back door of his apartment. It was a good exit for him—a tree-shaded wooden staircase rising thirty feet to the road behind his little building. His Vespa motor scooter was locked to a street sign, and he worked the combination quickly. The scooter started instantly, and he let the engine warm up for a moment before putting it into gear and starting down the hill.

He liked the scooter, partly for the anonymity—because there were so many scooters in the city—and partly for the wind in his face. Tonight, he made his way to a bar he liked at El Conquistador, a small but elegant hotel catering to upper-income international visitors. The hotel subsisted on word-of-mouth and relations with a couple of dozen travel agents in American and European cities. He liked it, too, for the occasional businesswoman traveling alone; he had gotten lucky there twice.

Teddy had heard the hotel might be for sale, and he had fantasized about buying it and becoming the genial host. He didn't have that much money, though, and he couldn't afford to become rooted, especially now when he had heard there was a man wandering around town showing a faded photograph of a middle-aged man and asking if he had been seen locally. He didn't much like the sound of that. The man was said to be staying at El Conquistador.

Teddy had chosen Panama City because he could flee north into Mexico or south into the southern continent very easily, and he could quickly disappear in either place. His Spanish had been pretty good when he arrived, and with work, it was much better now, so he was able to pass as an American who had made a career in the country and was now retired.

He parked the scooter and strolled through the lobby, making a show of looking at the expensive merchandise in the glass cases, the goods of nearby shops. The cases went through the wall and could be seen from the bar, too, and that allowed him to view the customers inside. He spotted the man almost immediately.

He was late thirties/early forties, medium height, pale skin, and thin blond hair, and he wore reading glasses on a string around his neck. He had apparently just arrived, because he was showing the bartender a photograph, and the bartender, after a cursory glance, was shaking his head.

Teddy walked into the bar and took a seat two stools down from the visitor, who was almost certainly American. "Fundador and soda," he said to the bartender.

"Ice, señor?"

"Yes, please."

"You're an American?" the man asked.

Teddy turned and regarded him for a moment. "How'd you guess?" he asked.

The man laughed. "Me, too. Can I buy you a drink?"

"You can buy me this one," Teddy replied, holding up his glass.

The man moved over a place; now there was only one stool between them. "Put that on my tab," he said to the bartender, who nodded gravely and did something with a pencil. "I'm Ned Partain," the man said, sticking out his hand.

"Larry Toms," Teddy said, shaking it.

"What brings you to Panama?"

"The canal, what else?"

"You work on the canal?"

"I did for twenty-seven years, until I retired two years ago."

"What did you do there?"

"Nothing glamorous like an engineer," Teddy replied. "I was an accountant." That information would stop any further conversation about his job.

"Oh."

"Yes, 'Oh,'" Teddy said. "How about you? What brings you down here?"

"An assignment. I'm a journalist."

"Now, that's a lot more interesting than accounting. Who do you write for?"

"A little rag called the *National Inquisitor,* maybe you've heard of it."

"When I'm in the States I see it at supermarket checkout counters, I think."

"That's the one. It's not exactly prestigious journalism, but it pays one hell of a lot better than the *The Washington Post* or others of that ilk."

"Good for you."

"You married?"

"My wife died last year in an automobile accident," Teddy replied. "You?"

"Divorced for two years. She's bleeding me white, of course." Ned dug into a pocket and came out with a well-worn photograph. "Say, have you seen this guy in your travels around town?"

Teddy took the photo and found his younger self staring back at him. Where the hell did this come from? He couldn't place it.

"He'd be older now, mid-fifties to sixty."

Teddy continued to stare at the photo. Chesapeake Bay, Fourth of July, eight or nine years ago: rented boat, girl with a camera, girl he'd picked up in a D.C. bar and seen for a few months before they'd tired of each other. "Looks familiar," he said. "Who is he?"

"Really?" Ned said, showing some excitement. "Where'd you see him?"

"I'm trying to remember," Teddy said. "He's older now?"

"Yeah, he was in his late forties when that was taken."

"Who is he?"

"Just a guy I'm looking for."

"Well, he must be a pretty important guy, if you've come all the way down here from the States looking for him."

Ned moved over another stool and leaned close to Teddy. "He's important to my story," he said.

"Let me buy you a drink," Teddy replied, signaling the bartender.

"If you could help me find this guy, there would be a reward," Ned said. "My paper is very generous."

Teddy looked at the photo again. "You know, I think I've seen this guy right here in Panama City."

"Larry, my friend," Ned said, "this could be the beginning of a beautiful friendship, as Claude Rains said to Bogey."

"You know," Teddy said, "it might be at that."

Teddy continued to drink with the man, but he would not answer the questions about the photo. Teddy badly wanted to know what Ned Partain knew.

It was dark outside now, and Teddy looked at his watch. "Want to get some dinner?" he asked.

"Sure," Partain said, "but the *Inquisitor* is buying."

"I don't mind that at all," Teddy replied. "Tell you what, there's a nice place in Balboa, sort of a suburb, called El Parador. I've got a quick stop to make, so why don't we meet there in half an hour? There's a cab stand outside the hotel."

"Good deal," Ned said. He was getting a little drunk.

# 31

EL PARADOR WAS PERFECT, TEDDY THOUGHT; IT WOULD BE CROWDED BEFORE THEY finished dinner, and they would blend in. And it was near the canal. They dined on the terrace, which sported a view of both the Gulf of Panama, where ships at anchor waited their turn for the canal, and the canal itself.

"Wow!" Ned said, as a huge tanker slid slowly past them.

"Pretty impressive, huh? Shall I order for us?"

"Sure, go ahead, and a good bottle of wine, too. The *Inquisitor* can afford it."

Teddy ordered the house specialty and a fine bottle of Chilean cabernet.

"Okay," Ned said, sipping his wine, "now, tell me where you've seen this guy."

"First I want to know who he is and what you want with him," Teddy said. "I don't want to get anybody in trouble. Did he skip out on his wife or something?"

"Nah, nothing like that." Ned looked around to be sure he wouldn't be overheard. "Did you ever hear of a guy named Teddy Fay?"

"Yeah, I have, but I don't remember where."

"Ex–CIA guy, an assassin, killed some people."

"Wait a minute, now I know who you're talking about," Teddy said. "Didn't I read that he went down with a boat somewhere in the Caribbean earlier this year?"

"That's the story everybody bought, but I don't think so."

"And there weren't any photographs of him, either," Teddy said. "So where'd you get yours, and how do you know it's him?"

"A girl he used to go out with a while back," Ned said. "She took the picture when they were out sailing, then forgot about it. A couple of weeks ago she was down here on a cruise and saw him, but he didn't see her. Since she was on a ship she didn't know who to tell, so she waited until she got home, found the old film, and had it developed. She was going to call the FBI, but she's a regular reader, and she figured she might as well make some money out of it, so she called the paper and asked for Editorial and I answered the phone. And here I am."

"So you're down here to get the guy busted?"

"Nah, I want to interview him, not bust him. I mean, eventually, we'll call the FBI, and when they grab him, my story and the interview will be ready."

"That's pretty neat," Teddy said, "but first you've got to find the guy."

"That's where you come in," Ned said. "If you can point him out to me, it'll be worth ten grand of the *Inquisitor*'s money."

"That's pretty inviting," Teddy said, grinning. "And when do I get the money?"

"It's in the safe at my hotel. You show me the guy, I'll talk to him, and we'll go back to the hotel for your money."

"Fair enough," Teddy said.

"Okay, where did you see him?"

"Right here, in this restaurant," Teddy replied.

Ned's eyes went left and right. "Holy shit! Is he here now?"

"He certainly is," Teddy said.

"Where?"

"You're looking at him."

Ned spilled his wine. Then he fished out the photo and compared it to Teddy. "Similar," he said.

"How about without the wig, the fake eyebrows, and the glasses?" Teddy said.

"That's a wig?"

"It certainly is." Teddy lifted a corner of the hairpiece, then stuck it back.

"I can't believe my luck," Ned said.

"I guess you're just a lucky guy."

"Wait a minute. Tell me the name of the girl who took the photo."

"Darlene Cole," Teddy said without hesitation.

"Son of a bitch, you *are* Teddy Fay."

"*Shhhh,*" Teddy said. "Finish your wine—we can't talk here."

Ned tossed back his drink and ordered the check. "Let's get out of here," he said, pitching some money onto the table.

A couple of minutes later they were walking down a path high above the canal that was lit by streetlamps, two of which were dark, because Teddy had thrown rocks at them before Ned had arrived. "Okay," Teddy said, stopping and leaning on the steel rail between the path and the canal, "let's talk turkey. If you're giving Darlene ten grand, I want fifty grand for the interview."

"Look," Ned said, "I've only got twenty-five thousand with me, but I'll send you the other half, I swear."

Teddy regarded him for a moment. "I believe you," he said. "What do you want to know?"

"God, I don't know where to start," Ned said.

"That's because you're drunk," Teddy replied. "Take a few deep breaths." He watched as another big tanker approached where they stood.

Ned began taking deep breaths.

"Oxygen, that's what you need," Teddy said.

Ned stopped taking the big breaths. "Jesus, I'm dizzy. I think I'm going to throw up."

Teddy took him by the shoulders and spun him around. "Over the rail," he said.

Ned leaned over the rail and vomited.

Teddy had a quick look around: nobody on the path, nobody on the foredeck of the tanker. He drew back, and, as Ned straightened up, Teddy struck him hard in the back of the neck with the edge of his hand. Ned collapsed onto the rail, and Teddy helped him over and watched him as he fell, struck his head on a crane on the foredeck, bounced off some pipes, then fell between them.

Teddy ambled away. Ned wouldn't be found before morning, if then, and by that time the ship would be at sea, and nobody would know when Ned Partain joined the cruise.

Then he remembered the photograph; it was still in Ned's pocket. And the negative was probably in the editorial offices of the *National Inquisitor*. Either that, or his old girlfriend Darlene, if she was smart, still had it.

Teddy unlocked his scooter from the rail outside the restaurant, started it, and headed back to Panama City.

He had a lot to think about.

# 32

WILL SAT ON *AIR FORCE ONE* AND WATCHED A TAPE OF HIS OPPONENT'S FIRST campaign speech. The man looked good: He had gray-streaked blond hair and wore a well-cut suit that complemented his tan, but there was nothing new in the speech. He turned to Moss Mallet, Tom Black, and Kitty Conroy.

"It's the same old speech," Will said. "I'm liberal, liberal, liberal, and he's more conservative than John Birch, Barry Goldwater, and Ronald Reagan put together."

"You're right," Moss replied, "but believe it or not, this speech did him a lot of good. For the first time, he's attacking you instead of his two opponents, and the guy looks great, you have to admit."

"I don't want to date him," Will replied. "I want to kick his ass in the election. How do we do that?"

"We'll attack his voting record, which is direly conservative," Tom said.

"Is that going to help us with independents and slightly liberal Republicans?"

"Sure it is," Tom replied. "In a lot of ways he's what they don't like about the Republican Party."

"Except," Moss said, "the electorate has always been partial to good-looking blond guys, like Jack Kemp and Dan Quayle."

"Kemp never got the nomination, and Quayle ended up as the poster boy for dumbness," Will pointed out.

"Yeah, but Quayle got elected, and more important, he didn't keep the first Bush from winning."

"So are we going to mount a campaign against Spanner's being pretty?"

"We won't have to do that," Moss said. "Every time he makes some sort of bone-headed remark, they'll remember Dan Quayle."

Will sat back in his chair. "Didn't Quayle have something like a three handicap?"

"Something like that," Tom replied.

"Do you have any idea how much practice it takes to have a three handicap?"

"A lot," Tom agreed.

"But he found time for it while he was in the Senate. Find out what Spanner's handicap his. God, I hope he's a scratch golfer. We could really make something of that."

"Who would that matter to?" Kitty asked.

"To everybody who doesn't play golf, or who plays but doesn't have time to practice to a low handicap," Tom replied. "Plus everybody who doesn't play golf and hates people who do. We could do a commercial with some guy who has a low handicap and ask him how much time he practices to stay so good. He'd say something like, 'Oh, at least four hours a day,' and I think people would get the idea."

"I like it," Will said. "I had a sixteen handicap before I was a Senate aide, and I had to play at least four times a week to keep that."

Kitty was banging away on her laptop. "Here we go," she said. "Bill Spanner is a member at Congressional and Burning Tree. His handicap is listed as nineteen."

"Never mind," Will said.

---

MARTIN STANTON WAS on television in Los Angeles with a room full of high school students, answering their questions.

A skinny kid stood up and said, "I'm confused. Last week you were governor. How'd you get to be vice president?"

Marty bestowed a smile upon the boy. "The Constitution says that if a vice president dies in office, the president appoints his replacement, with the approval of the Senate, so when Vice President George Kiel died, President Lee appointed me to the remainder of Mr. Kiel's term. That term expires next January, unless President Lee and I are reelected."

The boy sat down, and a Hispanic girl stood up and asked a question about the Democratic health care plan that was so sophisticated that Stanton was barely able to answer it. He was impressed.

Another girl stood up. "Mr. Vice President, how is it that, with a name like Stanton, you are supposed to be Hispanic?"

Stanton smiled again, relieved to receive a softer pitch. "Because my mother is Hispanic. She's a native of Mexico, and I spent a lot of time there as a child. My father was a soft-drink bottler in Tijuana. I'm proud to be thought of as Hispanic."


WILL FINISHED SPEAKING in Chicago and was driven in a motorcade back to the airplane. It always embarrassed him to drive down an empty street and see people stopped at every corner to let him pass.

Back on the airplane he got Kitty and the head of his Secret Service detail together. "I've told you both about this before," he said, "but nothing has changed. I'm still stopping traffic for miles around when I'm driven anywhere, and I want something done about it."

"Mr. President," the agent said, "we're doing the minimum we have to to ensure your safety."

"The minimum is an armored limousine, four Secret Service cars, half a dozen local police cars, and a platoon of motorcycle police?"

"The local cops *want* to participate in the motorcade, sir, and to tell the truth, I'm glad to have them clearing the way."

Kitty spoke up. "He's right, Mr. President. If we cut down the security and you were harmed it would be a stain on the Secret Service for decades."

"All that security didn't help Jack Kennedy," Will said, "and it didn't even help George Wallace."

"A lone gunman in a high place is always a problem, Mr. President," the agent said, "and the motorcade was traveling slowly, so that the crowds could get a good look at President and Mrs. Kennedy. Lee Oswald got a good look, too. That's why we have to keep up the speed of the motorcade. George Wallace was shot because he didn't follow the plan."

"What plan?"

"The first two rows at any event are always people we know or have cleared. Governor Wallace broke through the first two rows in his enthusiasm for shaking hands, and Arthur Bremer was waiting for him with a gun. If he had followed the plan, it wouldn't have happened."

"Look, Mr. President," Kitty said, "I know you feel embarrassed by this, but you can't ask the people who have the responsibility of protecting you to do less than what they feel is necessary. This is not going to change, and you just have to get used to it."

Will was relieved to see Moss Mallet standing at the door. "That's all, thanks," he said to the two people, while waving Moss in.

"Mr. President, we have the results of the first poll since Bill Spanner was nominated. You're favored by fifty-one percent of the American people to forty-five percent for Spanner."

"Moss, what is going on? Two weeks ago I had a sixty-two percent approval rating, and now there's only six points between me and the upstart?"

"He's a fresh face, Mr. President. He'll get old quickly, and the polls will reflect that. There's nothing to worry about."

"Then why do you look so worried, Moss?"

"I was just worried about telling you the news. Believe me, it will get better."

"Thanks, Moss. I'm going to take a nap now. Please put that DO NOT DISTURB sign on the door on your way out."

Moss left, and Will stretched out on the bed, but he didn't sleep.

# 33

LANCE CABOT GOT INTO HIS OFFICE AT CIA HEADQUARTERS IN LANGLEY, VIRGINIA, at seven a.m., as usual. He had been deputy director for operations for some months now, and he had just begun to feel he had a firm grip on the job when his direct line rang.

This line was there so that station heads and, sometimes, field agents could go directly to the DDO, in extraordinary circumstances, and whenever it rang, Lance got tense. He picked up the instrument. "Hello?"

"Lance, it's Owen Masters in Panama City. Can we scramble?"

Lance pressed the scrambler button. "Good morning, Owen, we're scrambled." Lance didn't like Masters a hell of a lot. As a young agent he had found the man to be opinionated and rude. The only reason he had left him as station chief in Panama was that the man had only a few months until his retirement.

"Something has come up I think you should know about. Yesterday morning a dead body was discovered on the deck of an oil tanker that had passed through the canal en route to Galveston."

"Anybody we know?"

Masters ignored the question. "The body was taken off by the

Coast Guard and flown to Panama City, which has the only medical examiner in the country. When an American dies in the Canal Zone I routinely get a call from a cop I know on the Panama City force, and this morning, on the way to work, I met him at the morgue and had a look at the body. It could be an accident, but it's more likely a homicide."

Lance was annoyed. Why on earth would a station chief take an interest in a local homicide? He repeated his question. "Anybody we know, Owen?"

"Not exactly, but he's an American journalist, in a manner of speaking, who works for a rag called the *National Inquisitor*, based in D.C. Know it?"

"Vaguely. It's gossip, isn't it?"

"Right."

"So how does this interest us, Owen?"

"I went through his effects. His name is Edward Partain, American. He had quite a lot of cash and credit cards on him, so it wasn't a robbery."

Lance was getting ready to hang up, when Masters stopped him.

"And he was carrying a photograph of Teddy Fay."

Lance was stunned. He took a moment to collect himself before he spoke. "There are no existing photographs of Teddy Fay," he said. "He removed them from all the databases before he started assassinating right-wing politicians."

"There's at least one photograph now," Masters replied.

"And how do you know the photograph is one of Teddy Fay?"

"Because I knew him when I was a field agent. He outfitted me for a couple of missions—fake passports, driver's licenses, credit cards—that sort of thing. He was the top guy in Tech Services."

"How long ago was this?"

"Twelve, fifteen years."

"And how old is the photograph?"

"I'm not sure. Five to ten years, I'd guess."

"Have you mentioned this to anybody in your station?"

"No. Nobody's in yet."

"Then don't. Scan the photo and e-mail it to me *now*."

"Will do."

"Did you get the original or a copy?"

"I got the only one on the body."

"Send it to me in an overnight pouch, and don't make any copies," Lance said.

"Okay. The e-mail just went out."

"Did the police know anything about this Partain?"

"He had a hotel bill in his pocket from a fairly elegant small hostelry, so they went there and turned over his room. The only odd thing was that he had a receipt for an envelope deposited in the hotel safe, and there was twenty-five thousand dollars in cash in it. It was odd, because he had another five grand in traveler's checks in his jacket pocket, plus a grand or so in cash and half a dozen credit cards. The police talked to the hotel bartender, who said Partain had a drink with a guy the night before last, somebody he met there in the bar."

"Description?"

"American, six feet, a hundred and seventy, fifty-five to sixty-five, and balding, with a comb-over, thick eyebrows, and mustache. Wore heavy-framed glasses."

Disguise, Lance thought. "All right, Owen, I'll get back to you." Lance hung up and sat, thinking, for a couple of minutes. This was trouble. He'd certified Teddy Fay as dead to the director, and since her husband was president and was running for reelection, she wasn't going to like hearing this report. Teddy Fay had "died" before, then turned up on the island of St. Marks in the Caribbean last year, before being thought dead again aboard a sunken yacht in deep water.

The president had withheld the information from the public that Teddy Fay had turned up alive twice after being confirmed dead, and if this broke now it could torpedo his reelection, which meant that Katharine Rule would no longer be director of Central Intelligence and, since Lance was her handpicked boy, his prospects for holding on to his career wouldn't be so hot, either.

Lance picked up the phone and called Holly Barker, whose office was adjacent to his own.

"Yes, Lance?"

"Come in here, please." Lance turned to his computer, found the e-mail from Owen Masters and printed out the photograph.

There was a knock on the door between their offices, then Holly walked in. Since he had been promoted, she had become his most trusted assistant. "Good morning," she said. Holly was tall and newly slender with short-cropped hair and a firm jaw. She was a retired Army officer who had been chief of police in a small Florida town when Lance had discovered her, recruited her, and seen her trained. She was also one of a tiny handful of people who had actually met Teddy Fay.

Lance handed her the photograph. "Do you recognize this man?"

Holly looked at it carefully. "No, who is he?"

"Owen Masters in Panama says it's Teddy Fay." Lance related Masters's phone call.

"It could be," Holly said, "but I never saw Teddy except in some sort of disguise, and he was very good at it."

"Owen knew him fifteen years ago, when they were both at Langley."

Holly shook her head. "I'm sorry, I just can't tell. I didn't know a photograph existed."

"Neither did anybody else. I want you to go to the offices of the *National Inquisitor* this morning, get the negative and any copies of the photograph, and scare the shit out of the editor. I don't care what you threaten him with or do to him, but see that his paper doesn't run a word about the photo or Teddy."

"What about freedom of the press and all that?" Holly asked.

"Fuck freedom of the press. You can shoot the guy, if you think you can get away with it. Now get moving."

## 34

HOLLY WENT BACK TO HER OFFICE, THINKING SHE HAD NEVER SEEN LANCE SO exercised about anything. Normally he was the coolest operator she knew.

Before she followed his orders she had some prep work to do. She began by going to the website of the *National Inquisitor* and finding the address of their offices and the name of their editor, Willard Gaynes, then she called Jeannie in Tech Services.

"Jeannie."

"Hi, Jeannie. It's Holly Barker. I need some quick work."

"Tell me."

"I want a general sort of court order from a federal judge requiring the *National Inquisitor* to divulge any and all information I request and to produce any documents and photographs I ask for, and a separate search warrant, signed by the same judge, allowing me to tear apart their offices if they don't give me what I want. Make the order unequivocal and eyes-only secret, with jail as an alternative and national security as a reason."

"How soon?"

"Yesterday."

"Gotcha. I'll get back to you."

Holly went back to her computer and began doing searches on the backgrounds of both Willard Gaynes and Edward "Ned" Partain. She found interesting stuff and began reading it. Then she called Owen Masters in Panama City.

"Masters."

"Owen, I'm Holly Barker. I work for Lance Cabot."

"I know who you are."

"Please call your police contact and ask him to see that his department doesn't call Ned Partain's editor until exactly noon today. I want to break the news to him personally."

"Anything else?"

"No."

Masters hung up without further ado.


FIFTEEN MINUTES LATER there was a knock on Holly's door.

"Come in."

A woman of about fifty walked in and handed Holly two envelopes. "Here you go," she said. "The court order has a reasonable facsimile of the signature of Judge Ezra Wolfe of the First District Court, and so does the search warrant."

Holly read the court order and smiled. "Nice work," she said. "Beautiful job on the letterhead, too."

"The letterhead is authentic," Jeannie replied. "We lifted a ream of it from the Federal Printing Office last year. And I made a call to the judge's clerk, who is on the payroll, so if anybody checks either the order or the warrant, he'll provide backup."

"Perfect," Holly said. "Thank you, Jeannie. I owe you one."

"It's what we do," Jeannie said, and with a wave, left Holly's office.

AT ELEVEN FORTY-FIVE, Holly walked into the editorial offices of the *National Inquisitor* and spoke to a woman at the reception desk. "My name is Branson. I want to see Willard Gaynes now."

"Do you have an appointment?"

Holly reached into her purse and removed an envelope. "Give him this," she said. "He'll see me." The envelope contained a business card identifying Holly as Assistant Director Hope Branson of the FBI.

"Just a minute," the woman said. She left the reception room and was back in less than a minute. "He'll see you," she said. "Through the door, down the hall to the corner office."

Holly followed the directions, opened Gaynes's closed door, walked in, flashed an FBI ID and sat down.

"So, what can we do for the FBI today?" Gaynes asked. He was a short, heavily jowled man with oily dyed-black hair.

"You have a reporter named Edward 'Ned' Partain?"

"Yes," Gaynes replied. "He's out of town on a story."

"I know," Holly replied. "In Panama. He's dead."

Gaynes's eyes widened. "Wait a minute," he said. He looked at the card Holly had sent him, then picked up the phone and dialed the number on the card, which connected him not to the FBI switchboard but to a facsimile at Langley. "Do you have an agent named Hope Branson?" he asked. "All right, Assistant Director Branson. Please connect me with her office." He waited, then listened. "Never mind," he said, and hung up the phone.

"Now," he said to Holly, "what the hell are you talking about?"

"The body of Ned Partain was found aboard a tanker bound from the Panama Canal to Galveston, Texas, yesterday. He appeared to have fallen from some place along the canal onto the deck of the ship."

"Was this a homicide?" he asked.

"Possibly. The autopsy is being conducted as we speak."

The phone on Gaynes's desk rang. "Excuse me," he said, and picked it up. He was on the phone for less than a minute. "That was the Panama City police. Apparently, what you told me is true."

"Tell me why Partain was in Panama," Holly said.

"We don't tell the FBI that sort of thing."

Holly handed him the court order. She waited while he read it, then said, "Tell me what I want to know, or you'll be in the federal detention center in twenty minutes."

"I've never seen a document like this," Gaynes said. "Hold on." He called the number on the letterhead, asked for the judge's clerk and questioned him, then hung up and turned back to Holly. "What do you want to know?"

"We don't like it when American journalists die in foreign countries," Holly said. "Tell me everything about Partain's assignment."

"Ned was in Panama to interview a man who is believed to be Teddy Fay."

Holly snorted. "Teddy Fay is dead," she said, "confirmed and reconfirmed."

"Maybe," Gaynes said.

Holly held up the e-mailed print of Teddy's photograph. "Is this the man you thought was Teddy Fay?"

Gaynes looked surprised. "Yes."

"This man is a CIA officer on assignment in South America. Where did you get the photograph?"

"From a woman named Darlene Cole, who works for a law firm in town. She knew Fay years ago."

"Which law firm?"

"Barton and Falls," Gaynes said.

"Give me all the copies you have of the photo and the negative."

"I don't have the negative," Gaynes said. "Ms. Cole was cagey about that."

"How many copies do you have?"

"Look, you're out of line here."

Holly handed him the search warrant. "I can have a team of agents here in half an hour to tear apart your offices, but of course, you'll be in detention by then."

Gaynes went to a safe in a corner of his office, punched a number into the keypad, and opened it.

Holly watched him and memorized the combination. It might come in handy one of these days.

Gaynes took out an envelope, examined the contents, and handed it to Holly.

She found half a dozen copies of the photo and tucked them into her purse. "Give me the card I gave you," Holly said, "and the court order and search warrant."

Gaynes surrendered the documents.

"You are under a federal court injunction not to speak of this to anyone," Holly said. "I was never here, do you understand?"

Gaynes nodded. "I understand."

"If you talk about this to anyone on your staff or off, bad things will happen," she said.

"All right, all right," he said, raising both hands. "Will you let me know more about Ned Partain?"

"The Panama City police will deal with you on that," Holly said. "Good day." She rose and walked out of the office, satisfied with her day's work.

As she passed the reception desk, a skinny, slightly disheveled young man wearing a backpack was talking with the receptionist. "But I have to see Gaynes right now," he said. "Ned Partain is out of town, and this is too important to wait."

"I told you, he's with somebody," the woman replied.

Holly pressed the elevator button. "Not anymore," she said. "Mr. Gaynes is entirely free."

"What is your name again?" the secretary asked.

"Felix Potter," the young man said.

The elevator arrived, and Holly got on.

"It's about some very important tapes," the young man said.

The elevator door closed, and Holly rode down.

## 35

FELIX SAT IN THE RECEPTION ROOM AT THE *NATIONAL INQUISITOR* FOR MORE THAN three hours, getting hungrier and hungrier but determined to see Willard Gaynes. Finally, the receptionist got up and went to the ladies' room, and Felix saw his chance. He was through the door and into the editorial offices before the woman had a chance to get her knickers down.

He stopped for a moment and assessed the layout of the floor. There was a sea of desks in a large newsroom, and offices, apparently for higher-ranking people, along the walls. Where would he sit if he were Willie Gaynes? he asked himself. The corner office, that's where.

Felix walked purposefully along one side of the newsroom, not dawdling but not hurrying, either. He was wearing a necktie and his best jacket, so he wasn't dressed too differently from how the other men present were dressed. The corner office was dead ahead, and the door was closed. He stopped, took a deep breath, let it out, rapped on the door, opened it, and stepped in.

Gaynes was sitting at his desk, talking on the telephone. He looked up at Felix and put a hand over the mouthpiece. "Who the hell are you?" he demanded.

"I'm one of Ned Partain's best sources, Mr. Gaynes, and Ned told me that if ever I couldn't reach him about something important I should come directly to you."

Gaynes pointed at a sofa. "Sit over there and shut up," he said, then went back to his phone conversation. "Señor, please give me the name and number of that funeral home," he said, then jotted down the information. "Can you tell me, señor, was this accidental or a homicide?" He listened. "All right, I understand that the official investigation will take some time, but can you give me your personal opinion, based on your experience as a police officer?" He listened again, and his face grew more serious. "Thank you, señor," he said. "Please call me at this number should you learn anything new about the case, and may I call you again, if I have any questions? Thank you, señor, and good-bye." He hung up and turned to Felix, but he said nothing. He seemed to be deep in thought.

Felix waited him out, and suddenly Gaynes seemed to snap out of his reverie.

"Who the fuck are you?" he asked, as if he hadn't asked before.

"I'm Felix Potter, Mr. Gaynes, one of Ned Partain's sources. Ned told me to contact you if I had something important and couldn't find him, and I can't find him."

"That's because Ned is in Panama, playing the role of corpse," Gaynes said. "I've never lost a man due to violence before, and I'm having a little trouble digesting it."

"Ned has been murdered?" Felix asked.

"It appears so. That's the opinion of the Panamanian police officer I just spoke to, anyway. You've worked with Ned, you say?"

Although Felix had set eyes on Ned Partain only once, in a coffee shop in the building, he saw an opportunity. "Yes, sir, and I'm extremely sorry to hear about Ned's death. Is there anything I can do?"

"You can tell me what's so important that you come barging into my office unannounced," Gaynes said, appearing to recover himself.

Ned held up his briefcase. "Mr. Gaynes, I have something in here of national importance, something that could have an important effect on the presidential race."

Gaynes sighed. "Spit it out, kid. This has been a bad day all 'round, and there isn't much of it left."

Felix opened his briefcase and took out a small CD player. He got up and walked toward Gaynes's desk. "I have a recording of two people here that's going to knock your socks off, Mr. Gaynes." He set the little machine on Gaynes's desk and switched it on.

"This better be two celebrities fucking," Gaynes said.

"Almost," Felix replied. The two voices began speaking, their conversation broken, then there was a gap, and they spoke again.

"What's with all the interruptions?" Gaynes asked. "And why do I care about this?"

"These people were on a cell phone and were recorded just outside the White House," Felix said.

"What, you're telling me they're White House staff? That's certainly not the president's voice. This guy doesn't have a southern accent."

"Sir, what does it sound like to you that they're doing?" Felix asked.

"Doing? They're certainly not fucking. I've heard a lot of recordings of people fucking, and that's not what they're doing."

"No, sir, but they're talking about fucking."

"Well, I guess you could draw that conclusion," Gaynes said, "but I wouldn't want to have to prove it in court. Why do you come in here with crap like this?"

"Because the man is the vice president of the United States," Felix said.

"The vice president is dead," Gaynes said. "Don't you watch TV?"

"Not that vice president, the new vice president," Felix said.

Gaynes squinted at Felix. "Play it again," he said.

Felix played it again.

"Well, he's got the deep voice and no accent," Gaynes said. "He sounds like Dick Nixon. Why do you think it's what's-his-name?"

"Martin Stanton, sir. I've had an expert compare this recording with Stanton's press conference on TV, after he was picked to be the veep. It's the same voice." This was a bald-faced lie, but Gaynes didn't know that.

"Well, Stanton is getting a divorce," Gaynes said. "Who's the woman?"

"I haven't been able to nail that down yet, sir."

"What city is she in?"

"I'm not sure about that, either."

"Who recorded this?"

"I did, Mr. Gaynes. My car is equipped to intercept cell-phone conversations."

"And you were at the White House?"

"I was driving around the neighborhood of the White House, sir."

"Play it again," Gaynes said.

Felix played it again.

"It does sound like Stanton," Gaynes admitted. "Who's your expert?"

"I'm afraid I have to keep that confidential, sir. He thinks this is too hot to touch."

"Well, it's hot only if it's Stanton and only if he's fucking this woman and only if we can find out who the hell she is."

"I think it's a pretty good start, sir."

Gaynes pressed the eject button on the machine and removed the disc. "You leave this with me, and I'll have it checked out by an expert I trust. If he says it's Stanton, then we'll talk."

"We need to talk now, Mr. Gaynes," Felix said. "We need to agree on a deal, if what I've told you is confirmed."

"All right, I'll give you a grand, cash, right now, and another ten grand, if it checks out."

"I'm going to need twenty-five thousand, if it checks out," Felix said.

"I'll pay you that when Stanton's voice is confirmed and the woman is identified," Gaynes said. He swiveled his chair around, opened a safe, and counted out some money with his back turned. "Here's your grand," Gaynes said. "Give me your phone number and get out of here."

Felix gave him a card, picked up the money, and got out of there.

# 36

HOLLY USED HER CELL PHONE TO GET THE ADDRESS OF THE LAW FIRM OF BARTON & Falls, which turned out to be in a seedy part of Washington in a commercial strip mall, next door to a bail bondsman. The plate-glass windows had been darkened with film stuck to them, and the door was locked, but there was a doorbell and intercom. Holly rang it.

"Yes?" a voice said.

"I want to see a lawyer," Holly said.

"What's your problem?"

"My husband has just been arrested for possessing a firearm and drugs."

A buzzer rang, and Holly pulled open the door. A woman of about forty, not unattractive, sat at a desk in the small reception room, filing her nails. The remains of a sandwich rested on a paper bag, next to a cardboard coffee cup, which was next to a large handbag.

"Everybody's at lunch," the woman said, shoving a sheet of paper and a pen across the desk before returning to her nails. "Fill out this form."

"That won't be necessary," Holly said. "Are you Darlene Cole?"

"Who wants to know?" the woman asked.

Holly held up her FBI ID. "FBI. Let me see some ID."

"What's this about?" the woman asked.

"Don't make me ask you again," Holly said.

"I don't have to show you any ID," the woman said.

Holly returned her ID to her handbag, set it on the floor, raked the sandwich and coffee cup off the desk, grabbed the woman's handbag, and turned the considerable contents out onto the desk.

"Hey!" the woman yelled.

"Shut up, unless you'd rather be handcuffed and interviewed at the federal detention center." Holly found a wallet amid the detritus of the handbag contents and inside that, a Maryland driver's license in the name of Darlene M. Cole.

Holly went to the front door, locked it, and returned to the desk. "Let's make this short and sweet," she said to Darlene, holding up the photo of Teddy Fay. "You met this man some years ago, and he told you his name was Fay, is that correct?"

"What if it is?"

"His name is not Fay—Fay has been dead for some time. This man is an American intelligence officer currently assigned to a foreign country. You made the mistake of believing him when he told you he was Teddy Fay and the further mistake of trying to expose him to Ned Partain of the *National Inquisitor.* As a result, Mr. Partain is dead, and the agent's life is in jeopardy, and you have committed a serious violation of the National Defense Act that could get you detained for up to a hundred and twenty days without being charged or seeing a lawyer. If you are convicted you'll do up to twenty-five years in prison."

"You're crazy, lady. I don't know anything about this," Darlene said, pushing her chair back against the wall.

"I want all the prints of the photograph, and the negative," Holly said, "and I don't have time to argue with you."

Darlene's eyes swiveled toward her wallet on the desk, then snapped back to Holly. "I don't know what you're talking about."

Holly produced a pair of handcuffs. "You are under arrest for a Title I violation of the National Security Act," she said. "You do not have the right to remain silent, and you do not have the right to an attorney for the first one hundred and twenty days of your detention. Stand up and put your hands behind your back."

Darlene sat wide-eyed and unmoving. Holly walked around the desk, jerked her out of the chair, threw her against the wall, and handcuffed her. "Sit down," she said, shoving her back into the chair.

Holly picked up the wallet and emptied it of its contents: credit cards and photographs. She flicked through the pile until she found a small envelope, which yielded a strip of thirty-five-millimeter negatives. Holding it up to the light, she compared the frames to the photo of Teddy Fay. "Right," she said. "Where are the prints?"

Darlene said nothing.

"All right, let's get out of here," Holly said. "We'll continue this discussion in a cell downtown."

"I don't have any prints," Darlene yelled, bursting into tears. "I gave them all to Ned Partain."

"If you're lying to me, I'll find out," Holly said. "Under the act, you're eligible for extreme interrogation techniques, and you'll tell me everything."

"I swear I don't have any prints," Darlene sobbed. "You've got the negatives, so take them and leave me alone."

Holly jerked her to her feet and unlocked the cuffs. "As I told you, Ned Partain is dead, murdered, and you could be next. You'd better not breathe a word to a soul about my visit, and you'd better forget you ever talked to Partain, or you could be joining him down at the morgue in Panama City, do you understand me?"

"Yes, yes, I understand," Darlene sobbed.

"If I were you, I'd move to another city far away and change my name. The people who killed Partain have long memories." Holly unlocked the door and walked to her car, laughing under her breath.

Back at Langley, Holly walked into Lance Cabot's office and deposited the prints and negatives on his desk. "I believe that's all there is," she said.

"I don't want to know how you got this stuff," Lance said.

"What stuff?" Holly asked, then she turned and went back to her office.

LANCE PUT the prints and negatives in an envelope, sealed it, and wrote "birth documents" on the envelope and locked it in his safe. No need to mention this to Katharine Lee, he thought. He felt comfortable in his skin for the first time since he had received the call from Owen Masters in Panama City.

Was Owen going to be a problem? Did he have an ax of some sort to grind? Or would he be the loyal time server he had always been and keep his mouth shut?

Lance resolved to think more on this when he was calmer and more relaxed.

## 37

MARTIN STANTON WAS STANDING BEFORE A BATHROOM MIRROR IN HIS PAJAMA bottoms when the phone began ringing. He shaved faster, hoping it would stop. It didn't. Finally, he grabbed the receiver next to the toilet in the giagantic bathroom. "Yes?"

"This is the hotel operator, Mr. Vice President. I have a gentleman on the line who says he is your attorney."

"Yes, I'll take the call." There was a click. "Jake?"

"Yes, Mr. Vice President. How are you this morning?"

"Nearly shaven. Can you hang on for a minute?"

"Of course."

Stanton went back to the mirror, moistened his beard, and completed the project. Rinsed and toweled dry, he returned to the phone, put down the toilet seat, and sat. "All right, Jake, what's up?"

"I've just been on the phone with Betty's attorney, and he says she says she wants another fifty thousand, to help her resettle. And the Cadillac."

Stanton tried not to scream. "Our settlement gives her fifty thousand for resettlement expenses already."

"She says it's not enough."

"She wants to reupholster, recurtain, recarpet, and repaint every square inch of the house," Stanton said. "I won't do it, not anymore."

"I don't blame you, Marty. We've already given her about sixty percent of your estate. It may be we've reached the point where we have to draw the line, tell them to accept what's on the table or we'll see them in court."

"I think you're right. Give her the Cadillac, tell her she can have it today, if she signs the settlement as is, but nothing else. This is the end of the line."

"All right, with your stated permission, I'll tell her attorney just that. He's smart enough to know that a judge, or even a jury, is not going to give her more than sixty percent of community property. She might even get less."

"Then do it, Jake, right now. Let me know what to expect. Oh, just to let them know I'm serious, tell them that if she doesn't sign, or if she signs and then complains about it, I'll release the settlement agreement to the press."

"All right, Marty. I'll get back to you." He hung up.

Stanton hung up, too. His blood pressure was up; he could feel it throbbing against his temples. How did what started out as an amicable attempt to settle turn into this? It was insane!

He put on his wristwatch and checked it. An hour until his first appearance. He chose a suit and tie and got dressed. As he finished, the doorbell rang, and the Secret Service agent in the living room answered it. Stanton walked into the living room to find an attractive woman standing in the foyer. "Good morning," he said.

"Good morning, Mr. Vice President," she said, extending a hand. "I'm Elizabeth Wharton, your campaign manager, if that meets with your approval."

"Please come in, Ms. Wharton. I didn't even know I had a campaign manager yet."

"The president, knowing that you had not had time to assemble a staff, directed his campaign manager, Senator Sam Meriwether, to appoint someone to help. If you would prefer someone else, that will be fine."

"Tell me about yourself . . . may I call you Elizabeth?"

"Liz will be fine, sir. I'm from the small town of Delano, Georgia, President Lee's hometown. I graduated from the University of Georgia with a master's degree in history. I taught history at Agnes Scott College in Atlanta for seven years, working on Democratic campaigns on the side, then I worked on Senator Meriwether's staff when he was in the House, and I managed his campaign for the Senate."

"Sounds like a good background, Liz. Let's see how it works out."

She opened a leather envelope and produced a sheet of paper. "Here's your revised schedule for today. You're speaking at a brunch this morning attended by members of the San Francisco alumnae association of Brandeis University. They're just about all Jewish, and we've included a statement of your support for Israel in your speech, which I wrote, myself, last night." She handed him half a dozen pages. "Please read it on the way to the event, and if you don't like any of it, please feel free to wing it, but remember to include your support of Israel."

"I'm sure it will be fine," Stanton said, tucking the pages into an inside pocket. She was very attractive indeed, he thought, and obviously very smart. The doorbell rang again, and a middle-aged Filipino man was admitted.

"This is your valet for the campaign," Liz said, "Alfredo Garcia. Alfredo will pack and unpack for you and manage your luggage in transit. The Secret Service wants someone who has been cleared by them."

"Good morning, Alfredo," Stanton said.

"Good morning, Mr. Vice President. May I pack your things?"

"Yes, please."

Alfredo disappeared into the bedroom.

"And I have some good news," Liz said. "Your campaign airplane has arrived, fresh from its annual inspection. It's a BBJ, Boeing Business Jet, which is based on the 737 series of airliners. It will carry you in comfort, along with half a dozen staff and a dozen or so press."

"Do I have half a dozen staff?" Stanton asked.

"You do, sir. When we arrive at Oakland to board the aircraft, you'll find two secretaries, Alfredo, representatives of the Mallet Polling Company and of Tom Black's political consultancies, and of course, me."

"Well, let's get started," Stanton said, rising. "After you." He took note of her breasts as she turned toward the door, then got a view of her stern on the way out. She was a tall, slender redhead, and very well put together, he thought.

IN THE ARMORED SUV that served as his limousine, Stanton quickly read the speech Liz had written. "Excellent," he said. "I'll use it as an outline to refer to, as I prefer to improvise a little as I go along."

"That's fine, as long as you remember to mention Israel favorably."

"That won't be a problem," Stanton said.

"Mr. Vice President," Liz said, "if you'll forgive my asking, do you have any personal difficulties that might bear on the campaign? I understand you're going through a divorce, for instance."

"Yes, I am, but I don't anticipate that being a problem. Just this morning my attorney is making my final offer in the settlement. I hope it will be signed before the day is out."

"I see. That's good news. May I ask, is there currently a woman in your life?"

"No," Stanton replied, "there is not." Not currently, anyway. "What about yourself? Are you married?"

"No, and there is no woman in my life, either. Nor a man of any importance."

"Good to know these things," Stanton said.

"Yes," she agreed.

Stanton picked up a newspaper and laid part of it in his lap, to hide what would be all too obvious.

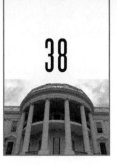

# 38

TEDDY FAY HAD DECIDED NOT TO LEAVE PANAMA CITY—NOT JUST YET, ANYWAY. HE had put away the gray-wig-and-mustache disguise and was now employing a red wig with a lower hairline and gray flecks, with eyebrows to match. He had kept his apartment, since no one had ever seen him leave or arrive there, and on the whole, he felt pretty comfortable.

There had been an item in the local English-language paper about Ned Partain's body being found on the tanker, but as he had expected, the police had not been able to ascertain where old Ned had boarded the ship. Eventually, they would get around to visiting El Parador, the restaurant where he and Ned had dined, and they might figure it out after that, so he would not return to El Parador. He had been back to the bar at El Conquistador, wearing the new disguise, and had detected no recognition in the eyes of the bartender, so he might go there occasionally in search of women.

He had considered paying a visit to Darlene Cole, in Maryland, but to remove her from the earth would just confirm her sighting of him. He had been reading the *National Inquisitor*, which, surprisingly, seemed to have a substantial circulation in Panama City, and there had been an article about the death of Ned Partain, quoting the local police as saying it was accidental in nature. No mention had been made of Ned's assignment, nor had the photo of Teddy run in the paper.

Teddy had felt the need of better cover, though, so on a moonless night he had let himself into the local personnel office of the Panama Canal Company, gone through the files of retirees and found an excellent match for himself, a retired gentleman with thirty years' service in payroll. He copied the man's file, substituted a photo of himself in his current disguise and returned the file to its dusty cabinet. Then, using the same photo, he made himself Canal Zone documents.

All this had kept Teddy entertained for a few days. Now, however, he had one more base to cover: the Panama station of the Central Intelligence Agency. If, somehow, the station chief had gotten wind of Partain's fate, he would have reported the incident to Langley, and one or more agents would have been assigned to see that the *Inquisitor* did not publish any stories about Teddy. That would not have been in the Agency's interests.

The website of the American Embassy had yielded the names of the principal officers of the embassy, and there, nestled in the list as deputy agricultural attaché, was his old acquaintance Owen Masters, so it was not hard to figure out who the station chief was.

Owen, apparently, had been shipped off to Panama to serve out his time before retirement, which, if memory served, would be in the not-too-distant future. Panama was hardly a plum assignment, and that meant that the other members of the station would be few in number, probably no more than half a dozen, mostly rookies. Owen's only real work in Panama would be training them to seem busy.

Teddy ran his agile intellect over the possibilities. Suppose, perhaps through an agency asset in the Panamanian government or police, Owen had been apprised of Ned Partain's demise. Teddy's one mistake had been not to remove his photograph from Ned's pocket before assisting him onto the ship. And that would have been found when the police went through his clothes and hotel room. Suppose, then, that Owen had seen the photograph and recognized Teddy from the old days. He would have alerted Langley, in the person of Lance Cabot, his boss, and by now Lance would have seen it.

This was all a worst-case scenario, of course. It was likely that Owen had never heard of Partain and that the photo now rested in some filing cabinet at police headquarters in Colón, at the other end of the canal, which would suit Teddy just fine.

The worst-case scenario, though, would suit him pretty well, too, because Lance Cabot, as soon as he saw the photo of Teddy, would have conducted an immediate sweeping-under-the-rug operation. Certainly, he would not have apprised Katharine Rule of the resurrection of Teddy Fay, since that would have reflected very badly on himself. Nor would he send people looking for Teddy, since that would mean looking for a dead man. Lance, for the moment, would serve very nicely as Teddy's new best friend.

Owen Masters, though, would have little interest in Lance Cabot's comfort. There had been, after all, a day when Owen's career track had aimed him, more or less, at Lance's job, and now he found himself moldering in the heat and humidity of Panama, grinding it out until his retirement clock reached the magic number of thirty, disaffected and thoroughly pissed off. Owen was the wild card in the worst-case scenario, and Teddy wanted to have sight of him, to assess his state of mind.

Teddy began by waiting outside the American Embassy in the late afternoon. He wanted to know what time Owen Masters called it a day, and he was gratified to see the aging spy wander out of the building at a quarter past four. He certainly wasn't working nights trying to find Teddy. Owen got into his car, a dusty embassy Chevrolet, and Teddy cranked his motor scooter and followed him.

The trail of Owen Masters led to a dimly lit cantina a mile or so from the embassy but probably near Owen's home. There he would be unlikely to encounter fellow embassy employees, so there would be no one to report back on how much he was drinking. And Owen was drinking much.

The man started with a tequila shooter and a *cerveza* chaser, just to get his alcohol blood level up, then switched to margaritas. Teddy witnessed all this from the far end of the bar, while he nursed his own drink. Owen spent an hour there, anesthetizing himself for whatever his evening promised.

What it promised, it turned out, after Teddy had followed him home and stationed himself outside a kitchen window, was five minutes of a monumental fight with Owen's wife, Estelle, whom Teddy had met once at a social gathering of spooks. The discussion covered the no doubt familiar ground of Owen's consumption level of alcohol, Owen's lack of career prospects, Owen's failure to save enough money for a decent retirement, and Owen's having got them sent to this godforsaken place.

This was followed, after Estelle had finally wound down, by a grimly silent supper and television viewing. Teddy was happy for Owen that he had a satellite dish.

Teddy wended his way to a favorite restaurant for dinner, feeling less worried about Owen Masters as a threat. He would stick around Panama City, albeit well prepared for flight, until he discerned some more threatening blip on his overdeveloped personal radar.

# 39

BARBARA ORTEGA LEFT THE DEPARTMENT OF JUSTICE FEELING VERY GOOD. SHE had spent a little over two hours with a three-person selection committee—two men and a woman—and had answered their questions directly, honestly, and sometimes bluntly. They had reacted with interest, seemed to appreciate her candor, and had, somehow, signaled the attorney general to join them for the last few minutes of the interview, which she took as a good sign. The AG had asked a few questions and had seemed happy with her answers, too.

Her résumé was great, the new vice president was her former boss, and she knew there was a letter of recommendation from the president in her file. There was nothing in her personal history that would count as a black mark. She had been outstanding as a student, as an ADA in Los Angeles and in the California AG's office, as well as in the state house. And she was a woman. What could go wrong?

She went back to her hotel, ordered a room-service dinner, and fell asleep with the TV on.

Martin Stanton was en route from Los Angeles to San Antonio when he got the call from the attorney general.

"Morning, Mr. Vice President."

"Good morning, General."

"My selection committee and I met yesterday with your former chief of staff, Barbara Ortega."

"I hope it went well."

"She was very impressive. I noted that there was nothing in her jacket from you about her candidacy, and I wanted to ask you why."

"I felt that I should not be seen to be promoting my former chief of staff for a high federal position at this time, that's all," Stanton said.

"So you asked the president to do it instead?"

"No, the first I heard of the president's involvement was when he mentioned that Barbara had given him as a reference."

"I suppose she had every right to do that," the AG said.

"Of course. She knows the president, and he knows her."

"What is your opinion of Ms. Ortega as a person and a candidate for the appointment?"

"Since you ask, I have the highest possible regard for her both personally and professionally. I think she's perfectly qualified for the appointment."

"I'm glad to hear that," the AG said. "Would you like to know my decision?"

"If you want to tell me, certainly."

"I've decided to hire her as head of the Criminal Division," the AG said.

Stanton tried to keep his voice neutral. "I'm sure you'll be very happy with Barbara," he said, "and I congratulate you on your judgment."

The AG laughed. "Thank you, sir. Would you like to give her the news?"

"No, I think she'd like to hear it from you, General. I'll drop her a congratulatory note when I get a chance."

"Thank you, Mr. Vice President, and good-bye."

Stanton hung up the phone, elated. He also found that he had an erection at the thought of having Barbara in Washington. It had been very tough to do without her during the past days.

At that moment Liz Wharton walked past his seat, and he watched thoughtfully as she made her way up the aisle. She stopped and bent over to speak to someone, and her skirt was pulled tight across her ass. Stanton's heartbeat increased noticeably.

SHELLY BACH PUT DOWN the phone, left her office, and walked a couple of doors down to Kerry Smith's secretary. "Does he have a minute?" she asked.

"He's alone," the woman replied. "Go on in."

Shelly rapped on the door and stuck her head in. "Got a moment?"

"Sure, come on in."

She walked in, took a chair, and noticed how carefully he watched her. They had made a point of being completely professional in the office, even when alone, but their evenings had been much more interesting.

"What's up?"

"Have you ever heard of an agent called Hope Branson?"

"No. What office is she in?"

"Well, the switchboard had a call this morning from someone asking for an Assistant Director Hope Branson, and after being told there was no such person he insisted on talking to an AD, and the call came to me."

"There's certainly no assistant director by that name," Kerry said. "What else did he say?"

"He said that she had come to his office yesterday and shown him FBI ID, and that he had called our switchboard to confirm her identity and reached her secretary. I told him I thought someone must be pulling his leg, and he hung up. I had the call backtracked and it was from the office of the editor of a horrible gossip rag called the *National Inquisitor*, a man named William or Willie Gaynes."

Kerry sat back in his chair and looked thoughtful. "And what do you divine from that?"

"Sounds like we have an impostor AD roaming the streets," Shelly said.

"Did you get a description of the woman?"

"No, he hung up too quickly."

"Maybe you'd better look into this," Kerry said. "Visit Mr. Gaynes and find out as much as you can about this woman."

"All right," she said, getting up and turning for the door.

"Dinner tonight?"

"Sure," she said, flashing him a smile.

WILLIE GAYNES SAT at his desk and thought deeply. What the hell was going on here? This woman had shown him a business card and federal ID that looked good to him and on top of that a court order and a search warrant, and the judge's clerk had backed it up. Now the FBI had denied all knowledge of this Hope Branson.

Of course, he no longer had the business card, the court order, or the search warrant; she had been smart enough to take all of that with her, along with all the photographs of Teddy Fay, if it was, indeed, Teddy Fay.

Willie had been mixed up in a lot of screwy deals in this job—that was the work, after all—but this one took the cake, and he was going to get to the bottom of it.

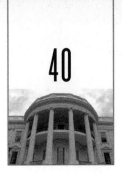

# 40

SHELLY BACH PARKED HER CAR IN THE BASEMENT GARAGE OF THE *NATIONAL Inquisitor* building and, as she walked to the elevator, noted the number of Porsches, Mercedes, and BMWs parked there. She doubted if the parking garage at *The Washington Post* sported so many.

In the reception room she showed her ID to the receptionist. "I'd like to see Mr. Gaynes," she said.

The woman dialed a number. "A lady from the FBI to see you," she said.

"Special Agent Shelly Bach," Shelly said.

The receptionist repeated this information into the phone, then hung up. "Through the door, down the hall to the corner office," she said.

Shelly followed the directions and found William Gaynes waiting for her at his open door, looking her up and down.

"Oh, a different one today," he said.

"You and I spoke on the phone yesterday," Shelly said, holding up her ID, "only you hung up."

"All right, come on in," Gaynes said resignedly.

Shelly took a chair and crossed her legs. "Tell me about this visitor you had," she said. "Start with a physical description."

"Tall," Gaynes replied, "like you. Short reddish hair, a good suit, great shoes, probably Manolos. On the whole, rather good looking."

"And what did her ID look like?"

"Like yours."

"You said she showed you a court order and a search warrant?"

"Signed by a federal judge. I called the number on his letterhead, and his clerk confirmed it."

"The judge's name?"

"I can't remember," Gaynes replied. "Not one I was familiar with."

"Someone went to a great deal of trouble and preparation to convince you of something," Shelly said. "What was it?"

"She told me that a reporter of mine, a valued reporter named Ned Partain, had died, was probably murdered in Panama. A moment later, somebody who said he was a Panamanian policeman called and confirmed it."

"My, what a coincidence. Well, if she wasn't FBI—and she wasn't—maybe he wasn't a Panamanian policeman."

Gaynes sat up. "You mean Partain might not be dead?"

"I have no idea," Shelly said, "but give me a minute, and I'll find out." She whipped out her cell phone and pressed a button. "This is Bach. Ascertain a reported death in Panama, name of Ned Partain, reporter, circumstances, too. Call me back immediately."

"How do I know *you're* FBI?" Gaynes asked.

"You called the Hoover Building yesterday and got me on the phone. I'm not the cleaning lady." She handed him her card. "You can keep this one."

Gaynes read it and dropped it into a desk drawer. "What do you want?"

"I want to know what *she* wanted," Shelly said. "She didn't turn up here with a lot of fake paper just to tell you your reporter was dead. She could have done that with a fake phone call." Shelly's phone rang. "Yes?"

"Death of Ned Partain confirmed," her assistant said. "Possibly accidental but probably homicide. Officer in charge of case: Sergeant Pepe Norte, Panamanian National Police, based in Panama City. Body iced and air-freighted to W. Gaynes, with a *y*, care of the *National Inquisitor*."

"Hang on," Shelly said. "Mr. Gaynes, Partain is dead, and his body was shipped to you this morning. I'd like to have an autopsy performed by our people. That all right with you?"

"What's it going to cost me?" Gaynes asked.

"It will be gratis."

"Gratis is good. Do your thing."

Shelly raised her pen. "Who is his next of kin?"

"He had an ex-wife, nobody else that I know of."

"Then I guess your permission will do." Shelly turned back to her phone. "Tell AD Smith I'd like the body met and taken to our ME for autopsy."

"Will do." She hung up.

"All right, Mr. Gaynes," Shelly said, "What did the fake FBI lady want?"

"Some photographs," Gaynes said.

"Of whom or what?"

"Teddy Fay."

Shelly stared at him, momentarily speechless.

"Allegedly," Gaynes said. "A woman named Darlene Cole called Ned and said she had taken the photo and that she had seen Fay in Panama while she was there on a cruise. We paid her for the shot, but she retained the negative." He read out the name of Cole's employer, address, and phone number while Shelly copied them down.

"Let me see the photograph," Shelly said.

"I gave all the prints we had to your supposed colleague," Gaynes said.

"*All* of them?"

"All of them. She said the photo wasn't of Teddy Fay but of an American intelligence agent on assignment in Panama, and she threatened me with all sorts of crap if I didn't forget she'd ever been here."

"Describe the man in the photo."

"Mid to late fifties, balding, gray hair, medium everything."

"This is preposterous," Shelly said, half to herself.

"Tell me about it."


SHELLY VISITED the law office where Darlene Cole worked and found her at her desk. Cole seemed happy to tell her everything.

"You didn't give her all the negatives, did you?" Shelly asked.

"She went through my wallet and found them. There were six, I think. I sold Gaynes a print of the best one."

"Do you have any other photographs of the man who said he was Teddy Fay?"

"No. I took those one afternoon eight or nine years ago, when Teddy—if that's his name—and I were sailing on Chesapeake Bay. Was he really Teddy Fay?"

"No," Shelly said. "Fay is dead."

"Was the guy I knew really an American spy?"

"Maybe." Shelly gave her a card. "If you should suddenly discover more negatives or prints, call me, please."

"Do I have to worry about Teddy Fay coming to see me?"

"I told you, he's dead."

"What about whoever the guy was?"

"I shouldn't think he'll be a problem," Shelly said. She stood up. "Thank you for your help."


SHELLY DROVE BACK to the Hoover Building, went to see Kerry Smith, and told him what she had learned.

Kerry picked up his phone, dialed a number, and asked for Katharine Rule.

# 41

WILL LEE GOT OUT OF *MARINE ONE* ON THE LAWN, WAVED AT THE GATHERED PRESS and staff, and made it into the White House just as rain began to pelt down. He reckoned the chopper had pretty good radar, if it had managed to avoid that. Lightning now joined the rain, illuminating the White House in flashes.

He walked into the upstairs family quarters and was surprised to find his wife already home from Langley, curled up on the living room couch, her feet tucked under her, watching CNN. He decided to play this as if nothing had happened the last time he saw her.

"Hi," Kate said.

Will was encouraged. He walked over and kissed her on the neck. "Hi."

"How was the campaign trail?" she asked.

"Spooky," he said. "I'm slipping in the polls for no apparent reason." He tossed his jacket onto a chair, loosened his tie, walked over to the bar, and made them each a drink. "Moss says there's nothing to worry about, but I don't believe him. I think Spanner is turning out to be a better candidate than we had given him credit for."

"I think Moss is right," she said, accepting her martini, muting

CNN, and patting a spot next to her on the couch all in one motion.

"You don't think the electorate doesn't love me anymore?"

"Don't be ridiculous," she said. "How could anybody not love you? I do."

He kissed her and tasted martini. "You certainly know how to welcome a weary candidate home," he said.

"And I'm not finished," she said, "but first I have to drink this martini and have some dinner, which I ordered as soon as I heard the chopper."

"All that beauty and efficient, too."

"I had a weird phone call today," Kate said.

"That can't be a new thing, in your job."

"No, this was way out there."

"Weird odd or weird funny?"

"Weird odd. You know that awful fucking scandal sheet, the *Inquisitor*, Charlene Joiner's best friend?"

Will rolled his eyes.

"Well, a woman visited their offices yesterday, claiming to be an assistant director of the FBI, showing ID, too. Turns out the Bureau never heard of this person. I got a call from Kerry Smith, telling me about it."

"Why would Kerry call you about this?"

"Because he thinks the woman was Agency, that's why, though he was too polite to say so."

"Are your people poking around in freedom of the press and all that?"

"Not on my orders, and Lance denied all knowledge, too, though I have to say he didn't seem terribly surprised when I asked him about it."

"Wouldn't be the first time a fellow hid something from his boss."

"Well, yeah, that crossed my mind."

"Why are you so concerned about this?"

"Well, suppose Lance is lying about having sent somebody over there. What the hell for? It would have to be connected to some sort of possible scandal, because that's what the rag does, right?"

"What sort of scandal?"

"I was hoping you didn't have any ideas," she said, looking carefully at him.

"You mean, do they have photographs of me being whipped by Charlene?"

She laughed. "Something like that."

He shook his head. "She hasn't whipped me in, I don't know, days," he replied. "And we were very careful to pull the blinds."

She elbowed him in the ribs. "Stop it! You know the mention of her name sets off a cherry bomb in my brain."

"You brought her up."

"Well, she's the only scandal I can think of."

"She's not a scandal," Will said.

"A scandal waiting to happen, then. How's the Charlene Watch doing?"

"I haven't heard anything, so she hasn't set off any alarms."

"I've got a funny feeling about this fake FBI lady," Kate said.

"All right. Tomorrow morning, call Lance in and read him the riot act. Demand to know what's going on."

"I'm not sure I want to know," Kate said. "He's a very smart guy, and if he's keeping something from me, he has good reasons. I think he might be trying to protect me and feels it might be better if I don't know."

"Well, that's a nice character trait. I've always had a hard time reading Lance, he's so smooth."

"I know what you mean," she said, "but I'm learning to figure him out, and mostly I like what I find."

"Do you think he might be protecting me as well as you?"

"We're the same person," she said, "to Lance, anyway. Anything that hurts you, hurts me, and anything that hurts me, hurts Lance."

"A daisy chain of hurt?"

"Well, yes."

"I don't . . ." Something on the TV screen caught Will's eye. He picked up the remote and unmuted it. A banner reached across the screen: BREAKING NEWS!!!

"What?" Kate asked.

*"Shhh."*

"Let's go to Jim Barnes in Atlanta," the anchor was saying.

The reporter stood in front of an Atlanta church that Will recognized instantly. "Less than five minutes ago, the Reverend Henry King Johnson made this announcement," he said.

The tall, handsome image of the Reverend Johnson appeared on screen, surrounded by a passel of admirers. "Today," he said, "I have resigned from the Democratic Party and am declaring my candidacy as an independent for president of the United States."

"Oh, shit," Will said, taking a gulp of his bourbon. The phone on the coffee table started to ring. He picked it up and said, "Hang on," then went back to watching CNN.

"For too long the current president has ignored the needs of black Americans," Johnson was saying. "For too long he has let us languish while other minorities crowd his thoughts."

"What the hell is he talking about?" Kate asked.

"Hispanics," Will replied. He put his ear to the phone. "Yes?"

"It's Kitty. You're watching?"

"I'm afraid so."

"This is not good."

"I can only agree," Will said.

## 42

LANCE CABOT HAD JUST FINISHED A MEETING WITH HIS NEWLY APPOINTED LONDON head of station, who was in town for a few days, when his phone rang.

His secretary picked up the line, then buzzed him. "The director would like to see you now," she said.

Lance got up from his desk, slipped into his suit jacket, adjusted his tie, and began the walk to the director's office, along the way composing himself into the attitude of glacial calm that he had learned over many years of practice. The secretary on guard told him to go in.

Lance knocked.

"Come in."

He took a deep breath, let it out, and opened the door. Katharine Rule Lee was at her computer, typing. "Have a seat, Lance," she said, without looking up from her computer.

Lance sat down and crossed his legs, waiting for her to finish typing.

The director finished, saved the document, and turned to face her visitor. "Lance, I had a very peculiar phone call yesterday from Kerry Smith at the Bureau."

Lance gazed at her and blinked very slowly but said nothing.

"The day before yesterday the editor of an execrable publication called the *National Inquisitor* was visited by a woman who showed him Bureau ID, a court order and a search warrant, all apparently bogus, all items we are capable of generating in-house. Do you know anything about that?"

"The national *what*?" Lance asked, to give himself time to think.

"Lance, you look well fed," the director said. "I'm sure that sometime in the past twenty years you must have visited a supermarket."

"Oh, *that* thing."

"Yes, that *thing*. Now what do you know about this incident?"

Lance gazed at her lazily but said nothing.

"Well?"

"Director, I recall that once you said to me something on the order of 'There will be times—rarely—when things will occur that I should not know about.'"

The director flushed slightly. "The description of the fake FBI agent closely resembles that of your assistant, Holly Barker," she said.

"Do you remember saying those words to me, Director?" Lance asked. "And if so, do they still apply?"

The director looked at him for a slow count of about five. "That will be all, Mr. Cabot."

"Good day, Director," Lance said, rising and walking to the door. He had the knob in his hand when she stopped him.

"Lance, is Teddy Fay still alive?"

Lance turned and looked at her. "Certainly not, Director," he said, then he opened the door, walked out, and closed it behind him. He was back in his office before he allowed himself to take a deep breath and expel it.

He hung up his jacket and sat down at his desk, then turned to his computer. He entered the code word for restricted personnel files, entered his personal code, then two other codes before he reached the security level he sought. Then he typed in the name Owen Masters. The computer responded by bringing up the restricted record of that agent, and it began with six rows of photographs of the man, one taken each year since he had been recruited from Brown University thirty years ago.

Lance studied the progression of the photographs. It was a pictorial biography, showing the years, cares, and shocks levied on the subject over an adult lifetime, and it revealed a sad decline.

Owen's file was 526 pages long. Lance placed the cursor in the search window and typed in the word *termination*. Almost instantly this produced the message "Not found." Clearly not specific enough, Lance thought. He typed in the word *assassination*.

This produced a dozen or so references, mostly political murders, of figures whose paths Owen had crossed during his career, but none of the deaths had been at Owen's hand. This was not good.

Lance gave it some thought, then typed in the words *assisted departure*. Two references popped up. Once, in 1979, Owen had "assisted the departure" of an African politician. Again, in 1984, he found the words "an assisted departure," this time in Egypt. Lance closed the file and exited the restricted records level.

He consulted his computer phone book, found a direct line to Masters in the Panama station and told the computer to dial it.

"Yes?" Owen's voice said.

"Scramble," Lance said.

"Scrambled," Owen said a moment later.

"Do you know who this is?" Lance asked.

"Yes," Owen replied.

"This is for your ears only," Lance said. "Forever."

"I understand," Owen replied.

"I hope you did not follow the instruction I gave you concerning the destruction of a photograph."

"I would have to check."

"He is alive and within your purview," Lance said, ignoring Owen's evasion, "and neither of those things is acceptable. Do I make myself clear?"

Owen was silent for a moment, then said, "What are your instructions?" He was going to make Lance say it.

"Give him every assistance in his departure," Lance said. "And ensure that he is not encountered by anyone again." He hoped that was clear enough. "And when that is accomplished, take some snapshots and prints and fluids."

"How much time do I have?"

"It must be accomplished at the earliest possible moment that it can be, while taking every care."

"I understand," Owen said.

Lance hung up.


OWEN SAT AT HIS DESK and stared out the window. It had been one hell of a time since he had received an order like that. Oh, what the hell, he thought. May as well go out with a bang, so to speak.

He opened his safe, extracted an envelope, and shook out of it the photograph that he had been ordered to destroy. He sat back in his chair, polished the glasses that hung on a string around his neck with a necktie, and put them on.

"Ah, yes, Teddy," Owen said aloud.

# 43

MARTIN STANTON FOLLOWED ELIZABETH WHARTON, A HOTEL MANAGER, A BELLMAN with his cart, and two Secret Service agents down the hall of the Mansion on Turtle Creek in Dallas. He was paying a lot more attention to the ass of Ms. Wharton than to anything else, and he was interrupted when the procession halted.

"Here we are, Mr. Vice President," the bellman said, inserting a key into the lock of a double door.

Liz turned to him while the attention of the others was absorbed with getting him into his suite. "I'm right next door, if you should need me," she said.

Beads of sweat popped out on Stanton's forehead. "Thank you, Liz," he said. "I'll keep that in mind." He walked into the suite and had a look around.

"I hope everything is to your satisfaction," the manager said.

"Yes, thank you." Stanton shook the man's hand, then turned to an agent. "Thanks, that will be all for the night. I'm going to order something from room service. I'll call you if I should want to go out again."

"Yes, sir," the agent replied, and after a moment Stanton was alone. He took off his jacket and necktie and hung them in the bedroom closet with the other clothes that his valet had pressed and put away in advance of his arrival, then he went into the large living room to the array of liquors that had been set out on the bar. He reached for a bottle of Scotch, then stopped.

Instead, he walked to a door on one side of the living room, put his ear to it, and listened, then unlocked the door and rapped on it with his signet ring. Nothing happened. He sighed and went back to the bar. Then he heard a sharp rap on the same door.

He went back and rapped again and got an immediate response, so he tried the knob. The door swung open to reveal Elizabeth Wharton, standing there, her hair wet, apparently wearing only a hotel robe.

"You rang?" she asked.

"I'm sorry. I didn't mean to disturb your shower."

"I just got out. You didn't disturb me."

"Can I buy you a drink?" he asked, nodding toward the bar.

"Oh, yes," she said. "I could use a drink." She stepped into the room in her bare feet. "Bourbon, please."

"Would you like anything in that?"

"Ice."

Stanton poured her drink and a Laphroaig, a single-malt Scotch, for himself. When he turned around, she was sitting on the sofa, her legs crossed, a satisfying amount of thigh showing. He took the drink over, sat down beside her, and handed her the drink.

"Tough day?" she asked.

"No tougher than yours." They clinked glasses and drank. In two weeks of campaigning, it was the first private, informal moment they had spent together, and neither of them seemed able to think of anything to say.

Liz reached out, took hold of his wrist, and pressed two fingers against it for his pulse.

"A little rapid, isn't it?" he asked. "How's yours?"

She took his hand and placed it on her left breast, under the robe. "You tell me."

"Very much like mine," he said, leaving his hand on her breast and rubbing a finger over the nipple, which sprang immediately to attention.

"I didn't think I could ever get you to do that," she said.

"I didn't think I could ever do it," he responded.

"I'm glad you did," she said, pulling the tie on the robe and allowing it to fall open.

He set both their drinks on the coffee table, then leaned over and kissed her, using his chilled drink hand to caress the other breast. He pulled her legs open and bent to kiss her delta and was surprised to find it completely bare. He explored with his tongue.

Liz raised herself and sat on the padded arm of the sofa, facing him and parting her legs. He buried his face in her flesh and parted the labia with his tongue. She took hold of his hair and held him in place, and in less than a minute, she came enthusiastically. He laid his cheek against her flat belly and panted.

"Does this suite come with a bed?" she asked, conversationally.

He got up, took her hand, and led her to the bedroom, where he allowed her to undress him, then they fell into the bed, locked in each other's arms and began what would turn out to be a full-inventory exploration of each other's body parts.

Stanton did not think of Barbara Ortega once.


BARBARA ORTEGA WALKED into the little town house in Georgetown and followed the agent around the place, the eighth one she had looked at this afternoon.

"It belonged to a congresswoman who decided to retire," the agent was saying. "It comes with everything you see."

The place was fully furnished, except for a lot of missing pictures, but Barbara had those in storage in Sacramento. The little two-story house even had linens, towels, and kitchenware in place, and it was decorated in a manner that she might have chosen herself, if she were doing it from scratch. "How much is she asking?" Barbara asked.

The agent mentioned a figure. "But I'm inclined to think she would be reasonable."

The figure seemed in line with other properties Barbara had seen or researched. She deducted twenty percent and spoke the resulting number. "Please phone your client now and tell her that this will be my only offer."

"What about financing?" the agent asked.

Barbara had inherited money from both her parents and grand-parents, and she had been frugal. "All cash," she said.

"Excuse me for a moment." The agent walked to the other side of the room and pressed a button on her cell phone. She spoke for a moment, then turned to Barbara. "When can you close?"

"Just as soon as she can furnish me with a successful title search."

The agent spoke again, then closed her phone and turned to Barbara, smiling. "You have yourself a house."

Barbara took out her checkbook. "I'll give you ten percent earnest money right now, and I want to sleep here tonight."

"I'm sure that will be fine, Ms. Ortega. When do you start at the Justice Department?"

"Monday morning," Barbara replied, tearing off the check and handing it over.

"The utilities and phone are still connected," the agent said. "As a courtesy, I'll have everything changed to your name, if that's all right."

"That would be perfect," Barbara said, holding out her hand. "Good night."

The agent left, and Barbara kicked off her shoes and made another trip around the jewel of a house. Then she went to the bedroom, took off her clothes, and lay on the king-size bed. She got her secret cell phone from her purse and called Martin, her pulse racing with the anticipation of telling him. No answer.

She closed the phone and touched herself, thinking of him, then she stroked herself until she came with a barely suppressed scream and lay, panting, on the bed until she fell asleep.

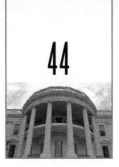

# 44

OWEN MASTERS FINISHED READING THROUGH THE FILES OF HIS FOUR RESIDENT agents. He had read them before, of course, but he was looking for something different this time, a kind of blind resolve. He thought he caught a glimpse of that in the report of a student's unarmed combat instructor. "At times," the man had said, "he seemed to want to kill his opponents." Owen put down the file and buzzed the young man.

Todd Bacon was ordinary-looking, Owen thought, except for his apparent fitness level. His blond hair was already going thin on top, though he was only, according to his file, twenty-eight. He sat in the hard, armless chair he had been offered, seemingly comfortable and calm.

"Where did you go to college, Bacon?" Owen asked him.

"The University of Alabama," the man replied with a soft southern accent.

Good, Owen thought, a state university man—something to prove to the Ivy League boys. "How long have you been with us?"

"Three and a half years," Bacon replied

"Are you enjoying the work yet?"

Bacon paused before he spoke. "Sometimes."

"Not getting into the field enough?"

"I could use more field time."

"You think you could handle yourself in a tough situation? Physically, I mean?"

"Of course," Bacon replied.

"You'd better give some thought to that," Owen said. "In this business, you don't get to square off with an opponent. It's not like at the Farm." The Farm was where agents underwent their first training. "Never let your guard down when you're in the field," Owen said. "You can be as easily killed by a small woman with a penknife as by a big guy with a gun."

"Good point," Bacon replied.

Owen noted that the man had never called him sir. "Do you think you might be just a tad overconfident?"

"I don't believe so." Bacon was looking a little less comfortable in his hard chair now.

"At your age and level of experience you don't believe you're mortal," Owen said, "but you are. I've seen young officers brought home in pieces and in body bags. I know two who, at forty, are in wheelchairs for the rest of their lives. Do you think you have the tradecraft and good sense to avoid that?"

"I hope so," Bacon replied, showing the first sign of any modesty.

"Hope won't be enough," Owen said. He was now ready to bring this boy into it, and he hoped, but doubted, that he had managed to put the fear of God into him. "I have a field assignment for you."

The young man leaned forward. "Yes, *sir*," he said.

Owen placed the photograph of Teddy Fay on his desk and pushed it across. "This man is an American, now in his sixties. This photo was taken some years ago. He is around six feet tall and could weigh anything from one-fifty to two-fifty, though I expect he has kept himself trim."

"Who is he?" Bacon asked, staring at the photo.

"He has a range of skills worthy of a good spy novel. He is expert in manufacturing identity documents, forging background paperwork, and creating legends. He is athletic, with many physical skills, and adept at flying, scuba diving, marksmanship, and all sorts of killing. He could end your life with a couple of fingers before you knew what had happened to you. His bland appearance lends itself to disguise, and he is a master at that."

"Any other photographs?"

"This one is, to the best of the Company's knowledge, the only one in existence."

"Is he in Panama?"

"He was; he may still be. He murdered an American reporter for a gossip rag—at least, it's thought he was murdered. His body was found on a tanker on its way to Galveston after passing through the canal. Do you see how clever that is? It prevents the police from knowing where he died. If he had been found a day later, the Galveston police would be wondering the same thing. Am I building a picture for you?"

"You certainly are," Bacon replied.

"Assume he is in Panama City," Owen said. "I want you to find him."

"And then?"

Owen ignored the question. "You will be at a great disadvantage: He will be disguised, you will not be. He will be ready for someone like you, you may not be. If you see him on successive days, he may appear to be another person, one you are unlikely to recognize. If you give him the slightest reason to suppose you may know who he is, he will kill you, and there will be little you can do to prevent it."

"Am I to kill him," Bacon asked, "if I can?"

Owen was so glad he had asked. "Please," he replied. "And if you are so fortunate, his body must never be found, and you must not be connected in any way with him or his death."

"I understand," Bacon said.

"Mind you, Bacon, should you find him you must be certain of whom you're dealing with. We don't want some businessman from home to meet an untimely end and stir up a lot of trouble for us because of mistaken identity. You must be sure."

"How am I to identify him?" Bacon asked.

"That will be the hardest part of all," Owen replied, "but he will probably be alone, or possibly with a woman, in a bar or restaurant. He likes the bar at El Conquistador and a restaurant called El Parador, across the canal, though I doubt if he will return there any time soon. He may look older or younger than he is. He will almost certainly bewig himself. Anything looking like a toupee will give you an indication. You were trained to look at subjects with your peripheral vision most of the time. See that you do. He must not know he has attracted your attention."

"Is that all you can tell me?"

"Look at the photograph, at the left ear, which is turned slightly toward the camera."

Bacon did so.

"Do you see it?"

"I'm not sure."

"It's a fold in the flesh, just above the earlobe, like a tiny gully."

"Yes, I see it now."

"We can't tell if this is symmetrical, if the right ear is the same, because of the way his head is turned, but that little mark will be present on his left ear. Unless, of course, he has filled it with spirit gum and makeup. But it gives us just a chance to identify him."

Bacon nodded. "May I keep the photograph?"

"No," Owen replied. "Take one last look at it, and give it back to me."

Bacon did so.

Owen returned the photo to his safe and removed a box with some gadgets in it. He removed two cell phones and handed Bacon one. "Memorize this number," Owen said, repeating it twice. "If you believe you have found him, leave the location in a taxi, call me at that number, give me any pertinent information—a companion, say. Then give me a meeting place nearby and return to his location by a circuitous route. Watch the place where you saw him and wait for me to turn up. Do not, repeat, *not* speak to him or confront him. If he speaks to you, be polite, then excuse yourself."

"Who is this man?" Bacon asked.

Owen sighed. "Whoever he says he is."

# 45

WILL SAT ON A SOFA IN THE OVAL OFFICE AND GAZED AT HIS POLLSTER. "ALL RIGHT, Moss, let's hear it." His chief of staff, press secretary, campaign manager, and political consultant were very still.

Moss consulted his papers. "In the first poll since Henry King Johnson announced, he appears to have attracted about a quarter of the black vote."

Will made a point of not showing a reaction. "Go on."

"Bill Spanner, as you know, is doing much better than expected, and the combination of those two elements means that if the election were held today, you would lose to Spanner by around five points."

Will turned to Tom Black. "Tom?"

"We have two commercials in the can showing you with civil rights leaders over the years. I want to punch up the voice-overs and rerecord, and we can have them on the air by the day after tomorrow."

Moss spoke up again. "Mr. President, I think you should know that as Reverend Johnson starts to campaign and get press coverage, the bleeding off of black voters is likely to continue."

"That's depressing," Will said.

"Unfortunately, we haven't yet reached a point in this country when voters will ignore race. He's going to get a lot of black votes simply because he's black, just as you're getting some white voters for the same reason."

Sam Meriwether spoke up. "In addition to running Tom's new commercials, we need to schedule more events with predominantly black audiences: schools, churches, wherever we can gather a crowd. Then we need to photograph those events and use them in advertising, particularly in southern states where black voters are a majority or nearly so."

"We can't just let the black vote slide to Johnson," Kitty said. "We have to stop the bleeding and as quickly as possible."

"Why is Henry doing this?" Will said. "I've always had a good relationship with him."

Tim Coleman, Will's chief of staff, said, "I've had word that Reverend Johnson has bought property adjacent to his church and plans to tear down the old building, which is in disrepair, and build a rather grandiose new church and an office building, most of which he will rent out to black-owned businesses. He's counting on the press exposure he receives during the campaign to put him over the top in his fund-raising."

"I've never heard of this plan," Will said.

"He's keeping it under wraps. He presented it to his board of deacons only a few days ago, and it will go unannounced until he feels the moment is right."

Kitty said, "Maybe we need to find him a big contributor, who . . ."

"No." Will cut her off. "The moment we do anything that smacks of bribing him to get out of the race, we'll take a big hit among voters at large, and justifiably so."

"I tend to agree," Moss said.

"Anytime a reporter raises the name of Henry King Johnson, we will use the opportunity to welcome him to the race and say good things about him," Will said. "If we criticize him, we show fear, and fear is contagious."

"The other polls will have this in a day or two," Moss said. "We're going to have to face that."

"I'll face it by saying that I've been down in the polls before, but I haven't lost an election so far, and I don't intend to start now."

"That's exactly what you should say," Tom Black agreed. "I want to talk to some of the black elected officials around the country and see if we can get them on record as supporting you."

"Don't go to anybody who hates Henry," Will said. "The tenor of any such statements should be that he's a fine fellow and an outstanding preacher but that he knows he isn't going to win this race, so why is he running? Tim, we need to get the plans for Henry's new church to a columnist who can break the story in a way so that it's on every front page the next day, and we don't want this traceable to us. Tom, you could let this slip when you're talking to black elected officials and let them do the leaking. Somebody won't be able to resist."

"Good idea," Tom replied.

"Ideally, the column would run on the day Henry announces his plans," Tim said. "If we can make his running look like a fund-raising ploy, then that might slow down the money to the point where he may wonder why he bothered."

"Maybe somebody could make it a church-and-state issue," Kitty said.

Sam Meriwether winced. "I don't know if that's a good idea," he said.

Will chuckled. "Kitty always wants to go for the jugular."

"Yeah, Sam," Kitty said, "you're way too soft. I think running for president in order to raise money for a self-glorifying church is a legitimate thing to attack."

"As long as the attack comes from just the right person," Tim said. "Every big daily has a black columnist these days; those people might be a good place to get the word out."

"Tom," Will said, "any efforts we make, like the two new commercials, are going to have to be on top of anything else we already have planned. We have to deal with Bill Spanner, win the independents and the few remaining moderate Republicans from him and win by a margin big enough to overcome any votes lost to Henry Johnson. We need people on every Sunday political show talking about that and ignoring Henry, except to answer direct questions."

"I'm doing two," Kitty said, "and so is Sam. I think we can get the message out."

"I haven't heard anything yet," Tim said, "but I'd be very surprised if the Reverend Johnson isn't on *Meet the Press* this Sunday."

"Then the day before would be an excellent time for the world to learn about Henry's fund-raising plans," Will said. "Russert would enjoy asking him about that. When should I do that program?"

"The week after Henry Johnson," Tim replied.

"Mr. President," Kitty said, looking at her watch, "your next appointment is camped outside the door right now."

"Let's break it up, then," Will said. "You all go out through my study, so that you won't bump into the Republican leadership. They want to talk about tax cuts again, so they can tell the press on their way out that I *still* won't cut taxes, even though we're running a nice surplus."

Everybody laughed and filed out.

# 46

WILLIE GAYNES WATCHED THE REPORTER ENTER HIS OFFICE. HE WAS NELSON
Pickett, whom Willie had recruited from a rival rag to replace Ned
Partain.

"Did you listen to the recordings, Nelson?" Willie asked.

"Yeah, I did," Pickett replied.

"Well?"

"The guy is certainly Martin Stanton, but in order to go with
that, we'd need to know who the woman on the recordings is," Pickett said.

"Tell me about it. Any candidates?"

"Three, sort of."

"What do you mean, 'sort of'?"

"I mean it could be one of the following: Jean Rodgers, with
whom Stanton was alleged to have had a long-running affair when
he was still practicing law in L.A. She is the wife of Elton Rodgers,
a very big real estate developer in southern California, and the two
of them were a presence on the charity-dinner circuit. She's twenty
years younger than Stanton, gorgeous, and has a reputation for lik-

ing lots of sex, some of it with more than one partner. Apparently, gender doesn't matter."

"That's juicy."

"Yeah, but we'd have to put half a dozen stringers on it, maybe for weeks, to nail it down."

"Who else is on the list?"

"His traveling campaign manager, Elizabeth Wharton. I've talked to two people on his campaign plane who say they've caught them looking hungrily at each other. Nobody, however, has been able to put them in the sack together."

"Okay, put on a stringer to shadow Stanton's campaign schedule. I want staff bribed at every hotel they stay at. I want to know the location of their respective rooms and the room-service delivery schedule to those rooms. I want to know how many Stanton orders for."

"Will do." Pickett made a note.

"Who's the third?"

"Barbara Ortega, who was Stanton's chief of staff the last two years he was governor. This is not the hottest tip, it's supposition based on proximity: she was there, so given Stanton's reputation for libido, he must have fucked her."

"That would be a legitimate basis on which to proceed," Willie said, "if we had six more months to nail it down, but we don't. Is this Ortega traveling with Stanton on the campaign? A threesome with Stanton and Wharton would be a nice thing."

"No, she's just been appointed head of the Criminal Division at the Justice Department. She's been living at the Ritz-Carlton for a couple of weeks, and she bought a house in Georgetown. They were seen together in Sacramento at the swearing-in ceremony for Mike Rivera, Stanton's successor, but not before or after. They can't be put together at any other time since Stanton got the vice-presidential nod."

Gaynes sat back in his chair and gazed out his window toward the Potomac River. "Tell you what," he said, "get recordings of the voices of all three women and have our guy compare them to the woman's voice on the Stanton recordings."

"Great idea!" Pickett said, sarcastically. "Any ideas on how I can manage that?"

"What do you think I'm paying you the big bucks for, Nelson? Do I have to do all the thinking around here? Now, get out and get on it! We're short of time!"

TODD BACON SAT on a bar stool at El Conquistador and sipped his third margarita. It was his third evening on the hunt, and he was with a code clerk from the embassy, a dish named Rita. He'd had his eye on her for a while, and now he had a professional reason for taking her out.

"When are we going to get some dinner?" Rita asked plaintively. "I'm going to topple off this bar stool in a minute."

"Just a sec," Bacon said. An elderly man with longish white hair and a Vandyke beard had just entered the bar, and Bacon's pulse was up at least ten points. The man was the right size and age, and the hair and beard were a good disguise. He rearranged himself on the bar stool so that Rita was between him and the mark. That way he could seem to be looking at Rita when he was actually looking past her.

"Todd, I'm not kidding," Rita said. "I'm drunk and hungry, and I'm going to faint any minute."

Bacon waved at the bartender. "Can we dine at the bar, señor?"

The bartender brought two menus.

"Can't we get a table?" Rita asked.

"Rita, baby, I'm working, here; you know about work, don't you? Order anything you like, and order one for me, too."

"You spooks are all alike," Rita said. "Work, work, work, day and night."

Bacon ran a hand up her skirt and found, to his surprise and delight, that she was wearing stockings and a garter belt, instead of panty hose. "Hey, hey," he said.

"Not now," she replied. "Not until I've had some food." She waved the bartender over and held up two fingers. "Dos specialitees," she said in mangled Spanish, "and a bottle of vino blanco primo."

Bacon snapped his attention back to the man at the bar to check out the left ear. Unfortunately, the man's hair covered the ear entirely. Just what the mark would do, Bacon thought.

Plates of guacamole appeared before them on the bar, and Rita dug in with a vengeance. "Oh, God, that's good," she said. "I might make it through the evening."

Bacon tried it, and she was right; it was good, and he was very hungry, too. The man with the beard was saying something to the bartender, and he strained to hear it. It was English, but that was the best he could do. Bacon was beginning to believe with all his heart that the man he was looking at was his mark. The man looked like a cross between Colonel Sanders and Grandpa on *The Waltons*. He had seen the reruns on Nickelodeon when he was a kid.

"So Toddy," Rita said, "where'd you go to school?"

"Alabama," Bacon replied absently.

"Joe Namath Alabama?"

"One and the same."

"So you're southern white trash, or what?"

Bacon fixed her with his gaze. "Southern white aristocracy," he replied, "not that you'd know the difference." The man at the bar reached under his hair with a finger and scratched at his ear, but there wasn't time for Bacon to fix on it before it was covered with hair again.

"You mean your people owned slaves and all that?"

"Lots of slaves and lots of all that," Bacon replied.

"So they were rich?"

"They were, for a time. They had to get it all back after the war."

"The Civil War?"

"The War Between the States," Bacon replied, "or the Struggle for Southern Independence, take your pick."

Then something awful happened. A pretty blonde in her thirties came into the bar and sat down beside the man with the beard, giving him a peck on the cheek. "Hey, sweetheart," she said.

"This is Mrs. Williams," the man said to the bartender. "We were married just before we left New York."

Mrs. Williams shook hands with the bartender.

"Is this your first time in Panama, señor?" the bartender asked.

"It certainly is," Williams replied. "We're taking a private tour of the canal tomorrow."

"I hope your rooms are satisfactory."

"Yes, we have a real nice suite on the top floor."

Bacon's heart sank. "Shit," he said under his breath.

"What?" Rita asked.

"Never mind, baby," Bacon said. "You just eat your dinner, then we'll go back to my place." At least the evening wouldn't be a total loss.

"Deal," Rita replied, mopping up the last of the guacamole and receiving a plate of some sort of stew.

"What the hell," Bacon said, starting on his stew. "You win some, you lose some. There's always tomorrow."


TEDDY FAY WATCHED the young couple at the bar from his table. "Mrs. Williams" was an American hooker he occasionally spent a night with in a hotel room, and he was looking forward to this night.

Teddy noticed the bartender head for the men's room. He excused himself from the table, walked over to the bar, to where the credit card machine was kept, and quickly fingered through the pile of receipts. Bacon—that was one of the names on the embassy's website. Bacon belonged to Owen Masters.

Teddy rejoined his date, but his mind was elsewhere.

# 47

TEDDY FAY LAY IN BED, SPENT BUT WIDE AWAKE, WATCHING CNN WHILE THE GIRL snored lightly beside him. He was profoundly disturbed by what he was seeing.

A tall, handsome black man in a gorgeously cut suit was speaking to a luncheon crowd of black businessmen in Birmingham, Alabama.

"It is time," the man was saying, "that we put America and the administration of President Lee on notice that *gradual* is not fast enough, that *transition* has gone on too long, that half a dozen black CEOs of large corporations is not full integration into the business life of this country, that new legislation is essential for the reinstatement of programs to help young black citizens participate fully in education and careers . . ."

CNN cut back to its correspondent. "There you hear the Reverend Henry King Johnson making an appeal to an influential and wealthy audience for campaign contributions. Meanwhile, at the White House, President Lee and his advisors are poring over opinion polls that have to be shocking to them, polls that for the first time actually put the president *behind* Bill Spanner in the election race and all because the Reverend Johnson is siphoning off enough black votes to make a loss for Will Lee a very real possibility."

Teddy's heart was pounding; it was time to go home. He switched off the TV, got out of bed, and got dressed. He left some money on the dresser for the girl, let himself out of the suite, and headed to his little apartment. There, he began by putting everything he no longer needed into a trash bag and leaving it outside for pickup. Then he packed some clothes and all the equipment needed to maintain his identities and disguises. From among his few weapons he chose the very small Colt Mustang .380 and slipped the holster onto his belt. He put the screw-on silencer and an extra magazine into his coat pocket and pulled a baseball cap on over his wig.

He packed his goods into the old station wagon he owned and drove them to the little airport outside the city where he kept his Cessna 182 RG stored in a ramshackle hangar. He packed the airplane carefully, then rolled the airplane out with the tow bar and over to the fuel pumps, where he filled the wing tanks and the ferry tank in the rear seat that doubled the airplane's range. Then he returned the aircraft to its hangar, closed it, and drove back to Panama City.

He parked the station wagon near where he kept the scooter and wiped it clean of fingerprints, then he started the scooter and drove to within a few blocks of the American embassy. The sun was well up now, and rush hour had started. He parked near the embassy and looked for transportation to steal. He found an elderly but well-kept Honda light motorcycle and spent no more than a minute getting it started. That done, he drove to within fifty yards of the embassy and pulled into a side street that allowed him a view of the area.

He had not been there for more than half an hour when he saw young Bacon get out of a taxi and start up the front steps of the embassy. Teddy held his position. For sentimental reasons, he did not wish to harm a bright young man just starting his career with the Agency.

He waited another forty-five minutes before he saw Owen Masters get out of a cab across the street from the embassy and start picking his way through traffic. Teddy started the motorcycle.

Masters paused on the center island of the wide street to wait for the light to change, and, when it did, he started across. In company with half a dozen others, Teddy pulled into traffic, and, when the flow stopped for the light, he continued through the crosswalk, which took him within six feet of Masters's back. He stopped. "Hello, Owen," he called out.

Masters turned and looked behind him. With his left hand, Teddy pulled off the Vandyke beard, and he saw recognition in Masters's eyes. Teddy shot him once, in the middle of the forehead, then gunned the motorcycle and raced off.

He made his way back to near where he had parked his scooter in an alley; abandoned the motorcycle; then stripped off his coat, wig, and baseball cap, and put on a windbreaker and a different cap that he kept in the scooter's storage compartment. In a moment, he was on his way.

He drove by the embassy again and was made to turn off the main drag by the police, but he got a good look at the scene: Owen crumpled in the street, while two policemen tried to keep the curious crowd away from the corpse while they waited for backup.

An hour later, Teddy put the scooter inside the hangar, rolled the airplane out, and closed the door. He did a cursory preflight inspection, then got the engine started. He taxied to the end of the three-thousand-foot grass strip, did a brief run-up of the engine, and ran through his takeoff checklist, then he shoved the throttle in all the way and began to roll down the runway.

He needed nearly two-thirds of the airstrip to gain enough airspeed to rotate, and when he did, the Cessna climbed strongly. He flew north at five hundred feet to stay below canal radar and held that altitude until he had cleared Panamanian waters, then he climbed to eight thousand feet, leaned the engine, and settled in for the long flight. His fuel totalizer told him he had plenty for his plan, and he had a thirty-knot tailwind, to boot.

Four hours later he landed on a small strip in the Cayman Islands and took a taxi into George Town, where he visited his bank and replenished his funds. He also turned in his credit card and received a new one, usable anywhere and paid directly from his Cayman account; it was untraceable. He had some lunch, then returned to the airport, fueled his airplane, and filed a flight plan for Key West, using a false tail number.

He took off and flew north, contacting Cuban air traffic control for clearance to cross the island nation, which was granted. With Key West in sight he switched off his transponder, descended to wave top height, and flew northeast to Marathon, where he began a climb and contacted Key West approach. "November one, two, three Tango Foxtrot, off Marathon, VFR to Sarasota," he told the controller.

Now he was just another American light-aircraft pilot, wending his way home. Well after dark, he landed at Covington, a small-town airport east of Atlanta. He had some dinner at a local restaurant, then checked into a motel and fell gratefully into a deep sleep.

Tomorrow he would begin his research on the Reverend Henry King Johnson and his movements, and within a few days, he was confident, their paths would cross.

# 48

TODD BACON STOOD AT THE WINDOW OF THE OFFICE HE SHARED WITH THREE OTHER young CIA officers, sipping coffee and looking idly into the busy street below. He was, as usual, the first one in, so he had time to drink his coffee and take a look at the *International Herald Tribune*.

As Todd watched, he saw Owen Masters get out of a taxi on the opposite side of the street and start across. Owen limped a little and seemed older than his years, Todd thought. Would he end up like the older man? Station chief in some backwater, serving out his time? The traffic light changed, and Owen started across the street.

Todd was about to turn away when he saw something moving fast between the cars stopped for the light. He watched, thinking the motorcycle was going to plow into the crossing pedestrians, then it suddenly stopped in the middle of the crosswalk. Owen stopped, turned, and looked back. Then the man on the motorcycle held out his arm, and there was a wisp of smoke. Owen went down, and the motorcycle moved on.

Todd was horrified, but he had the presence of mind to watch the motorcycle, and he recognized the suit and the longish gray hair protruding from a baseball cap. It was the man from the night before.

He looked back at Owen. A police officer was bending over him, then putting fingers to his throat and shaking his head, while another officer waved the crowd away. Todd set down his coffee cup, went to his desk, and retrieved a typed list of telephone numbers. He found the number he wanted next to the words "Pizza delivery," and he dialed it, while trying to control his breathing.

LANCE CABOT WAS GOING OVER some equipment orders with Holly Barker when his phone rang and his direct field line started flashing. "Hold on," he said to Holly and picked up the phone. "Yes?"

"Sir, it's . . . I'm sorry, scramble."

Lance pushed a button. "Scrambled."

"Sir, it's Todd Bacon, assistant station chief in Panama City."

"What is it?"

"I'm in my office. I saw Owen Masters get out of a cab and start across the street. A man on a motorcycle shot him in the head, then made his escape. Owen is dead."

Lance thought he was going to throw up. "Is Owen's office secure?" he was finally able to ask.

"Yes, sir. He never arrived for work to open it."

"Hold on." Lance turned to his computer and pulled up a secure file. "Write this down: The combination to the lock on Owen's door is 66759, the combination to his safe is 797461. Did you get that?"

"Yes, sir."

"You're acting station chief until somebody can relieve you. Do not, repeat, *not* call the police. They will contact the ambassador's office and be given Owen's cover story. You are not to speak to them unless they seek you out, which is unlikely. If they do, stick to the cover story, understand?"

"I understand, sir, but there's something you ought to know."

"What's that?"

"I know the man who shot Owen."

"What?"

"Owen gave me an assignment to find him, and I found him last night, but I didn't recognize him, since he was disguised."

"What is the man's name?"

"Owen didn't tell me, he just showed me a photograph and gave me a lecture about how dangerous the man was. I saw him in a hotel bar last night and overheard his conversation with the bartender. He was with a younger woman he introduced as his wife. He said they were from New York and were taking a private tour of the canal tomorrow—today, rather—and I bought it. Do you know who this man is, sir?"

Lance ignored the question. "Did Owen assign anyone else to this operation?"

"No, sir, just me."

"You are not to tell any of your Agency colleagues or anyone else at the embassy or the Agency of your conversation with Owen or your assignment, is that clear?"

"Yes, sir, if you say so."

"How long ago did this happen?"

"About one minute before I called you. I want to track down this man and kill him."

"You are not to do that, Todd. The man is already on the way out of the country, and looking for him would be a waste of time. He'll be somewhere in South America by lunchtime."

"But I know what he looks like."

"You know what his disguise looks like, and he has already changed that."

"Then what am I supposed to do?"

"Hang up, go to the ambassador's office, and tell him personally what you saw happen. Tell him your instructions are to stick to Owen's cover story. Tell him that this incident will be dealt with from Langley and to direct police inquiries to me through the State Department switchboard. Have you got that?"

"Yes, sir."

"Then I want you to go back to work, doing what you would ordinarily be doing. When you get into Owen's office, I want you to search his desk and file cabinets for any reference to the assignment he gave you. If you find anything referring to it, I want you to scan it and e-mail it to me, then shred any documents and, particularly, the photograph of the man. We already have that."

"Who is he, sir?"

"Whoever he says he is," Lance said, then hung up.

Holly looked at Lance expectantly but didn't ask any questions.

"Teddy Fay has killed Owen Masters in Panama City," Lance said.

"Oh, shit," Holly said.

"Yes, exactly," Lance replied. "Who do we have of station head rank, currently unassigned?"

"You want to promote somebody, or do you want another Owen Masters?"

Lance thought about that for a moment. "Another Owen Masters," he said.

"There's Terence Cotten. We pulled him out of Madrid a month ago, and he's sitting downstairs in a transient office, working his way through a book of *New York Times* crosswords, waiting for his pension."

"Perfect. Get him up here in half an hour. Right now, I have to go and see the director."

"Are you going to tell her Teddy's back?"

"Teddy who?" Lance asked, getting into his jacket.

# 49

LANCE HAD TO WAIT FOR TEN MINUTES WHILE KATHARINE RULE LEE FINISHED A meeting, which gave him more time to think. Finally, he was told to go in.

"Sit down, Lance. What is it?" the director asked.

"Director, I've just had a call from the assistant station chief in Panama City. Owen Masters has been shot in the street by an assassin. He's dead."

"Good God!" the director replied. "I knew Owen when he was a top agent."

"He was, for quite a long time."

"How long before retirement?"

"Four months, give or take."

"What's your theory of this, Lance?"

"I haven't spoken to the police yet, but I don't think this is Agency related. Owen wasn't working on anything that would have gotten him killed."

"You're sure about that?"

"I am, unless he was working something on his own, and frankly, I think Owen was too tired to go chasing hares. Unless . . ."

"Unless what?"

"Unless he went off the ranch—trying to make some extra retirement money."

"Drugs?"

"Possibly. From what I've been told, the killing sounded professional. He must have pissed off somebody."

"Have you talked to his widow?"

"Not yet. I want to let embassy and State Department protocol run its course first. I should be able to speak to her before the day is out."

"What insurance will Owen have?"

"He'll have the standard Agency policy, based on his pay grade."

"What about line-of-duty fatality?"

"If he was really off the ranch, he wouldn't qualify for that."

"I'd like Mrs. Masters to have that, if we can manage it."

"Then I'll manage it," Lance said. That was a fairly direct order to cover up any off-ranch activity, he thought.

"Keep me posted," the director said, then turned to answer her buzzing phone.


LANCE WENT BACK to his office, where Holly was still waiting. She handed him a phone slip. "You had a call from the Panamanian police on your State Department line," she said.

Lance picked up the phone, then paused and put it down again. He had an idea.

"Okay."

Lance phoned Capitán López.

"Señor Cabot," López said, "I believe you may have already been notified of the death of your diplomat, Señor Owen Masters."

"Yes," Lance replied. "We're all deeply shocked. What can you tell me of his death?"

"Señor Cabot, do you have any reason to suspect that Señor Masters might be involved in any . . . financial activity not related to his work at the embassy?"

"No, do you?"

"The nature of his death suggests other connections."

Oh, come on, say it! Lance wanted to scream at the man. "What sort of connections are you referring to, Capitán?"

"The means used to end the gentleman's life are often associated with the drug trade in this country, señor."

Lance paused meaningfully, then said, "I see."

"I do not wish you to think I am making any accusations, Señor Cabot," López said. "I am merely making an observation based on my long experience as a police officer."

"I understand, Capitán," Lance replied. "Perhaps you could tell me, privately, what chance you believe you might have to find this killer?"

"Oh, we will make a thorough investigation, señor, you may believe that. But . . . at the end of it all it is unlikely in the extreme that we will be able to make an arrest, let alone secure a conviction. In cases like this, you see . . ."

"I quite understand, Capitán, and while we would, of course, be glad to hear that Mr. Masters's killer had been caught and punished, we are cognizant of the difficulties involved in such a case. I would be grateful if you could forward a copy of your final report to me through the embassy."

"Of course, señor."

"I would ask you, in your report, to be aware that his widow will read it and not to include any unsupported supposition that might cause her distress."

"Of course, Mr. Cabot. You may be assured that I will be discreet."

Lance thanked the man and hung up, still thinking fast.

"Terrence Cotten will be here shortly," Holly said.

"Call him and tell him to go back to his crosswords," Lance said. "There's no point in sending another man down there for just a few months." He got on his computer and consulted his classified telephone directory, then made the call.

"Todd Bacon," the youthful voice said.

"Scramble," Lance replied.

"Scramble."

"Todd, it's Lance Cabot."

"Yes, sir."

"I've talked with the chief investigator from the Panamanian National Police," he said, "and I'm afraid we're in something of a bind, here."

"How can I help, sir?"

"Let me explain. The chief investigator believes that Owen was involved in some nefarious activity that resulted in his murder."

"No, sir," Bacon said. "He wouldn't have assigned me to find that man, if that were the case."

"Todd, have you been through Owen's desk and files yet?"

"I'm in the middle of that now, sir, and I'll be finished shortly."

"So far, have you found any written reference to your assignment in his papers or on his computer?"

"Ah, no, sir," Bacon replied.

He's beginning to get the picture, Lance thought. "The man Owen assigned you to find is known to the Panamanian National Police," he said, "though not by name. It is their view, though not officially, of course, that Owen was in business with this fellow and that the deal went south. Owen's next step would have been to eliminate the man, which may be why he ordered you to find him, but the tables were turned and it was Owen who was killed. It's possible that, in observing the man last night, you inadvertently did something that tipped him off that Owen was after him. So . . ."

"God, I hope that's not the case," Bacon said, sounding shocked.

"Don't worry about that, Todd. At least you didn't become involved in Owen's extracurricular activities. There's something else to consider, as well. While Owen had Agency life insurance, there is a much larger payment to be made to his widow, if this were a line-of-duty matter. Since we have no hard evidence that it wasn't line-of-duty, the director is desirous of Mrs. Masters receiving that payment, as it would make a substantial difference in her standard of living."

"I believe I understand, sir."

"Good. This is going to require great discretion from all of us. And since I believe I can count on your discretion, I've decided not to send a replacement to fill Owen's position. Instead, I'm appointing you station chief for Panama and the Canal Zone."

"Why, thank you, sir," Bacon responded, obviously stunned.

He would be less stunned after he had thought about it, Lance thought. "I'll send you another man to fill in, Todd. He'll probably be right off the farm, so he'll be green, but I'm sure you can bring him along. Pick another of your personnel to fill your assistant station chief's job, and let me know whom you've chosen."

"I'll do that, sir. It will probably be Nesmith, since he's next senior to me."

"Fine, I'm sure he's a good man and a good choice. I'll be in touch Todd, and my congratulations." Lance hung up.

Holly was looking at him. "You think that's going to do it?"

"It fucking well better do it," Lance replied.

# 50

KATHARINE RULE LEE LEFT HER OFFICE FOR THE DRIVE HOME A LITTLE AFTER SIX. Normally, she worked on papers and reports during the drive, but she had left all of that on her desk or in her safe. She had something else to think about, and she didn't want to be distracted, not even by the thought of sixty people en route in the black of the Afghan night to the Pakistani border. Her driver seemed to sense that she was deep in thought and did not wish to be disturbed with chat.

Kate was now able to admit to herself that Teddy Fay was still alive, and she was pretty sure he had killed Owen Masters, but she didn't know why. Lance Cabot knew, but he wasn't going to tell her unless she pressed him, and she couldn't afford to press him. She couldn't afford, in fact, to know that Teddy Fay was alive.

TEDDY WAS SUPPOSED to have died in a small aircraft crash off the coast of Maine, but the FBI had tracked him to New York, where he was supposed to have died in the collapse of a building under construction. Later, he had been rumored to be on the island of St. Marks, in the Caribbean, and Lance Cabot had dispatched a team to find him and, presumably, kill him.

She had thought the Fay problem had ended when the small yacht he had owned was witnessed in a sinking condition, and no body had been found. But now he had been spotted in Panama by a tourist who knew him, and she had produced an old photograph. She presumed that no copies of that photograph existed, since Holly Barker had confiscated all the copies and the negatives while posing as an FBI assistant director.

The only official threat now was Assistant Director Kerry Smith of the FBI, and he couldn't prove that Teddy was still alive. No one, in fact, could prove it, and Teddy wasn't going to turn himself in. Her only choice seemed to be to sit on the Teddy Fay problem until after the election. If it came out then, well, she was good at damage control.

Her husband didn't know any of this, of course, and she had to keep it that way. By the time she reached the White House, she had made and reconfirmed that decision.

At least, she thought, Teddy Fay was out of the country, and nothing he could do there would affect the election.

TEDDY FAY, MEANTIME, was working on his laptop in a Covington, Georgia, motel room, reading the schedule of the Reverend Henry King Johnson on his very nicely constructed and informative website. One question that lay heavily on Teddy's mind was: Did Johnson have Secret Service protection? His guess was that Johnson did not, because he had not run in the primaries and didn't loom large enough in the polls.

Johnson was traveling a lot now, raising money and working to get on the ballot in as many states as possible. That made him a moving target, but his published schedule also made him predictable, and that was good enough for Teddy.

He noted that the Reverend Johnson was due on Amelia Island, Florida, for a convention of black undertakers in a week. He knew something about Amelia Island: it was a golf-oriented upscale community near Jacksonville.

Then he noticed something else on the reverend's website: he was to perform a marriage ceremony the day before on Cumberland Island.

Teddy Googled Cumberland Island.


MARTIN STANTON CHECKED into the Brown Palace Hotel in Denver, which dated from its days as a cow town, and rapped on the door to the adjoining room. Liz opened it and gave him a big, wet kiss. "More later," she said. "I have some phone calls to make."

"Before you do that, order yourself dinner from room service," Stanton said. "We don't want them delivering two dinners to my suite."

"Right," she said.

Stanton closed the door, ordered his own dinner, and went to get a refill for his pen from his briefcase. As he opened it, he heard his secret cell phone vibrating, and he picked it up. "Yes?"

"It's me, baby," Barbara said.

"Good to hear from you," Stanton replied, not entirely convincingly.

"That sounded like something you'd say to a campaign contributor," she pointed out.

"I'm sorry, hon. It's just that they've had me on a breakneck schedule for three weeks, and I'm sort of operating on autopilot. How are you? What are you up to?"

"Well, I've started my new job at Justice, and now it's up to you and Will Lee to get reelected, so I won't get fired by a Republican attorney general early next year."

"We'll do our best," Stanton said. "We've got to keep you in work."

"And I bought a house," she said proudly.

"Well, that was fast. Where?"

"On a beautiful block in Georgetown," she said. "It's tiny, having been previously occupied by a Republican congresswoman who didn't think she could be reelected, and you're going to love it. It's the sexiest place you ever saw!"

"Then I look forward to sex in it!"

"Oh, me too, baby! I'm aching for you."

"Then let's not wait. What's wrong with now? Are you alone?"

"No, I'm with you."

"Then get your clothes off," he ordered.

"You, too."

"Are you naked now?"

"I am. How about you?"

"I am." He was not, but the two of them proceeded to have phone sex until Barbara climaxed noisily. Stanton had to pretend, because his mind and his cock, which were co-located, were both in the room next door.

The doorbell rang. "Kid, there's somebody at my door," he said into the phone. "Gotta run."

"Bye," she had time to say before he ended the connection.

Stanton went to the door and let the room-service waiter in, signed the ticket, and went to wait for Liz to wheel in her dinner.

He had been turned on, in spite of himself, during the phone sex, and now he would spend that pent-up energy on Liz.

When she rolled her tray in, she was naked, and they dined that way.

---

TODD BACON SAT at his new desk in Owen Masters's old office and leafed through a file marked "Golf in Central America," and looked at the photograph of Teddy Fay. Todd had lied to Lance Cabot when he had told him that he had destroyed it. Who was this guy? he wondered. Some drug dealer, like the cops said, or just some hit man? But if he was any of that, why would Owen care about him? It seemed obvious to Todd that Owen had wanted the man killed, so he must have been a danger of some sort, but what sort?

He pored over the two pages of notes that Owen had kept in a haphazard way and found references to Ned Partain. He was the reporter from that tabloid who had been found dead on the ship. Owen hadn't mentioned him, but Todd had seen a reference to it in the daily news digest circulated inside the embassy.

Then, down at the bottom of one page, he saw the entry, in block capitals: PARTAIN/TEDDY?

Teddy? Teddy who? And then something clicked in Todd Bacon's mind.

## 51

WILL WAS FINISHING A MEETING WITH THE SECRETARY OF AGRICULTURE WHEN HIS phone buzzed, contrary to his instructions. "Yes?"

"Mr. President," his secretary said, "the director of Central Intelligence and the chief of naval operations are here to see you urgently."

Will didn't like the sound of that combination. He checked his schedule. "All right, just push everything back as necessary and send them in." He shook hands with the secretary of agriculture and apologized for the interuption.

Kate and Admiral Halstead entered the Oval Office and were waved to a seat.

"All right," Will said.

"Mr. President," Kate said, "we have received pretty good intelligence that the missing Pakistani nuclear warhead is in one of a group of eight villages, all within fifty miles of each other, in extreme western Pakistan, along the Afghan border." She spread a map on the coffee table and pointed.

Will sat up straight. "Isn't that the area where you think bin Laden and his top people are hiding?"

"Yes, sir," Kate replied. "And we have refrained from send-ing people in there because of the objections of the Pakistani government."

"Well, the presence of a nuclear warhead in that area would place a different color on those objections, wouldn't it?"

"I should think so," Kate replied, "but Admiral Halstead and I have a suggestion, and we both believe the Pakistani government should not, in this case, be consulted."

Will sat back and looked at the two people before him. "And what is your suggestion?"

"We have enough people within chopper range—a combination of Navy SEALs and CIA operatives—to put eight small reconnais-sance teams on the ground there to investigate the report of the pres-ence of the warhead. We'd like to put them in there at the earliest possible moment to check this out."

"How soon is the earliest possible moment?"

"If we go now, before dawn tomorrow morning. They would be choppered to the border on the Afghan side and hike it from there."

"And when would the teams be in place?"

"By dawn on the following day, without complications."

Will didn't need to ask about the complications; the possibilities were multitudinous. "What are their chances of getting in there, get-ting the intelligence, and getting out without detection?"

Kate and Halstead exchanged a glance. "Better than fifty-fifty," Halstead said. "Maybe as good as seventy-thirty."

Will's stomach felt funny. "If any of those people were captured . . ."

"In the circumstances," the admiral said gravely, "their orders would be not to be captured."

Will stared at the admiral, then back at Kate, whose gaze was steady. "I've never given anyone an order like that," he said.

Kate spoke up. "It's my firm belief that the circumstances re-quire it."

"But there's no time for preparation, is there?" Will asked.

"All these men and women have run multiple rehearsals for missions such as this," Halstead said. "They are equipped with the latest surveillance and communications equipment, which, I might add, would be destroyed in the event of the threat of capture."

"The alternative," Kate said, "is to share our intelligence with the Pakistanis and let them send their people in. They would have the advantage of blending in with the population and would be able to travel openly in daylight."

"I seem to recall," Will said, "that a couple of years ago we requested a similar mission from the Pakistanis. How long did it take them to mount it? Does anyone remember?"

"Three weeks," Kate said.

"And that warhead could be anywhere in three weeks," Will replied.

"Exactly. It's entirely possible that we are already too late, that the warhead has been moved."

"Then we'd better find out," Will said. "Send them in. I know I don't have to tell you to take every possible precaution for their safety."

Kate and Halstead stood up. "Thank you, Mr. President," she said. "The order will go out within minutes." They shook hands and left.

Will watched them go and tried to reorder his mind for his next meeting, but it didn't work.

# 52

NELSON PICKETT ANSWERED THE PHONE IN HIS OFFICE AT THE *NATIONAL Inquisitor*. "Yes?"

"Nelson, it's Jimmy Pix." Jimmy Pix (the only name by which Pickett knew him) was a slimy little guy who did dogwork for publications like the *Inquisitor*, and Nelson had assigned him to follow Martin Stanton's campaign plane around the Southwest, where Stanton had been assigned to bring in the Hispanic vote.

"Where are you, Jimmy?"

"In Denver. Stanton spoke here yesterday, and he has another appearance today."

"What have you got for me?"

"I've got this: Stanton and his road manager, the lovely Liz Wharton, are in adjoining rooms at the Brown Palace. Stanton has a suite, Liz has the room next door."

"Are the two connected?"

"They sure are, by a door that needs to be unlocked from both sides."

"Good start. What else?"

"They both ordered a late dinner last night from room service, and within a minute of each other. The two dinners were delivered to their separate rooms at the same time, and the trays were left in the hallway a couple of hours later."

"I want photographs of the suite and the other room and the connecting door," Pickett said.

"Hey, come on, Nelson, we're talking Secret Service protection here. I can't get past them and into their rooms, and if I did, I'd end up in a federal prison."

"All right, then, bribe a room-service waiter or, better yet, a chambermaid to photograph the rooms. Stained sheets would be nice. Tell them to squirt some ketchup on the bedding."

"That might be possible," Pix said. "Let me work on it."

"Do it fast, Jimmy—I'm running out of time."

"Will do."

Pickett hung up and phoned a technically oriented man he knew, and gave him an assignment.

GENE PEARCE HUNG UP the phone and began checking the gear in the work case he traveled with. It contained an assortment of electronic tools and gear, and half a dozen kinds of pickup devices.

He got into his van, which was disguised as that of a plumber, and drove from his Silver Spring, Maryland, home to the Georgetown neighborhood of Washington, D.C. It was late morning, and he had been told the mark would be at work.

He parked a couple of doors down from the address he had been given, walked to the house, carrying a bag of plumber's tools and his work case, and rang the bell. He didn't want to stumble upon the cleaning lady. No answer.

Gene looked carefully around the block. Not much traffic and no one at all on foot. The curtains were drawn on the house directly across the street. He dug out a set of lock picks and went to work on the front door. He was inside in less than a minute.

The first thing he saw inside was an alarm control box. He stared at the thing, waiting for it to start beeping. It did not. The lady had not set her alarm before leaving home. Sweet of her.

He set down the plumbing tools in the entryway, then entered the house. Cute. Two floors, the master bedroom and a guest room upstairs. A cursory glance told him the master had been occupied.

Gene placed three microphones in the bedroom, one by the bedside where the phone was, one by the dressing table, and one high, on top of a picture, that would bridge any gaps between the other two. When he finished there he went downstairs and placed one under the living room phone. As an afterthought, he placed one in the kitchen, as well. You never knew.

He was done and back in his truck in under an hour. He dialed the number and listened on his equipment for it to ring. It worked perfectly. As a final touch, he placed a voice-activated tape recorder in what appeared to be an electrical box, and fixed it to the outside of the house behind some azalea bushes. He would collect the tape every day.

Gene called Nelson Pickett. "Nelson, you're up and running in Georgetown," he said.

"Send me your bill," Pickett said.

"I have to pick up the tape every day," Gene told him.

"You do that, and be sure you pick it up tomorrow," Pickett said.

"Something special about tomorrow?"

"You bet your ass," Pickett replied.

# 53

TODD BACON LOCKED HIS NEW OFFICE DOOR AND TOOK A SANDWICH AND A SODA TO his desk. He had a couple of more files to read from Owen Masters's safe before he would be done. The first was a kind of telegraphic diary, documenting Owen's joining the Agency right out of Yale, his training, and every assignment he had been given during the ensuing thirty years. Interesting, but not very. Owen must have been planning to write an autobiography.

The second file was clearly labeled "Teddy Fay." That name rang a distant bell for Todd, then the whole thing flashed in his frontal lobe. Teddy Fay was the former Agency employee with liberal political leanings who had vanished after retirement, then emerged as the assassin of several right-wing political figures, among them a blowhard talk show host and the speaker of the House, one Eft Efton, both deceased. Before leaving the Agency, Fay had deleted all his personal records from every computer he had access to, so there were no photographs of Teddy extant. Todd suddenly knew he had what was probably the only one.

He read slowly through the file, which contained a number of newspaper clippings, and he formed the opinion that Teddy, who had been reported dead a number of times, was Owen's man in Panama, the one he had assigned Todd to find. The last item in the file was a large clipping from the *International Herald Tribune*, originally printed in *The New York Times*, about a man named Henry King Johnson, a black preacher from Atlanta who had announced his candidacy for the presidency as an independent and who had become a threat to the reelection of President Will Lee.

Todd had heard Owen make a number of favorable remarks about Lee and his wife, Katharine Lee, who was director of Central Intelligence, and Todd was, himself, favorably disposed to both of them, having joined the Young Democrats organization in college. He noted, too, that all the people Teddy Fay had assassinated were outspoken opponents of President Lee and his moderate Democratic policies.

Todd then asked himself two questions: (1) What had Teddy Fay been doing in Panama? Answer: Hiding, obviously, since if it were known that he was still alive, all sorts of agencies would be hunting him. (2) If Teddy had left Panama, then where had he gone? Answer: Unknown. Lance had said Owen's assassin would be in South America by now, but Teddy seemed to have a record of going where there were people he wanted to kill.

Todd scanned the article on the Reverend Johnson again. "Teddy would not like this guy," he said aloud to himself.

Something else in the file reminded him of what Owen had said about the man in his briefing: He flew airplanes. Todd was a pilot, too, having grown up with a father who flew and having earned his private license in the family Beech Bonanza when he was in college and his instrument rating not long afterward.

Todd knew the private-pilot mind-set well enough to know that pilots, when they traveled, much preferred flying themselves to flying the airlines or driving. Teddy Fay had faked his death in an airplane, and it stood to reason that, if he were out there and on the run, a light airplane would be his transport of choice.

Todd got onto his computer and logged into the Agency's mainframe. He did a search for "Reported aircraft incidents" and narrowed it by date. He got a list of fifteen incidents. In one a small Piper had flown too close to a nuclear power plant in New York state; in another, a Beech Baron had made a wrong turn on departing Santa Monica Airport, in Los Angeles, and had had a near miss with an airliner. And in another, a light aircraft had filed a flight plan from the Cayman Islands, across Cuba and to Key West, then had disappeared from approach radar when only a few miles from its destination. A search had been conducted by the Coast Guard, but they found nothing.

Todd did a little more searching and found the daily logs of Key West Approach Control, which was operated by the Navy at its base on Boca Chica. There was a note that a Cessna had reported taking off from Marathon, fifty miles up the Keys from Key West, and was flying under visual flight rules to Sarasota. Todd then found the Sarasota Tower logs and noted that no light Cessna had landed there within the time frame for the flight from Marathon.

Todd went to the FAA registry, online, and entered the tail number of the Cessna: It had been registered to someone on Long Island . . . until the airplane had been totally destroyed while landing at East Hampton in fog.

Todd got out his atlas and checked the route. From Panama, it was due north to the Caymans, then to Key West, and he calculated the mileages. It was possible for a light Cessna, particularly with some ferry fuel aboard.

Todd left his office and walked down the hall to the embassy library, where he found an aeronautical chart for Panama. He found the international airport at Panama City, then, a few miles north, a private grass strip. He dug a large-scale map of the area from the stacks, then went back to his office, locked his safe and the door, put on his jacket, and took a cab home, where he had left his car.

Half an hour later, he found a little dirt road off the Colón highway, with a sign with the outline of an airplane painted on it. He drove through the jungle for five minutes and emerged into a large, elongated clearing containing a grass airstrip of four to five thousand feet. There was a cluster of hangars at the near end of the strip, and in one of them Todd found an attendant, his feet on his desk, his head thrown back, a flying magazine resting on his chest, snoring loudly. He pinched the man's toe, and he woke up, startled.

"*Buenos días,*" Todd said, smiling.

"*Buenos días,*" the man replied. He looked as though he may have had a few beers, and a glance into his trash can confirmed that.

"Speak English?" Todd asked.

"Yes, I speak," the man said sleepily.

"How many airplanes are based here?"

"Maybe twelve, sometimes," the man replied.

"How many Cessnas?"

"A twin, over there," the man said, pointing at a tied-down aircraft, "one 172, over there," pointing at another, "and one 182, in the hangar, there," he said, pointing again.

"Can I see the one in the hangar, please? I'm interested in buying a 182."

"Okay," the man said. He led the way to the hangar, took hold of the door, and pulled up on it. "She's out," he said. The hangar contained only a motor scooter.

"When?"

"Dunno. They come, they go, sometimes when I'm not here."

"You have fuel here?"

The man pointed at a pump.

Todd nodded and walked into the hangar and over to the scooter. He inspected it closely. It was very clean, as if it had been wiped down. He opened the little storage compartment and found a rag and a bottle of Windex. Then he walked around the hangar slowly, finding only two cans of motor oil and a few basic tools, which also looked very clean. He turned back to the attendant.

"What is the tail number of the airplane that lives here?"

The man shrugged. "N something," he said. "I don't remember the rest."

N meant American registration. "Thank you very much for your help," Todd said. "If the owner returns, would you ask him to call me about his airplane?" He scribbled his number on a page of his notepad and ripped it out.

"Sure, señor," the man said.

Todd drove back to Panama City, thinking all the way. His guess was that Teddy Fay was in Atlanta, looking for the Reverend Henry King Johnson, who was now a threat to the reelection of President Will Lee.

Todd went home and packed a bag, then called the international airport and chartered a CitationJet from a service the Agency did business with. He was now station head, and he had that authority. He called his number two and told him he would be away for a few days on business and available on his BlackBerry, then left a similar message with the ambassador's secretary. No one would miss him, or even question him.

Todd strapped on a compact SigArms 9mm semiautomatic, got into his car, and left for the airport.

# 54

BARBARA ORTEGA LEFT HER NEW OFFICE AT THE JUSTICE DEPARTMENT A LITTLE after six and drove toward home. She stopped at a supermarket on the way and stocked up on groceries for her new house, and as she was waiting her turn at the checkout counter a headline in a tabloid newspaper on the rack next to her caught her eye.

VEEP AND HOTTIE CAMPAIGN MANAGER
IN TRAVEL TRYST?

Barbara wanted to read the newspaper then and there, but she tossed it onto her pile of groceries and checked out. Once at home, she made herself wait until the groceries were put away before she opened the paper and read the text of the article.

"VICE PRESIDENT MARTIN STANTON, who has long had a reputation with the ladies, has been raising eyebrows among the press and staff on his campaign plane, and rumors are circulating about his relationship with his traveling campaign manager, Elizabeth Wharton. The lovely Liz, who is at least fifteen years younger than her boss, has been quartered nightly in several cities in a room adjacent to the veep's suite, with a connecting door, and room-service deliveries to their separate rooms seem to have been coordinated.

"Vice President Stanton, until recently governor of California, has been rumored to have had regular liaisons with at least two California women over the past few years, and is in the middle of what some say is a contentious divorce from his wife of many years. Has Marty been seeking solace in the arms of the nearest beautiful woman?"

BARBARA PUT DOWN the paper, dug her secret cell phone out of her purse, sat down on the living room sofa, and called her lover. The phone rang a number of times before it was answered.

"Yes?" Stanton said.

"I think you know who this is," Barbara said.

"Yes?"

"Have you seen this rotten . . . *paper*?"

"What are you talking about?"

Barbara picked up the paper. "The *National Inquisitor*."

"I don't know . . ."

"According to this vile rag, you are fucking your campaign manager, somebody named Elizabeth. Is that true?"

"I, ah, can't really talk right now," Stanton said. "Can I call you back?"

"I just want you to deny it," Barbara said, seething. "Will you deny it right now?"

"I'm afraid I'll have to call you back, and what with my schedule, it might be a couple of days before I can do that," he replied.

"Don't bother, you son of a bitch," she said. "Don't bother *ever* to call me again. I've torn my life apart for you, Marty Stanton. I've moved across the country, bought a house, found a new job—all just to be near you—and this is how you treat me?"

"I'll have to say good-bye for now," Stanton said, then hung up.

Barbara threw the cell phone at the opposite wall as hard as she could, shattering it.

THE FOLLOWING AFTERNOON, Gene stopped at the Georgetown house, collected the tape from the recorder, inserted a new one, then drove to the offices of the *National Inquisitor*. He put the tape in the envelope, wrote Nelson Pickett's name on it and left it at the reception desk.

The envelope was sent to the *Inquisitor*'s mail room, and shortly before the office closed, it was left on Pickett's desk. He returned from the men's room to find the envelope there. The cassette had no name on it, just the date and time of collection.

Pickett took a small tape player from his desk drawer, inserted the cassette, and pressed the play button. Then he listened, with increasing interest, as he heard the conversation between Barbara Ortega and the vice president of the United States. Before he had finished he was on his way to the office of William Gaynes.

He burst into Gaynes's office to find him on the phone. Gaynes pointed at his sofa and put a finger to his lips. Pickett waited impatiently while Gaynes continued his conversation. Finally, he hung up the phone. "What?" he said to Pickett.

"Running that story in yesterday's edition did the trick," he said. "Listen." He played the tape.

Gaynes waited until it was finished before he said a word. "Brilliant!" he said, finally. "She actually used his name!"

"And he didn't deny it," Pickett said. "Do you realize what effect this could have on the national election?"

"I don't give a flying fuck what effect it has on the election," Gaynes said, "I'm Australian. All I care about is circulation."

"Well, before you make a decision to run this story, let me explain something to you about this woman. She is the head of the Criminal Division of the United States Justice Department. Do you understand what that means?"

"All right, tell me," Gaynes said.

"It means that all the United States attorneys report to her on criminal matters."

"So?"

"Making this recording is a criminal matter—it's against the law. Do you see where I'm heading here?"

"I think I get the picture," Gaynes said. "If we run it, we get busted by the feds."

"That's exactly right."

"So we can't run it."

"Not as such. We can't even allude to this conversation, because if we do, Ortega will immediately know that we could only have gotten it by taping her phone conversations. Not only would we be charged with illegal wiretapping, but she would have her house swept for bugs in a flash, and no more telephone tapes."

"So how are we going to handle this?" Gaynes asked.

"The story that ran yesterday, which was just supposition, set her off and made her get indiscreet on the phone. We need more stuff about Stanton and Wharton, stuff we can back up. If we can get that, then Ortega might get even madder, and who knows where that could lead. We've got a couple of weeks before the election, so let me put more people on Stanton and Wharton, and more people on Stanton and Ortega when they were in Sacramento, and we'll see what we come up with. If we can get something more concrete we can name Ortega and blow the lid off the whole thing."

"Well, get your ass on it!" Gaynes said. "Spend whatever you have to!"

# 55

TODD BACON LANDED HIS AIRPLANE AT PEACHTREE DeKALB AIRPORT, AN ATLANTA general aviation field, then rented a car and drove to the Ritz-Carlton Buckhead, only ten minutes away. He ordered some dinner from room service, set up his laptop, and got online.

He had no evidence of where Teddy Fay was or what his plans were, but the Reverend Henry King Johnson was easier to find, since he published his travel schedule, like any candidate, on his website. Johnson was traveling, mostly in the Southeast, and Todd tried to put himself in Teddy's shoes. If I were Teddy, he asked himself, where would I kill Johnson? He'd worry about how later.

Todd looked for locations that were outside large population areas like Atlanta and Charlotte; Teddy would find smaller venues easier to deal with and, most important, easier to run from. His airplane was likely to be his escape vehicle, so Todd went through Johnson's schedule, looking for smaller cities with airports nearby. There was only one stop on the reverend's campaign trail that fit the bill.

Amelia Island was an expensive resort community near Fernandina Beach, just east of Jacksonville, Florida. Todd, being a southerner and the son of a flying southerner, had visited there with his father as a teenager. They had landed at Fernandina Airport and spent a weekend playing golf.

Then he noticed something even more attractive on the schedule. The reverend was to perform a marriage ceremony on Cumberland Island, the next up from Fernandina Beach. Todd had visited there once, too, with his parents. They had stayed at Greyfield Inn and had taken a nature tour with a guide in an old truck. The place was mostly national seashore now, so the number of visitors was restricted to the inn and a campground that had a capacity of a couple of dozen. The marriage was to take place in the old slave village, now mostly deserted but maintained. Todd remembered that John F. Kennedy, Jr., and his wife had been married there, in the tiny village church, which Todd had visited with his parents.

He found a map of the island on the Internet and, right in the middle of it, the grass landing strip where his father had landed the family Bonanza. He remembered that they had had to buzz the strip before landing, to clear away the wild horses and feral pigs that foraged there. The inn was south of the airstrip, and the slave village was north of it. Teddy could get in there in his airplane, do what he planned to do, and get out in a hurry, and, flying low, he would be virtually untrackable.

Todd went through Johnson's schedule once more, which ran right up to election day, and Cumberland Island seemed Teddy's best choice. Amelia Island would do for a backup, but the place was fully built up, and there would be other people at the Fernandina Airport.

The wedding was three days away, and Todd started looking on the Internet for an airplane to rent at Peachtree DeKalb Airport. He jotted down a couple of numbers and would phone them in the morning.

Todd watched a movie on TV and got to bed early, tired from his long flight. He fell asleep and dreamed of stopping one murder and committing another.

---

MARTIN STANTON WAS RATTLED, first by the appearance of the *National Inquisitor* article and then by the phone call from Barbara. And as if that were not enough, he had a phone call from his lawyer.

"This is not good, Marty," Jake said. "I was supposed to get the signed settlement from Betty's attorney today, and it hasn't arrived."

"Shit," Stanton said.

"I have no way of knowing whether either of them has seen the *Inquisitor* piece, but I think we should assume that they have."

"Jake," Stanton said, "I give you full authority to deny the *Inquisitor* thing on my behalf. It's nothing but scurrilous supposition, based on nothing but hunches. I am not having an affair with anybody. I go to bed, exhausted, every single night after half a dozen campaign appearances and speeches. I have neither the time nor the inclination to be screwing anybody."

"I'll do what I can, Marty. If I don't hear from her attorney, I'll call first thing tomorrow morning and have at him."

"If they don't deliver by noon, sue. Thanks, Jake, and good night." Stanton hung up and looked at the naked Liz, propped up on an elbow beside him in bed. "You and I have to deny everything," he said.

"Well, of course we do, sugar," she said, dallying with his crotch.

The phone rang.

"I'd better answer this," Stanton said, picking it up. "Hello?"

"This is the White House operator," a woman's voice said. "I have the president for you."

"Yes, of course." He covered the receiver with his hand. "It's the president," he whispered to Liz.

She lay back and pulled the covers over her head.

"Marty?"

"Yes, Will. How are you?"

"I've been better. I suppose you've heard about this *Inquisitor* thing."

"Somebody showed it to me late this afternoon. I'd never even heard of that publication until that moment."

"I've heard of it, and it can be troublesome. It's not so much that anybody really believes what they write, it's the fact that the mainstream press, once they've seen something there, have a basis to start asking questions."

"Well, if they start asking, I'm prepared to answer them."

"I'm glad to hear that. Worse comes to worst, we have on our side that you and Betty are practically divorced, so both you and Liz are single. You are practically divorced, aren't you?"

"We are. In fact, we were supposed to get the signed settlement today, which is the last step before getting a decree from a court."

"That's good. I'm prepared to back you with the press, Marty, but I think it's in your interest to tell them the truth. We don't want this to come back and bite us on the ass later."

"I understand, Will, and I appreciate your confidence."

Liz was making her way across the bed and was now exploring Stanton's crotch with her tongue.

Stanton gave a little gasp.

"Sorry, Marty," the president said. "What was that?"

"Mosquito, Will."

"I didn't know they had mosquitoes in Denver in late October."

"It's probably been trapped in this hotel since August," Stanton said, running his fingers through Liz's hair.

"We'll talk again," the president said. "Good-bye for now."

"Bye, Will." Stanton hung up and gave his undivided attention to what Liz was doing to him.

# 56

TODD BACON BEGAN MAKING PHONE CALLS FIRST THING IN THE MORNING, AND HE
soon found a late-model Bonanza for rent. He called Greyfield Inn
on Cumberland Island, where he knew the owners. He managed to
book a room for two nights and got permission to land on the grass-
and-sand strip near Stafford Beach, in the middle of the island. He
also got their help in renting an old pickup truck that a local owned
and arranged for them to leave it for him at the strip.

He checked out of the hotel, drove out to the airport, and presented his pilot's license and medical certificate to the renters of the
Bonanza. Then he took half an hour's checkride, to show them he
could handle the airplane.

"You'll do," the other pilot said, and Todd performed a respectable landing. He gave the people his credit card number and was
given the keys to the airplane.

He turned in his rental car, tossed his bag into the rear of the
Bonanza, started the engine, and took off in perfect weather. He
didn't file a flight plan; instead, he flew toward Stone Mountain,
the second-largest piece of granite in the world, at two thousand feet
above ground level, in order to stay under the Class B airspace of

Atlanta, then, when he was clear, climbed to twelve thousand and leaned out the engine. The airplane would do better than 180 knots, and he had a decent tailwind, too.

As he flew south and east the landscape flattened and became more agricultural, and two hours later he was descending, with Cumberland Island in sight. The island was the typical leg-of-lamb shape, with the pointed end at the south, and he was at two thousand feet when he spotted the airstrip. As he anticipated, half a dozen of the island's wild horses were grazing on the strip, and he flew over at fifty feet to scatter them before he turned and lined up for landing. He had to dodge a couple of potholes left by the rooting feral pigs that were common on the island.

He saw the rented pickup at the end of the field, taxied up to it, and cut the engine. He locked the aircraft and looked around for others. There were none in sight. He got the pickup started and drove slowly around the perimeter of the field, checking to be sure that no airplane was tucked away in the trees.

Satisfied, he drove south on the island's only road toward the inn. Cumberland Island had been bought after the Civil War by Thomas Carnegie, brother of the steel magnate Andrew Carnegie, as a family retreat. Carnegie built a large mansion for his family, manned by a village of three hundred workers who tended to the house and the island. He had no sons, but as his daughters grew into womanhood, he built a house for each of them, one of which, Greyfield, was now the inn.

He parked in front of the colonial house, with its huge live oak trees out front, dripping with Spanish moss. He checked into his room, found a book in the inn's library, and sat in a rocker on the front porch reading and listening. Any airplane landing on the island could be heard from here.

A young woman brought him a glass of iced tea, which he accepted gratefully. "Tell me," he said, "have any other airplanes landed on the island today or yesterday?"

"None at all," she replied, "though we're expecting a couple tomorrow, carrying a wedding party. The wedding is day after tomorrow, and some of them are staying here."

"Thanks," he said, and went back to his book.

As midafternoon passed, Todd got into the pickup again and drove north. Using a local map he found the slave village, where he stopped and got out. There were a few tiny cottages, all unoccupied, and the church. Todd walked around it, looking underneath, where there was only a crawl space behind latticework. He walked into the church and found an elderly black woman sweeping it out with a homemade broom.

"Good afternoon," she said to him.

"Good afternoon, ma'am. You getting ready for the wedding tomorrow?"

"That's right, suh," she said in the low-country accent of the locals.

"It's a pretty church," he said, looking around.

"We likes to think it is," she replied.

"Good day, then," he said, and left.

"And de same to you, suh," she replied, and went back to her sweeping.

She was the only person Todd had seen on the island outside the inn, and he didn't think Teddy Fay was good enough at disguises to pass for an old black lady.

Todd drove on north, stopping once to watch a couple of good-sized alligators in a stream. He passed Plum Orchard, a Palladian mansion built by Carnegie for one of his daughters, now unoccupied. He saw deer, armadillos and other small wildlife, and hundreds of birds. He reached the beach and drove farther north, passing what must have been a flock of five hundred brown pelicans grouped on the beach.

He turned around and drove south on the beach at thirty miles an hour and saw not a soul until he reached the turnoff for the inn, where he saw a man filling potholes on the narrow road. He was back at the inn in time for a nap, and he left his window open to catch the sound of an airplane, which didn't arrive.

He had an excellent dinner at a long table in the dining room with other guests and chatted with a few people. He had an after-dinner brandy, then retired to his room and his book.

Todd dozed off, then woke and switched his bedside light off and slept.

He was wakened in the night by the sound he had been waiting for. A small airplane was flying over the island to the north. He checked the bedside clock: three-ten a.m. Todd got out of bed, dressed, strung his holster on his belt, and crept out of the inn. He got the pickup started and drove north. There was a moon out, and he didn't need headlamps, so he switched them off.

He stopped the truck in the trees a hundred yards from the airstrip and got out, taking care not to slam the door. He walked to the edge of the moonlit field and looked around. No sign of an airplane. He stood still and listened. No sound of anyone walking or coughing or talking. Taking his time, he walked the perimeter of the field, staying in the trees. Once he awakened a rattlesnake a few yards away, which gave its warning noise, then slipped away into the woods. He was glad he hadn't stepped on it.

It took him an hour to walk around the whole field, but finally he was satisfied that no airplane had landed there. He walked back to the truck and drove back to the inn, then returned gratefully to bed.


TEDDY, ON THE OTHER HAND, was still at work. Judging the airstrip to be too far from the slave village to carry his equipment, he had landed on the beach in the moonlight and had pushed the aircraft between two dunes and partially covered it with brush.

Then he had picked up his case and the other gear and begun

walking up a rutted road that led to the slave village. He did his work there, then returned, less burdened, to the airplane, where he got out a sleeping bag and made his bed under a wing, having first slathered himself with mosquito repellent and donned a sleeping mask.

It was mid-morning before he woke, ready to do what he had come to do.

**57**

WILL LEE SAT UP IN BED, A BREAKFAST TRAY IN HIS LAP, AND WATCHED CNN. THE news network had somehow gotten hold of a videotape of a closed talk given to a group of his faithful by the Reverend Henry King Johnson, who was nakedly gouging them for money for his new monument to himself. This went on and on, for some twenty minutes, before they cut back to the anchor.

"Also on the campaign front," the anchor was saying, "our investigative reporter Jim Barnes has unearthed a document from public records showing that the Reverend Johnson had legally changed his name when he was in his early twenties, adding the middle name King. Many people had apparently thought that he was somehow related to Dr. Martin Luther King, Jr., which is not the case. Members of the community in Reverend Johnson's neighborhood are expressing shock that he had never denied the relationship."

Will switched channels to find the same stories playing elsewhere.

Kate came into the room, still dressing. "That's good timing," she said, fastening her belt. "I hope it will have the desired effect."

"The name-change thing won't make much difference," Will replied, "but after that tape has been played a few hundred times on TV and the Internet, Moss Mallet thinks it's going to have a very big effect. I think that now we can concentrate on Bill Spanner's lack of a record, without worrying so much about Henry Johnson."

"You think there's anything to those death threats from white supremacy groups Johnson says he's been getting?"

"They may be real enough, but I think it's just hot air."

"It would be awful if he were assassinated this close to the election."

"You think people would think I had something to do with it?" Will asked.

"People are crazy."

"Not crazy enough to try and kill Henry Johnson, I hope. I think after this he'll be back to his preaching and out of politics."

"I wouldn't count on it," Kate said. She was about to walk out the door when her bedside phone rang, and she picked it up. "Yes?" She listened for three or four minutes. "Right, I'll be there in half an hour." She hung up and turned to Will. "There was a weather delay in launching our reconnaissance missions in Afghanistan, but they're in the air now."

"The sooner the better," Will said.


WILL SAT in the Oval Office an hour later, listening to his campaign staff.

Moss Mallet was up. "It's too early to see any effect from this videotape of Johnson," he said, "but my polling shows that, if he gets out of the race or suddenly becomes less of a factor, it will put you within two points of Bill Spanner. That's within the margin of error."

Tom Black spoke up. "I'm hearing that a liberal group has got hold of some tapes of some of Johnson's sermons where he's being blatantly anti-white," he said. "Word is, they're going to run TV commercials using the tapes."

"You're staying away from that, I hope," Will said.

"Wouldn't touch it with a fork," Tom replied. "These are just rumors, of course, but I wouldn't be sad to see those commercials happen."

"Don't let anybody ever hear you say that," Will said. "I want us to run our own campaign, without any attacks on anybody."

"Spanner seems like the kind of guy who would have something in his background that would come out in a campaign," Sam Meriwether said.

"If that's so, then let it come out without our help," Will said.

"I'll bet there's something sexual," Kitty Conroy said. "He's too good-looking not to have dallied with the ladies at some point in his marriage."

"Let's not count on anything like that," Will said. He wanted terribly to tell them about the Afghanistan mission.

Tom Black was looking at him oddly. "Mr. President," he said, "you look worried. Is there something you want to give us a heads-up on? Something that might affect the election?"

Will took a beat to think about that, then replied, "No."


TODD BACON SAT in his rented pickup at the edge of the landing strip on Cumberland Island and watched a King Air, a twin-engine turbo-prop, set down on the grass-and-sand strip, followed a few minutes later by a Cessna 340, then a Beech Baron. These aircraft disgorged their passengers who were met by cars ferried from the mainland in the inn's old World War II landing craft and then driven north toward the slave village.

The reverend's published schedule on the Internet said that he was leading a prayer service on the front lawn of Plum Manor, the empty Palladian mansion on the north end of the island, immediately before the wedding, so Todd got the pickup started and drove toward the slave village.

TEDDY FAY HAD some breakfast from a cooler aboard his airplane, then slipped on a light backpack and began hiking toward the slave village. After half an hour's walk, he sat down on a fallen tree and checked his equipment. His transmitter had a range of a mile, but he had stopped half a mile from the village. He could do everything from here, guaranteeing himself a clean getaway. Television news had told him that the Reverend Henry King Johnson had not requested Secret Service protection, and Teddy was relieved about that.

TODD REACHED the deserted slave village and got out of the pickup. He walked from cabin to cabin, checking each one thoroughly, then walked to the church and went inside. Two ladies, one white and one black, were arranging flowers at the altar, and they greeted him politely.

"Are you part of the wedding party?" one asked him.

"No," Todd replied, "I'm a guest at the inn, and I was just taking a little tour of the island. Is there a wedding today?"

"Yes, and they should be arriving any minute," one woman said, consulting her watch.

"I wish the couple every happiness, then," Todd said, and left the church. He walked slowly around the little building. It was set on stone pilings about four feet high, elevating the building over the rest of the village. The area from the floor of the church to the ground was covered with wooden latticework. Everything looked in order here, but Todd wanted to walk the perimeter of the village and check for intruders. He pulled the Sig pistol from his belt and checked its readiness, then kept it in his hand as he walked. From what the late

Owen Masters had told him, his chances in an encounter with Teddy Fay would be poor, and he wanted to improve the odds.

He walked as silently as he could, looking as far into the trees as he could see, looking for wires on the ground or anything that could mark a danger.

He heard car doors slamming and looked toward the village to see the tall, handsome Reverend Johnson get out of a car and walk toward the church. He went inside, followed by the small procession of the wedding party, no more than a dozen people.

As Todd watched, rays of sunshine broke through a cloud and illuminated the building. The effect was theatrical, as if God were personally blessing this union, turning his own spotlight upon it. And then Todd saw, under the building, illuminated by the sunshine, the tank.

# 58

FOR JUST A MOMENT, TODD FROZE. HE MUST GET THOSE PEOPLE OUT OF THE church, he thought. Then he changed his mind and began running. He tore around the church to the rear of the little building and began pulling at the latticework surrounding the crawl space. It was nailed firmly on, but by bracing a foot against a post he got a corner loose.

A large black man in a suit and tie came around the corner of the building. "Hey, what are you doing there?" he yelled.

"Help me get this off!" Todd yelled at him.

"What are you doing?"

"There's a large bomb under this church, and if I don't get to it in time, we're all going to die."

The man grabbed the latticework next to Todd, and they pulled together. The extra weight and strength did the job, and the latticework came away, dumping both men on their backs.

Todd scrambled to his feet and dove under the church, crawling as fast as he could.

"What can I do?" the man behind him yelled.

"Get those people out of the church and as far away from it as possible!" Todd yelled back. He reached the propane tank and found something electronic fastened to it with duct tape. The device had a flashing light and a short antenna. Todd got his Swiss Army knife out of a pocket and a blade open, and with one hand, he grasped the antenna in his fist, hoping that would keep it from receiving. With the other hand he sawed at the duct tape.

TEDDY HAD GOTTEN close enough to the church to hear the cars stop and the wedding party walking up the wooden steps of the building. He gave them another two minutes, then held up his remote control and flipped a switch. To his surprise, nothing happened. He flipped the switch off, then on. Still nothing. Teddy didn't understand; he had built these two devices himself and had tested them thoroughly the day before. Maybe he had miscalculated the range. He started walking toward the church, switching the remote on and off.

TODD WORKED HIS WAY through the tape, and finally the device came away in his hand. He could hear running feet above his head as the wedding party fled the church.

Still grasping the antenna, he scurried from under the church on his knees and elbows, got to his feet, and began running away from the building. When he was fifty yards away, he flung the device as far as he could and kept running. It exploded before it hit the ground, sounding like a big firecracker and pelting Todd with bits of plastic as he ran toward the pickup truck. He had no wish for a conversation with either the wedding party or the law enforcement people who would, eventually, show up.

He got into the truck, started it, and backed down the road for fifty yards before he could turn around and start back toward the airstrip. Then, suddenly, he slammed on the brakes and came to a halt.

Teddy Fay had *not* landed on the Cumberland Island airstrip, Todd was certain of that. But if not, then how had he gotten here? By boat? Todd doubted it. Then it came to him: the beach. Teddy had landed on the beach. There were eighteen miles of firm sand with nothing to impede an airplane.

Todd got the truck going again, then, as he approached the landing strip, he turned left on a road that led to a beach house.

TEDDY HEARD THE BANG and saw smoke rise from the charge, but it was not from the direction of the church, and the propane tank had not exploded. He could hear shouting ahead of him, and he turned and ran back toward the beach at a fast jog. He had most of a mile to go, and he didn't want to exceed his fitness level. He ran along on some sort of animal path, which helped him move faster, sending a scared armadillo scurrying off into the brush.

He reached the airplane out of breath, and he stood, leaning on the fuselage and taking deep gulps of air until his blood began to reoxygenate. When he was steady on his feet again he tossed his backpack into the Cessna and began throwing aside the brush and palm fronds that hid the airplane.

When he had cleared everything away, he ran forward and grabbed the tow bar that was still attached to the nosewheel and started to pull. It took all his remaining strength to get the airplane rolling, and it was slow going. As he got onto the firmer sand of the beach, the towing got easier, and the airplane moved faster. The tide was out, and Teddy pulled the aircraft onto the packed, wet sand left by the outgoing sea.

He got the tow bar undone from the nosewheel, placed it in the rear seat of the airplane, and got in. He sat, breathing hard and sweating from the exertion, trying to keep the sweat out of his eyes while priming the airplane's engine.

He checked that the mixture was on full rich, cracked the throttle a quarter of an inch, and turned the ignition key. The propeller began to turn slowly, but the engine did not catch. He primed it a little more, then tried again. This time there was a cough from the engine, and it began to run roughly. He leaned it a little, until it ran smoothly, then got the airplane rolling along the wet sand. It was slow to pick up speed, but then the airspeed indicator came alive and read thirty knots. Then, to his astonishment, he looked down the beach and saw a pickup truck, all four wheels in the air, rocket over the crest of a dune, then hit the ground and wallow through the loose sand toward the beach.

What the hell? Teddy thought. Who was this? He shoved the throttle all the way in and added a notch of flaps. Forty knots.

The pickup reached the packed sand and turned north, toward the airplane, which was running south on the sand.

Fifty knots. He put in another notch of flaps for a soft-field take-off and pulled the yoke back into his lap. Sixty knots. The airplane struggled off the sand and into the air, but Teddy kept it inches off the sand, in ground effect, while it gathered speed. He retracted the landing gear to decrease drag. The pickup truck was upon him, the fool at the wheel obviously planning to ram him. Then, for a split second, Teddy clearly saw the driver. It was that kid, Bacon, from Owen Masters's staff.

Teddy jerked back on the yoke and cleared the pickup by inches, then he got the airplane into ground effect again, retracted a notch of flaps and let the airspeed build.


TODD BRAKED TO A HALT, PANTING. He couldn't believe he had tried to drive the truck into a spinning propeller; if he had been successful, he would have been mincemeat. He spun the truck around and floored it, chasing the airplane. It was flying just above the beach and not all that fast. Maybe he could clip the tail with the front of the truck and crash it. Now he was gaining on the Cessna. Since he was behind it he couldn't see the registration number, but he saw that it was a retractable. He was forty feet behind the airplane and closing fast, his speed nearly a hundred miles an hour on the speedometer.

THERE IS NO REARVIEW MIRROR on airplanes, so Teddy could not see the pickup coming. At ninety knots he pulled back on the yoke, and the airplane pulled away from the beach. Then, to Teddy's astonishment, he saw the pickup in front of him, out the right side window. He retracted the last notch of flaps and kept climbing. Then he heard shots.

Todd was leaning out the window of the pickup, his pistol in his left hand, firing at the airplane as it pulled away from him. He emptied the magazine, and he had no idea if he had hit the thing.

TEDDY REACHED THE END of the island and kept going straight. He checked his fuel: both tanks were at three-quarters, and he had some in the ferry tank, too. He flew straight down the coast at five hundred feet, passing Fernandina Beach and Amelia Island. When his GPS told him he was thirty miles from Cumberland Island and well out of sight of the pickup, he went to the flight-plan page of the GPS and tapped in the code for a little airstrip he knew in the Bahamas. Then he descended to around twenty feet, set the altitude hold on his autopilot and the navigate button, and took his hands off the yoke.

He had over two hundred miles to go, but he had the fuel, and if he didn't turn up on somebody's look-down radar, he would be fine.

———

**TODD BACON STOOD** on the beach beside the pickup and watched the airplane disappear to the south. Then he reloaded his pistol, got out his BlackBerry, and dialed a number.

**TEDDY WAS AN HOUR** from the coast, with another hour to go when he noticed that the right wing tank was nearly empty. He looked out the right window and saw what appeared to be smoke trailing from the wing; it was a mist of fuel. The son of a bitch had gotten lucky and hit a tank, and a quick calculation told him it was unlikely that he would make the Bahamas. And he had no life raft aboard.

# 59

LANCE CABOT WAS WALKING INTO HIS OFFICE WHEN HE HEARD THE CHARACTERISTIC ring of his direct telephone line. He picked it up. "Yes?"

"It's Bacon," a voice said. "Scramble."

Lance pressed the Scramble button. "I'm scrambled. What's up?"

"I'm in Georgia," Todd said.

Lance's jaw dropped. "What the hell are you doing in Eastern Europe?"

"Not that Georgia, the other one, the one in the United States."

"Same question," Lance said, feeling his gorge rise, "and your answer better be good."

"I'm at a place called Cumberland Island," Todd said. "I pursued Teddy Fay here."

"*What?*"

"I figured out where he was going and what he was going to do when he got there, so I followed."

"You followed him back to the United States?"

"Yes. I figured out that he was in Atlanta or nearby and that he was going to assassinate the Reverend Henry King Johnson. Do you know who that is?"

"Of course I know who he is," Lance snapped.

"Teddy has mostly killed right-wing political figures, but he figured Johnson was a threat to the president's reelection. After killing Owen, he had to get out of Panama, so he went to Atlanta."

"Todd, Teddy Fay is dead, and I don't want you ever to mention his name to me or anyone else again. Is that clear?"

"No, he's not dead. I saw him less than five minutes ago."

Lance was speechless.

"You'd better let me tell you what's happened, because I think you need to know about it before it hits the papers. Teddy tried to blow up a little church on this island where Johnson was scheduled to perform a wedding ceremony. He placed a propane tank with a detonator on it under the church, but I managed to find it and disable it before it went off. I pursued Teddy to the beach, where he had an airplane. I tried to stop him, but he managed to get the thing in the air and flew south."

"Jesus H. Christ," Lance said.

"I was unable to see the registration number, but it was a Cessna 182 RG, mostly white. I fired at it, emptied a magazine, but I don't know if I hit it."

Lance began to regain himself. "Now you listen to me very carefully, Todd," he said.

"I'm listening."

"I don't know how you got to the States, but . . ."

"I chartered a small jet."

"I don't care about that. Your orders are to get your ass back to Panama City immediately, if not sooner, and to stay there. You are not to discuss where you've been with anyone, nor are you to mention any theories you might have about Teddy Fay. Do you understand my orders?"

"I suppose."

"Well, you'd better do more than suppose, or you're going to find yourself in a much less attractive station than Panama City and at a much lower salary level than you are now. That, or you'll find your-self on the street, and I can promise you that the street will be an inhospitable place. Am I beginning to get through to you?"

There was a brief silence. "Yes, sir," Todd replied. "I think I understand perfectly."

"Good, and you'd better go on doing so. Was anyone hurt in the explosion?"

"No, sir. Everybody got out of the church safely, and the church was undamaged."

"Did anyone see you?"

"One man, a black gentleman, who helped me a little."

"You were never there, do you understand?"

"Yes, sir. I understand."

"How long ago did this happen?"

"Twenty minutes, maybe half an hour."

"Call me when you're back in Panama City, and it had better be soon." Lance hung up and thought for a moment. He turned to his computer and pulled up a classified list of every cell-phone number in the United States. He did a search and found one for Henry King Johnson, then dialed it, using an untraceable line.

The phone rang half a dozen times before it was answered. "Hello?" a deep, rich voice said.

"Mr. Johnson?"

"Yes? Who is this?"

"It's very important that you not know," Lance said. "In fact, this call never happened."

"What are you talking about?"

"I'm aware that, a few minutes ago, you had a very close call."

"How could you know that?"

"Have you called the local police yet?"

"No, but I'm certainly going to the moment I'm back in a place where there *are* police."

"That would be very unwise," Lance said.

"Are you insane?"

"Certainly not, but I must tell you that you are in no immediate danger. I must also tell you that, if you bring the police into this or if you continue to be a candidate, it will no longer be possible to protect you."

"Protect me? Did you send the man who saved us from the bomb?"

"Suffice it to say that you were saved."

Johnson was quiet for a moment. "Well, whoever you are, I thank you for that. What is it you want me to do?"

"Continue with the wedding, swear everyone present to secrecy, and forget this ever happened."

"You want me to drop out of the race, don't you?"

"I cannot tell you to do that. I can only tell you that you will be in very great danger if you continue. Now, I must say good-bye." Lance hung up.


MARTIN STANTON WAS alone in his Scottsdale, Arizona, hotel suite, dressing for a campaign appearance, when his secret cell phone began ringing. He walked to his briefcase, hesitated, then picked it up. "Yes?"

"So Marty," Barbara Ortega said, "how are things in Scottsdale? Getting hot out there?"

"It's comfortably warm," Stanton said warily.

"Well, it's going to get a lot hotter," Barbara said.

"What are you talking about?" Stanton asked.

"I thought I'd join you on the campaign trail."

"Barbara . . ." Then he realized he had used her name and she had used his. "Baby, you've got to relax and get a grip."

"I've got a grip, sweetheart, and I'm packing it as we speak."

"Don't do anything foolish, baby."

"Oh, I don't want to do anything foolish, I just want to do *something*, like tear her face off."

"Baby, you're not thinking clearly."

"Sweetheart, I'm thinking more clearly than I have in my entire life, and I'm going to go on thinking clearly. Do you realize what I can do to you?"

Stanton began to sweat, and he fought to control his temper. "Baby, I'm going to say something to you, and I want you to think about it very, very carefully after I hang up."

"Go ahead."

"We *both* have a lot to lose." He took a breath and broke the connection, then he went to his luggage, found a shoe with a shoe tree in it, took it and the phone into the bathroom, placed the phone on a marble countertop and began banging on the instrument with the shoe, smashing it into little pieces. He swept up the pieces in his hand, dropped them into the toilet, and flushed.

Then he went to his toiletry kit, found a Valium, and washed it down. By the time he was dressed he was calm again.

## 60

WILL LEE WAS WORKING AT HIS DESK ON *AIR FORCE ONE* WHEN HIS POLITICAL consultant, Tom Black, knocked and entered.

"What's up, Tom?"

"There's news," Tom replied, "good and bad."

"Sit down and start with the good news," Will said.

Tom sat down. "The Reverend Henry King Johnson just spoke to a crowd in Amelia Island, Florida, and announced that he was no longer a candidate for the presidency."

Will stared blankly at Tom. "How come?"

"His stated reason was that he wanted to devote himself full-time to the completion of his new church project in Atlanta."

"I thought his whole reason for running was fund-raising for that project."

"That's our supposition," Tom replied.

"Then why stop now?"

"Frankly, I don't know."

"It bothers me that you don't know, Tom."

"It bothers me, too, but I just don't know."

"Well, that is certainly good news," Will said.

"Moss has already started on a poll to see how this will affect the race."

"I'll look forward to the results. Now give me the bad news."

"One of my people, who's traveling with Marty Stanton, was taken aside this morning by a character, improbably named Jimmy Pix, and told that there's going to be a major exposé of Marty."

"Exposé of what?"

"Three things: One, that Marty is having an affair with Barbara Ortega. Two, that Marty is having an affair with Elizabeth Wharton. And three, that Marty's wife, Betty, who was thought to be on the verge of a settlement in their divorce, has hired both a forensic accountant and a publicist."

Will frowned. "All three of those at the same time?"

"I'm afraid so."

"And where is this exposé being exposed?"

"I'm not sure, but this Jimmy Pix guy works as a stringer, both reporter and photographer, for anybody who'll put a buck in his pocket, and that includes the supermarket tabloids."

"I see," Will said.

Tom sat silently.

"And do you have a proposal for dealing with any or all of these calamities, Tom?"

"Not yet."

"That's unusual for you, Tom."

"I know. The situation is a little overwhelming, I guess."

"I've never known you to be overwhelmed, Tom."

"Well, the election is the day after tomorrow, and I'm tired, and I'm thinking about getting out of this business as soon as we're done."

"What were you thinking about doing, Tom?"

"I don't know: chicken farming, llama breeding, something pastoral."

"Tom, you're the best there is at this business and one of the few honest men in it. It's what you were meant to do."

"That's what I thought until the past few days, but . . . "

"Tom, don't make any decisions. Just get us through Tuesday, then take a long vacation very far away, and leave your BlackBerry at home."

"That's good advice, sir," Tom said. "If I could parachute out of this airplane and start now, I'd be happy."

"Let me give you something to do, instead," Will said.

"I'd be grateful for some orders."

"Find someone who's very close to Governor Mike Rivera, in Sacramento, ask him to have Mike call somebody who's very, very close to Betty Stanton and have that person go see Betty and persuade her that it's time to wrap up her settlement talks and sign the papers. Have that person make Betty aware that her decision will be for the good of the country, and let that person know not to leave her presence until she has done so."

"Can we offer her the post of ambassador to the Court of St. James's?" Tom asked.

"I think she might need something quieter and more soothing, like the Bahamas."

"Yes, sir." Tom got to his feet and started out.

"And Tom, on your way out, will you please tell Cora to get me Barbara Ortega at Justice?"

"Yes, sir."

"And get back to me soonest on the Betty Stanton situation."

"Yes, sir."

Will sat and worked for the half a minute it took the phone to buzz. He picked it up.

"Barbara Ortega on the line, Mr. President," Cora said.

Will took a deep breath. "Hello, Barbara."

"Mr. President," she said guardedly.

"Barbara, I'm sorry to have taken so long to call you, but I heard about your appointment at Justice, and I just wanted to congratulate you."

"Thank you, sir."

"I know you'll do a wonderful job there, and I look forward to hearing about your successes—and I'm sure there will be many—during the next four years."

"That's very kind of you, Mr. President."

"You know, Barbara, in spite of our best efforts, we aren't always able to attract the very best people to government work, even in jobs as important as the one you now hold, jobs that make it possible for someone to actually make a difference in this country. That's why I'm so pleased that we were able to appoint you. Everything I know about your background, your work experience, and your work ethic tells me that we can expect great things from you.

"After this next term you're going to be able to write your own ticket: a partnership in a major law firm or, even better, I think you'd make a fine choice for attorney general for the next Democratic president."

"Well, I'm overwhelmed, Mr. President, and I'm very grateful for your confidence."

"I hear you've bought a beautiful house in Georgetown."

"Yes, that's true. I think I'll be very happy there."

"I'm sure you will. And I want you to know that we're very happy to have you aboard."

"Thank you, Mr. President."

"And now, I'd better get back to work and make sure you'll still have a Democratic president to work for after Tuesday's election. Good-bye, now."

"Good-bye, Mr. President."

Will hung up, then buzzed Cora again.

"Yes, Mr. President?"

"Tell Kitty Conroy to come and see me," he said.

Kitty appeared in seconds, and Will told her to sit down.

"Kitty, I'm sure you've already heard about the situation with Marty Stanton, his two girlfriends, and his soon-to-be-former wife."

"Oh, yes, sir."

"I want you to pick a columnist, preferably somebody from *The Washington Post* or *The New York Times*, and tell him the whole story, off the record, of course."

Kitty blinked. *"What?"*

"I'd like to read that column in tomorrow morning's paper or, better yet, tonight on the paper's website."

"Mr. President . . . "

"That'll be all, Kitty." He turned his attention to his paperwork until she had left the office.

LATER THAT AFTERNOON, as *Air Force One* was approaching Los Angeles for landing, Tom Black knocked on Will's door.

"Come in, Tom."

"Just an update, Mr. President," Tom said. "Judge Alvin Friedman, in Sacramento, has received the signed settlement agreement from Betty Stanton, and, as a favor to . . . somebody or other, he immediately signed the divorce decree."

"That's good news, Tom, and good work," Will replied. "Where is Marty Stanton at the moment?"

"In New York, sir. He has an important speech tonight at the Cooper Union."

"Thank you, Tom."

"Also, I'm told that Dick Thompson, of the *Post* has filed a column for tomorrow's paper revealing the vice president's, *ah*, difficulties. It'll be on their website by nine tonight, when the vice president will be speaking. When he leaves the hall, the press will be all over him."

"Thank you, Tom," Will said. "See you on the ground."

Tom left, and Will picked up the phone.

"Yes, Mr. President?"

"Cora, please get me the vice president."

Thirty seconds later, the phone buzzed, and Will picked it up.

"The vice president for you, sir."

"Marty?"

"Yes, Will."

"How are you?"

"Ready to wrap this thing up."

"Have you heard from Betty's lawyers yet?"

"No, and I'm afraid she's going to be difficult."

"I wouldn't worry about it, Marty. In fact, I'm glad to be the first to tell you, you are officially a divorced man. The judge signed the decree a few minutes ago."

"Are you sure, Will?"

"Absolutely sure, Marty. Also, I wanted to let you know that I have reason to believe that Barbara Ortega is not going to be a problem for you anymore."

"Well . . . I'm certainly glad to hear that, but how . . ."

"Don't ask, Marty. Now, may I give you some personal advice?"

"Of course, Will."

"I think you've been single for too long. I think you should get married."

"What?"

"Or at the very least, engaged. I'm told that the jewelry stores in New York are very good and that they will actually deliver a selection of rings at the request of an important customer."

"Oh?"

"Certainly. Now make an honest woman of that lovely girl. And, by the way, I think it would be a very good idea if you made the public announcement at the earliest possible moment, no later than six o'clock, say. I'm a romantic, Marty. I'd like to see this on the evening network news shows."

"That soon?"

"I have it on good authority that Dick Thompson, at *The Washington Post*, is going to run a column about you, Barbara, Elizabeth, and Betty tomorrow morning. I think it would be nice if everything it says has already been negated."

"I think that's a very good idea, Mr. President, and although I'm a bit befuddled, I thank you for it."

"Let me be the first to congratulate you, Marty, and please extend my wishes for her every happiness to Elizabeth." Will hung up, got into his jacket, and walked forward in the big airplane, ready to greet the crowds in Los Angeles.

# 61

NELSON PICKETT WAS SNUGGLED UP TO HIS NEWEST BOYFRIEND IN BED, WATCHING an interesting video that featured two other boyfriends, when his bedside phone rang. Busy as he was, he ignored it, until he heard the voice on the answering machine.

"Goddammit, Nelson, pick up the phone!" Willie Gaynes shouted.

Pickett immediately stopped what he was doing and grabbed for the phone. "Yes, Willie?" he panted.

"Have you seen the website of *The Washington Post*?"

"No, Willie, it's not part of my regular reading."

"Well, if you'll get off your ass and get onto your computer, you can read tomorrow's big fucking front-page story. Your story!"

"I don't understand," Pickett said.

"The *Post* has scooped you! Do you know how much I hate being scooped by a straight newspaper?"

"That doesn't seem possible, Willie."

"Not only is it possible, it's a fucking fact! I'm at the office, ripping out our front page and trying to find something to replace your story!"

Pickett's heart sank. "Do you want me to come down there, Willie?"

"No, don't you come down here, not ever again. You're fired!"

The noise of the phone slamming down caused Pickett's ear to ring.

"What's the matter, sweetie?" his friend asked.

"I've just been fired," Pickett said in a hollow voice.

"Really?"

"Really."

His friend looked at the bedside clock. "Oh my God, I've got to get out of here!" he said, leaping out of bed and grabbing his clothes.

"I could use a little consoling," Pickett said.

"Sorry, baby, I forgot about another appointment."

Then he was gone, and Nelson Pickett was left alone to contemplate his job prospects.

# 62

WILL STOOD ON THE PODIUM, LETTING WAVES OF APPLAUSE AND WHISTLES WASH over him. It had been his best speech of the campaign, he knew, and those who did not see it on live television would be bombarded with half a dozen carefully constructed sound bites the following day, the last before the election.

He shook hands on the podium and in the green room for half an hour, then was whisked back to the Presidential Suite at the Hotel Bel-Air. As he walked into the suite he saw Kitty Conroy standing, holding a telephone. Half his campaign staff was assembled in the room.

"It's Kate," Kitty said. "I mean, the director of Central Intelligence."

Will took the phone from her. "Yes?"

"Mr. President," Kate said, "one of our Navy SEAL teams now in Pakistan has apparently located the warhead."

"Is it secure?"

"No. A team of eight is on the ground in a village hardly big enough for that name. Apparently, there are more goats than people, but we know it's a hotbed of Taliban and Al Qaeda activity. They estimate fifty men in the village. We have a live feed from the team right now. A Lieutenant Parsons is the leader, code name Striker."

Will pressed the speaker button on the phone and hung up the receiver, motioning everybody to sit down and listen. The voices were low, but intense.

"This is Striker. I'm twelve yards from the house, and my readings have doubled. This is definitely ground zero. There's a window, and we're going to approach." There was the sound of feet on gravel, running.

"Striker, this is Hitman. Do you require support?"

"Negative, Hitman. We're planting the charge now. Start for base camp, we'll catch up. Hang on, a vehicle is approaching the house."

"I see it, Striker. It appears to be a large flatbed truck, covered with a tarp."

"They're going to move it," Striker replied.

"The tarp is off. There is what appears to be a missile on the bed, but there is no warhead."

"Hitman, start your stopwatch on my mark—detonation in three minutes. Fire a Hellfire at the vehicle five seconds early."

"Roger, Striker."

"Three, two, one, *mark*." Again, the sound of running feet.

"Kate," Will said.

"I'm here."

"What kind of charge is he planting?"

"C-four."

"And a Hellfire missile to be fired at the truck?"

"Correct. It's shoulder-mounted."

"Is the combination of the two explosions going to endanger the team?"

"They have three minutes to put ground between them and the village, and there is available rocky cover. They'll be all right if the warhead doesn't detonate."

"Are you telling me that one or both of those explosions might detonate the warhead?"

"We don't know for sure. I'm told that the people holding the warhead may have modified it. The standard warhead is set for airburst. If they've altered it for a contact burst, then the force of the explosion could set it off."

"And we have no information on whether they've done so?"

"None."

"I would have liked to have had the opportunity to consider that possibility," Will said.

"I'm sorry, Mr. President, but we've been listening to this mission for less than four minutes, and, in any case, we have no direct contact with the team leader. We're listening on a one-way relay, and in order to contact them, we would have to call the base in Afghanistan, they would call a chopper, and the chopper would contact the team."

Will heard somebody at Kate's end say, "Ninety seconds." He stood and listened, straining for any sound. All he could hear was heavy breathing and running footsteps.

"Keep going, Striker," a voice said into the radio. "I'll be right behind you after I fire the missile."

"Roger, Hitman," the panting Striker responded, and the footsteps continued.

Will looked around the room. Everybody was staring at the telephone, rapt.

"Thirty seconds," a voice at Kate's end said.

"God help them," Kitty said, then was shushed.

"Ten seconds, Striker," a male voice said.

"Take cover!" Striker shouted, abandoning caution.

A *whoomp* sound came from the other end. "Missile fired," a voice yelled, followed a second later by a large explosion.

"Three, two, one," Kate said. There was a noise, then another explosion, followed a fraction of a second later by a shrieking noise, followed by silence.

"Their radios are fried," a voice from Kate's end said somberly.

"What does that mean, Kate?"

"Charlie, call downstairs!" Kate yelled. "I want a tremor report instantly!" She came back on the line. "This is not good, Will."

Will could hear a telephone ringing at her end. "What's happening?"

A male voice replied. "Detonation confirmed."

"Will," she said, "the warhead detonated. The team on site is dead, along with everybody else in the village, and maybe some of the other villages and other teams, too."

Other voices were shouting information at her.

"Will, I'm told that a chopper was in the air between ten and twenty miles from the village. That will be gone, too."

"How soon will you have a casualty and damage estimate?"

"Everybody here is on that," she said. "I'll have to call you back, and I don't know when."

"I understand," Will said. "I'll be here. I'm sorry about your team, Kate. I'll want to call their families myself."

"I know you will. Good-bye for now."

Will hung up and looked around the room at the shocked faces. "You know everything I know," he said. "You'd better all get some sleep."

"Mr. President," Kitty said, "you're going to have to throw me out of here." There was a murmur of assent from the rest of the people present.

"All right," Will said, "Somebody send out for some coffee and sandwiches. It's going to be a long night."

WILL WAS DOZING in an armchair, his jacket off and his tie loose. Daylight was filtering through the blinds, and the clock read a little after seven a.m. The phone rang. He jerked awake and pressed the speaker button. "Yes?"

"Mr. President, I have a preliminary report," Kate said.

"Go ahead."

"The base in Afghanistan has made contact with all but two of the teams. The first we know about, the second was in a village four miles away. Both teams, one Navy SEAL, one Agency, comprising a total of nine men and two women, are presumed dead. All the other teams witnessed the detonation from a greater distance and from cover and have reported no casualties. They have all withdrawn to their base camps in Afghanistan and will be choppered out during the next twelve hours or so. An estimated one hundred to one hundred fifty villagers are presumed dead."

"I've heard nothing from Pakistan," Will said. "Has their government been in contact with anybody there?"

"Our station in Islamabad has canvassed its sources, and their estimate is that the Pakistani government believes that the people in possession of the warhead inadvertently set it off. It appears that we can, if you wish, deny involvement."

"No. I won't do that," Will said.

"There is one other report that you may find interesting," Kate said. "One of our sources has reported a gathering of more than a dozen top Al Qaeda and Taliban leaders in the region. There is some reason to believe that they may have been meeting in the village where the warhead detonated."

"I want every effort made to confirm that, and I want names as soon as possible," Will said.

"We're working on it, Mr. President."

"Call me back when you have more details," Will said. "I'm going to ask for network time at eight."

"Yes, sir."

Will hung up and turned to Kitty. "I want five minutes on all the networks at eight o'clock," he said.

"I'm on it," Kitty replied.


AT SEVEN-THIRTY A.M., Will spoke to President Khan of Pakistan. It was a tense conversation, but Khan seemed to grasp that what had occurred may have solved more problems for him than it created. He told Will that he had already dispatched troops. At eight a.m., Will broadcast from a conference room at the hotel. In a somber voice, he divulged every detail at his disposal, except the names of the dead, pending notification of their families.

At noon, as he was returning to Washington to pick up Kate, Will received another call from President Khan, confirming half a dozen names of those leaders killed in the detonation, and Will released them to the press on *Air Force One*.

He spent the remainder of the flight speaking to the families of the American dead.

# 63

THAT AFTERNOON, LANCE CABOT GOT INTO THE ELEVATOR AND PRESSED THE basement button. As the doors were closing, Katharine Rule Lee stopped them and got on board.

"Good afternoon, Director."

"Good afternoon, Lance."

Lance glanced at his watch. "I haven't often seen you leaving this early."

"My husband and I are flying down to Georgia, so we can vote bright and early for the TV cameras tomorrow morning."

"Oh, yes. From what I hear, his prospects have recently improved."

"That's what I hear, too," Kate replied.

"I wish you both the very best of luck," Lance said.

"Thank you," she replied. "Lance, would you tell me something, please?"

"Of course, Director."

"Is Teddy Fay still dead?"

Lance blinked. "Oh, yes, Director," he managed to say.

Then the elevator doors opened on the ground floor, and Kate got off. Lance continued toward the basement. He pressed his forehead against the cool doors and heaved a great sigh.

## AUTHOR'S NOTE

I am happy to hear from readers, but you should know that if you write to me in care of my publisher, three to six months will pass before I receive your letter, and when it finally arrives it will be one among many, and I will not be able to reply.

However, if you have access to the Internet, you may visit my website at www.stuartwoods.com, where there is a button for sending me e-mail. So far, I have been able to reply to all of my e-mail, and I will continue to try to do so.

If you send me an e-mail and do not receive a reply, it is because you are among an alarming number of people who have entered their e-mail address incorrectly in their mail software. I have many of my replies returned as undeliverable.

Remember: e-mail, reply; snail mail, no reply.

When you e-mail, please do not send attachments, as I *never* open these. They can take twenty minutes to download, and they often contain viruses.

Please do not place me on your mailing lists for funny stories, prayers, political causes, charitable fund-raising, petitions, or sentimental claptrap. I get enough of that from people I already know. Generally speaking, when I get e-mail addressed to a large number of people, I immediately delete it without reading it.

Please do not send me your ideas for a book, as I have a policy of writing only what I myself invent. If you send me story ideas, I will immediately delete them without reading them. If you have a good idea for a book, write it yourself, but I will not be able to advise you on how to get it published. Buy a copy of *Writer's Market* at any bookstore; that will tell you how.

Anyone with a request concerning events or appearances may e-mail it to me or send it to: Publicity Department, Penguin Group (USA) Inc., 375 Hudson Street, New York, NY 10014.

Those ambitious folk who wish to buy film, dramatic or television rights to my books should contact Matthew Snyder, Creative Artists Agency, 9830 Wilshire Boulevard, Beverly Hills, CA 98212-1825.

Those who wish to make offers for rights of a literary nature should contact Anne Sibbald, Janklow & Nesbit, 445 Park Avenue, New York, NY 10022. (Note: This is not an invitation for you to send her your manuscript or to solicit her to be your agent.)

If you want to know if I will be signing books in your city, please visit my website, www.stuartwoods.com, where the tour schedule will be published a month or so in advance. If you wish me to do a book signing in your locality, ask your favorite bookseller to contact his Penguin representative or the Penguin publicity department with the request.

If you find typographical or editorial errors in my book and feel an irresistible urge to tell someone, please write to Rachel Kahan at Penguin's address above. Do not e-mail your discoveries to me, as I will already have learned about them from others.

A list of my published works appears in the front of this book and on my website. All the novels are still in print in paperback and can be found at or ordered from any bookstore. If you wish to obtain hardcover copies of earlier novels or of the two nonfiction books, a good used-book store or one of the online bookstores can help you find them. Otherwise, you will have to go to a great many garage sales.